D0049437

JA 12 77

SUMMER on
EAST END

DOUBLE
ECLIPSE

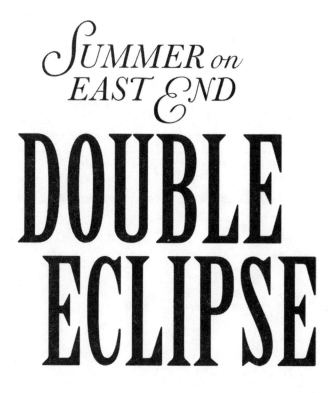

SUMMER on EAST END

DOUBLE ECLIPSE

melissa de la cruz

G. P. Putnam's Sons

G. P. PUTNAM'S SONS
an imprint of Penguin Random House LLC
375 Hudson Street, New York, NY 10014

Printed in the United States of America.
ISBN 9780399173561
1 3 5 7 9 10 8 6 4 2

Text set in Zapf Intl Light.
This is a work of fiction. Names, characters, places, and incidents
either are the product of the author's imagination or are used fictitiously,
and any resemblance to actual persons, living or dead, businesses,
companies, events, or locales is entirely coincidental.

For the amazing Moretz family:
Teri, Trevor, and Chloë

Thank you for loving the East End coven

LOCKED OUT OF HEAVEN

From the Diary of Molly Overbrook

$\mathcal{D}$ear Diary,

That's how these things usually start, right? "Dear Diary"? I'm only asking because it seems kind of strange to pretend that I'm writing a diary, which should be, you know, *private*, when what I'm really writing is a "therapy assignment" that's going to be read by Dr. Mésomier and my dad and aunts and Odin-knows-who-else. But since right now I'm not really speaking to any of those people, I'm just going to pretend that none of them are going to see this, because if I think of them reading these words, then I'm never going to be able to write down what happened this summer. And although I want to make it clear that I think this is a *totally lame assignment* and it's not really *anybody's business but mine and Mardi's*, I do actually want to write it down. Because, well, it was pretty freaking strange, and maybe writing it down will help me figure out how the Hel, I mean, the Underworld, things could have gotten so messed up between me and my sister.

And since maybe this is going to be read by people who have never met me, I suppose I should catch you up on a few things that happened before summer even started.

So:

Most people know me as Molly Overbrook, but in certain *very* select circles, I'm also known as Mooi, and my twin sister, Mardi, is called Magdi. Most people see us as two fairly normal seventeen-year-olds, albeit ones from privileged backgrounds: Mardi's normal ride is a vintage Ferrari, while I usually go for something with a chauffeur (I like a chauffeured Navigator or Escalade preferably, but a Town Car will do, or even a taxi— although as I learned this summer, nothing beats a Maybach), so I can sip on some bubbly and check my social media feeds while someone else does the driving. Shopping means department stores and individual designers (although in our case, the department stores are Barneys and Jeffrey and the designers are 5:31 Jérôme and Kim'Haller). Good hair is an obsession, and we own approximately one hundred different hair care products between us; of course mine gets a little assistance from the Frédéric Fekkai salon. Like everyone our age, we sweated over the SATs, and we'll soon be waiting on pins and needles to see which colleges will let us in.

HOWEVER:

Despite the outward appearance of quasi-normality, we are in fact the daughters of Thor, a.k.a. the god of thunder. No, not the one played by Chris Hemsworth. Our dad doesn't wear a red cape and silver armor, although he *does* have a hammer, which he doesn't swing around as much; he keeps it hanging on a couple of hooks above the mantel in the living room of our Park Avenue penthouse while he jets around the world buying and selling skyscrapers and companies and, I don't know, *islands.* By which I mean that, yes, our father's a genuine Norse god, which makes us goddesses—Mardi's the goddess of rage and I'm the goddess of strength. But we're a little different from our dad and his ex, Ingrid, a.k.a. Erda, the goddess of the earth, and her sister Freya, the goddess of love. They were all born thousands of years ago in Asgard, which is our real home and where we're supposed to live, coming to Midgard (the place humans call Earth) only when they mess things up and need our help.

But Thor (whom we call Troy, when we're not just calling him Dad) and Ingrid and Freya and a few other Aesir and Vanir (which is what the gods call themselves in Asgard) ended up getting trapped here after the rainbow bridge that connected Asgard to the rest of the nine worlds was destroyed almost five hundred years ago, leaving them pretty much stuck here. Like, *forever*.

Literally.

Despite the fact that Thor and Tyr—the god of war (a.k.a. Trent, whom we'll meet later)—and Ingrid and Erda and about a half dozen other gods have been trapped here for so long, none of them ever had any children—that is, until Mardi and I came along seventeen years ago.

To be sure, our births were prophesied a long time ago, but that was before the Bofrir was destroyed, and everyone figured those prophecies had been canceled when the link between the nine worlds was cut— especially because in the legends our mother is supposed to be a Jotun (a giant) from Jotunheim, a world that was also cut off from Midgard by the destruction of the rainbow bridge. And as far as everyone knows, there aren't any giants here on Earth. But then one day our dad showed up with a cute little bundle of joy in each arm (so we're told anyway; we may be goddesses, but you can't expect us to remember things from when we were a couple of months old, let alone a couple of days), and judging by the way glass shattered when we cried for our bottles and the trays on our high chairs would break into a million pieces when we threw temper tantrums, it was pretty clear we were the goddesses from the ancient prophecies. Needless to say, our appearance on the scene raised a lot of questions, but one of them was kind of more important than all the others:

Where was our mother? And who was she?

Well, we'll get to that, but first I want to tell you about this dream I had around the start of the summer. Not once, but every night for more than a week. I know, it's the twenty-first century and no one really cares about dreams anymore besides Jungian analysts—and how can you take someone seriously when their job is to sit on a couch and listen to people talk? Except gods' dreams aren't like humans' dreams—our unconscious is plugged into the magical currents that govern time itself, as in, they're prophetic. (How do you think they came up with the prophecy about Mardi and me all those thousands of years ago? It wasn't from gazing into a crystal ball. It was a dream.)

So:

In the dream, I'm at Fair Haven, which is this beautiful colonial-era mansion on Gardiners Island, just off the East End, where Mardi's boyfriend, Trent, lives. Besides being the Gardiners' ancestral home, Fair Haven also happens to sit on what's called a "seam" between our world and the Land of the Dead, also known as Niflheim, the most fearsome and inhospitable of the nine worlds, with a cold white sun that's not even as bright as the full moon and covered in endless sheets of ice—including Hel, the vast city where dead Vikings are banished if they fail to die a heroic death.

The reason why I'm telling you all this background stuff is because I didn't know it in my waking life—I found it out in the dream. And only after I did a little digging around did I realize it was all true. Which is why I knew this dream was important.

Important, and terrifying.

In the dream, I'm walking toward Fair Haven across the front lawn. In real life, that lawn is as flat and manicured as a croquet pitch or tennis court, every single blade of grass perfectly trimmed to 1.5 inches. But in the dream, the yard is a swampy, cratered mess, alternating puddles of sludge and muddy mounds the size of muskrat nests. Plus, it's raining. Plus, the puddles of water are freezing cold.

Now, I'm a serious shoe girl, and a muddy lawn is not my normal habitat. (Not good for the Zanottis!) Yet in the dream, I'm barefoot and wading right into this vast field of sludge like it's the Mediterranean lapping on the Côte d'Azur, plopping one foot into six inches of ice-cold muck and then the other, as I charge toward Fair Haven. I don't know why, but I have to get to the mansion, and I have to get there soon, or it'll be too late. And so I'm splashing through the mud as fast as I can, slipping every other step and falling on my hands and knees and splashing my face with brown goo. I don't even care what my hair looks like—so you know I must be *completely out of my mind.*

I'm so caught up with just trying to get across the lawn that I'm not really paying attention to my destination. But then, after what seems like hours, I manage to climb onto one of those muddy but still comparatively dry mounds, and when I pause to catch my breath, I look up for the first time, to see how far I am from my destination.

That's when I see the mansion—which just last year was described by *Architectural Digest* as "not only the most beautiful, but the most elegant home on the whole of the East End." Except in my dream it's not beautiful at all, let alone elegant. It's a ruin. Every single pane of glass in every single window has been smashed, and two out of every three of the thousands upon thousands of cedar shingles that normally cover the house have been blown off, and the simple white Ionic pilasters and window frames have been ripped away or hang in splinters from the walls—and that's only what I can see of the house, because the whole enormous building is covered in dark, droopy tangled vines that look more like seaweed than ivy or creeper. The vines cling to the house not like they're growing up its walls but like they're trying to pull them down, and there are big holes in the roof with tree branches growing through them, as if the house had been abandoned for a hundred years or more. Which is impossible. I was there just last summer. The house was in perfect condition. I played croquet with Mardi on this very lawn.

And I mean, I know it was a dream, so the normal rules of reality don't apply. But the thing is, I *knew* I was dreaming, and in the dream I *wasn't surprised* to see Fair Haven looking like this. It was exactly what I expected to see. It was only the part of me that was watching myself dream that was confused. Was I seeing the future? Or maybe some alternate version of the past? And if so, how? Though it was said that the Aesir possessed magical artifacts that allowed them to change time itself, all those were trapped on the other side of the destroyed rainbow bridge. So how was I seeing this vision?

But before the not-dreaming part of my brain could ask the dreaming part of my brain for the answer to this question, I noticed something off to my right, in the east wing of the mansion. The east wing was built in the early seventeenth century, and Trent always said it was the strongest part of the house. Its posts and beams had been cut from solid tree trunks two feet thick and had stood for nearly four hundred years. But now the whole wing swayed like a poorly built tent in a hurricane, and much of the roof had caved in, and some kind of vast . . . mound rose from the hole, like one of those creepy termites' nests in Africa, but a hundred times bigger. But it was only when it flashed a second time that I realized it wasn't the mound that had caught my eye, but a pulse of light somewhere deep within the crumbling walls of the east wing: a thick greenish-yellowish glow that pulsed on and off. And each time it shone on, it cast a shadow that, though monstrously distended, was still recognizable as human, and female.

And even though I didn't know who this woman was, I knew I had to get to her, I had to save her.

2

O MOTHER, WHERE ART THOU?

Mardi-Overbrook-Journal.docx

*L*et me guess: the first thing Molly wrote in her diary was "Dear Diary," wasn't it?

Gods, she can be so predictable, not to mention conventional. That's the difference between us. I like to surprise people. When Molly got extensions in fifth grade so she could look like every other Britney-Christina-Beyoncé-Gaga-Katy wannabe, I went all Sinéad (or Amber Rose, if you don't remember Sinéad) and buzzed my long wavy locks down to the skull. And when it grew out, I dyed my hair black to make sure I'd stand out from the basic bimbos of the world even more. I pierced my tongue when I was thirteen and tattooed the rainbow bridge on my neck when I was fifteen. Troy, a.k.a. Thor, a.k.a. Daddykins, says I do these things because I grew up without a strong female presence in my life, but he doesn't know what he's talking about.

I do these things because it's fun.

I do them because I *can*.

No doubt Molly will tell you everything started to go wrong or, I don't know, weird between us, when Janet Steele (yes, *the* Janet Steele) dropped her little bombshell after winning the French Open this past May (yes, *the* French Open), but I don't think that's true. I think everything changed last summer, after Troy booted us off to the East End to get away from a little trouble in Manhattan—trouble that was not actually our fault, as later events made clear. Neither Molly nor I was particularly *thrilled* about spending the summer babysitting for one of Dad's old exes, Ingrid, but Ingrid turned out to be pretty cool, and her sister Freya makes the best cocktail-cum-love-potion you've ever guzzled.

But of course what really made last summer interesting was meeting Trystan Gardiner, a.k.a. Trent, a.k.a. Tyr, the god of war. (Molly mentioned him, right?) Although it wasn't as simple as just meeting him—when you're a goddess masquerading as a witch pretending to be a normal human, nothing ever is.

Molly and I both met Trystan Gardiner in different places, at the same time. If that sounds fishy, that's because it was. See, the Trystan I met—who called himself Trent—was the real Trystan, whereas the Trystan Molly met—who called himself Tris—was really this evil shape-shifter named Alberich who was just trying to steal our ring, which happens to be made out of Rhinegold and has all kinds of magical powers.

Anyway, when all was said and done, Alberich had been defeated and banished, the Rhinegold was safely locked away in Hel, and Trent and I were the only couple left standing, while poor Molly realized she'd been dating an absolute troll all along.

But wait, you're asking, isn't Tyr one of the multi-thousand-year-old gods? What's he doing dating a seventeen-year-old? Isn't that a little, you know, *ew*? That's a very good question, and I'm going to get to it eventually, but for now let me just explain that the gods trapped here in Midgard are a little different from the gods who still live in Asgard. See, Asgardians are immortal. Like, they really live forever and ever, and pretty much nothing can kill them, and if they do get killed, then they stay dead. But here in Midgard, the gods' bodies are practically as vulnerable as human bodies, which means they *can* be destroyed. But only the flesh: the soul sticks around and migrates to a newly conceived body. Joanna, Ingrid and Freya's mother, who was also trapped here in Midgard with her children, has not only had to watch each of her children die, in some cases more than once, she's also had to give birth to each of them two or three times, which has got to be pretty weird, not to mention kind of horrible, since when they first come out, they're like any other baby: crying, breast-feeding, diapers, the whole nine yards, with no knowledge of who they used to be. It's not until puberty that their powers start to manifest and their memories return to them, a drawn-out and not-particularly-fun process known as the Reawakening—although I imagine it still beats dying.

And so Trent got himself into a little trouble about nineteen years ago, and he ended up burning his mortal body (his second, if I've got the count right). I used to ask him what happened, and he'd go silent. At first, I thought he was trying to hide the fact that he'd done something shady, but then I realized he actually didn't remember—all his memories had died with his old body and haven't returned yet. Or rather, hadn't returned as of the beginning of this summer, although by early June that situation had changed.

In fact, that's when everything changed, but that's getting ahead of the story.

So here we are, in our second summer on the East End. Molly and I ended up liking the place so much that it was pretty much taken for granted that we'd come out and stay with Ingrid and her mortal husband, Matt, and their two kids, Jo and Henry, as soon as school let out. Except this year, only Molly was going to be crashing at Ingrid's cute but kind of small beach house (only 3,000 square feet), while I was going to stay with Trent in Fair Haven, his family's grand home on Gardiners

Island, just off the coast of North Hampton. You could drop Ingrid and Matt's house in Fair Haven's ballroom and still throw a raging party for a hundred of your closest friends in the space left over.

Dad sort of raised his eyebrow at the whole thing, but I raised my own back and that was that. This is the man who used to give us cereal for dinner and left us with a succession of girlfriends over the years.

The day everything began to happen, however, I was over at Ingrid's house to watch the French Open final on TV. I know what you're thinking. *Tennis.* Who watches tennis except for old British people and wannabe Anglophiles? And I'm not even a tennis fan. That's Molly. (Or that was Molly. Something tells me she's not too big on it now.) She'd gotten into it a little during our sophomore year, when she went out for the team, but then Dad made her quit because even though she'd never picked up a racket before, she had this funny way of winning *every single match* she played, and he was pretty sure she was using magic to help her out. Molly claimed she wasn't, and who knows, maybe she wasn't doing it on purpose, but my sister is just about the most competitive person I know—after me—and sometimes when a goddess wants something, she's just going to get it.

So anyway, she quit the team, and destroyed all her gear, including an adorable platinum tennis bracelet that quite frankly looked better when it *wasn't* worn with a tennis skirt. But by then she'd started watching matches on TV—she even made Dad add the Tennis Channel to our cable package—and she'd become obsessed with Janet Steele.

In case you live under a rock, Janet Steele is the number one female tennis player in the world, which is amazing, given that she's something like thirty-seven or thirty-eight years old, which in tennis years is *ancient*. She was once a teenage prodigy, but then something happened when she was twenty or twenty-one and she vanished into the Outback, that big desert in the middle of Australia, which is where she's from. Some kind of "family crisis" was all she'd say—or all her publicist would say, since Janet simply disappeared. She was gone for thirteen or fourteen years, until about two years ago, when she suddenly showed up and started playing again, at around the same age that most tennis players retire. And not just playing: winning. By the end of her first year back, she was in the top ten. By the end of her second year, she was number one. She even almost won the Grand Slam last year (Serena Williams beat her at Wimbledon) and, what with the fact that she's a six-foot-two Glamazon with three feet of lustrous dark hair and legs that would make Giselle jealous, she became the highest-paid female athlete in the world. According to reports, she pulls in more than a $100 million a year in endorsements and prize money. That's Michael Jordan money, people. That's LeBron James money.

So, Janet started the year by winning the Australian Open and cruised right to the French Open final, where she was once again facing Serena Williams. I didn't watch last year's Wimbledon match, but I guess it was a real slugfest, and according to the tabloids, whatever friendship might've existed between Janet and Serena was dead and gone by the time it was over.

"Rumor has it she can be a bit of a bitch," Molly said as she settled onto a couch with a bottomless bowl of Parmesan-dusted popcorn, courtesy of Ingrid's magic and culinary prowess.

The TV was on, but it was just the announcers, droning away about things like "first-serve percentage" and "forehand volleys" and "hitting a clean, flat ball." I would've rather been at the beach, or with Trent, but it was pouring rain outside, and Trent was busy. So I was stuck with the fam.

"Molly, please," Ingrid said. "Little pitchers have big ears." She nodded at Jo, who was sitting a few feet away on an easy chair.

"Oh, Mom, puh-lease!" seven-year-old Jo said, snacking on her own bottomless bowl of crunchy kale chips. "I totally know what a bee-yotch is!"

Ingrid shook her head in defeat.

"Who's the b?" I asked Molly. "Janet or Serena?"

"Puh-lease," she said in her best imitation of Jo. "Janet Steele basically shows up, plays her matches, crushes her opponents, then leaves. Never talks to anyone, doesn't socialize or practice with any of the other play-ers, nothing. Back when she was a teenager, she was supposed to be a real party girl, but now she says all of that is 'beneath her.'"

"Like, literally," I said, pointing to the screen. That woman was tall.

The players were walking out onto the field, or court, or whatever it's called. Serena Williams is like five foot ten or something, with guns like an NBA star, but Janet Steele towered over her by a good four inches. She was more lithe than Serena, but you could see the strength in her shoulders and legs, all three or four feet of them, which were fully on display in a skimpy white tennis dress that barely covered her butt cheeks.

"My Lord," Ingrid said from the other side of the kitchen island. "Is that what they're wearing these days? I have bathing suits that cover more than that!"

"Mo-om!" Jo groaned. "You are em-bar-ras-sing me!"

"Watch it, young lady, or I'll turn those kale chips back into plain old kale, and make you eat till you turn green. Mardi, here are your spicy wasabi peas," she said, proffering an antique earthenware bowl with a bright red stripe around the rim. "I've put a bottomless hex on them, so pace yourself or you're going to end up with a tummy ache."

Tummy ache. Ingrid's fought demons and giants, visited six of the nine worlds, and helped raise peo-ple from the dead, but she still talks like a children's librarian (which, btdubs, is what she is in her human guise). You gotta love her.

Just then, Freya burst through the front door. She was rocking a typical Freya look (not that anything Freya wears is "typical"): cutoff denim shorts that were definitely shorter than Janet Steele's tennis dress, and a sleeveless, backless, semi-see-through blouse that showed off her arms, which glittered with bracelets, including an asp coiled high up around her toned left biceps.

"Hey, Molls, what's shaking?" she said before turning to me. "Mardi, I was going through my closet this morning, and I saw something that made me think of you."

She tossed me a little box; inside I found a thick black leather belt. When I uncoiled it, I saw that the chunky silver buckle read *BOY TOY*.

"Oh, my gods, it's awesome!" I practically squealed. "Is it vintage?"

"It's more than vintage," Freya laughed. "It's Madonna's. I borrowed it from her at a club in New York in like 1982, and then when she got famous, I kind of sort of forgot to give it back." She winked mischievously.

Molly tried to hide her disappointment at not getting anything, but you could tell she was upset. This was the third item of clothing Freya had given me since we'd arrived last week, and just the day before, Molly had complained that Freya liked me best and she felt left out. I tried to tell her it was just because Freya and I have the same taste in clothes, not because she liked me better. I mean, Molly's a label queen, and everything she wears has to be right off the runway or she won't even look at it. I don't mean that as a dig or anything. Just stating the facts.

When Molly puts on the same Herve Leger you've seen on a thousand different celebrities, she works it out. But Freya and I are more rock 'n' roll. And besides, I told her, Ingrid clearly preferred Molly to me. This didn't make Molly feel any better, though. "Ingrid dresses more like a librarian than any librarian in the history of libraries," she'd whined.

Now, however, before she could say anything, Freya exclaimed, "Is that *Janet Steele*? She's back?"

Molly immediately perked up. "Do you know her?"

"Know her?" Freya said. "I held that girl's hair out of her face while she puked her guts out. We used to party like it was 1999 when it was only 1995. She used to hang around—"

"Janet's a big tennis star now," Ingrid said in this bland but curiously sharp tone of voice. When I looked over at her, she was frowning at Freya, and her face bore a clear shut-up expression. Like I said, Ingrid's a librarian, so she can make a shut-up face like nobody's business.

"Right, she was always a big tennis star, even then," Freya said, oblivious to her sister's warning. "I always thought it was a little suspicious myself."

"Why?" Molly asked. "I think she's amazing. She's beautiful and talented, and she doesn't care what anyone thinks about her."

"I'm sure Freya's just exaggerating," Ingrid said, coming around the island with a bottle of white wine in one hand, seltzer in the other. "Sis," she said in a not-very-sisterly tone, "why don't you make us some spritzers to drink while we watch the game?"

"It's called a match," Molly said. "A game is, like, I don't know, *baseball*."

"Yes, Mother," Jo echoed drolly. "*Baze-bowl.*"

Ingrid and Freya exchanged a significant look, and suddenly Freya's eyes went wide. She opened her mouth, then snapped it shut. With a false smile on her face, she ran to the kitchen, and Ingrid sighed in relief.

I looked back and forth between them, then glanced at the TV. Janet Steele was unzipping her warm-up jacket and shaking out her legs prior to the start of the game, or match, or whatever you call the whole tennis experience. It seemed pretty clear that Freya and Ingrid knew something about her that they weren't saying, and I was determined to get it out of them, if only so I'd have something to talk to Molly about while two grown women spent the next two hours hitting a ball back and forth with giant flyswatters.

But as it turned out, I didn't have to get it out of them. Janet told us herself.

* 3 *

YOU DROPPED A BOMB ON ME

From the Diary of Molly Overbrook

$\mathcal{F}$reya came around the counter with a tray of ice-filled glasses and a fat pitcher full of golden liquid.

"Those don't look like spritzers," Ingrid said, frowning in the way that only a woman who knows she's magically immune to frown lines would dare to risk.

Freya laughed. "It's the French Open; I made Pimm's Cups."

"Um, I think that's Wimbledon," Ingrid said.

"Um, what is a Pimm's Cup?" Mardi said.

"Pimm's Cups are traditionally associated with Wimbledon, which starts in three weeks," I added.

"Oh, my gods, this is going to happen *again*?" Mardi said, waving a hand at the screen, where Janet and Serena were warming up. "You've had that TV on twenty-four seven for the *past two weeks*."

"A Pimm's Cup," Freya said before I could inform Mardi that not only was there still Wimbledon to come, but also the US Open at the end of the summer, "is muddled cucumber, lemon, mint, candied ginger, and a liqueur called Pimm's No. 1, which is basically an herb-infused gin. Plus some bubbles to give it fizz. Of course it's me, so I added a little twist of my own—and I don't mean the lemon peel," she said, winking.

I *almost* forgave her for not giving me any presents when we arrived, like she did Mardi.

She handed the first glass to me, and I took an experimental sip. Unsurprisingly, it was delicious—herbal and cooling, becoming warmer as it hit my stomach. It pays to have an aunt who's a world-class mixologist with a sideline in magic potions, even if she gives all her clothes to my sister.

I sniffed at the glass. "Is that elderflower?"

"Nice nose, Molls," Freya said. "I infused the Pimm's with it a few days ago. Gives it a nice mellow finish."

"It's fantastic," I said, taking a longer sip. Then, glancing at Mardi, I added as innocently as I could, "So tell me more about Janet Steele. Where did you guys meet?"

Like Mardi, I had noticed the looks they had exchanged earlier. Freya glanced over at Ingrid, whose frown had gone even deeper. Then she turned back to me, an awkward smile on her face, before her eyes drifted to the TV.

"Whoa, who's the weirdo in her player's box?" Freya asked.

I turned to see the camera focused on a twentysomething guy with pale skin that seemed even whiter next to his jet-black hair, which was parted in the middle and fell past his shoulders like Jared Leto used to wear it. His most striking feature, however, was a Fu Manchu mustache that fell a good three inches past his chin.

A name and caption appeared on the screen below him:

IVAN
J STEELE HITTING PARTNER

I've seen Ivan a hundred times before, of course, but as I stared at him this time, I felt a strange chill. In fact, I've always thought he was a little creepy in a way that reminded me of vampires I've met—his hair too dark, his skin too pale, his eyes too, well, empty. But today was different. Today my dream popped into my head, so palpably that I could smell the stale salt water and feel it swirling icily around my ankles. As I looked into Ivan's dark, empty eyes, I felt as though I was looking into the broken windows of Fair Haven.

"That's Ivan," I heard Mardi say, shaking me out of it. "Guess he doesn't have a last name."

"'Hitting partner.'" Freya giggled. "Is that a euphemism?"

I laughed, shaking off the last images of my dream. "Some people think so; some people think he's gay.

He's actually kind of a mystery. Even though he's been following Janet to every major tournament for the past two years, no one even knows his last name."

"Ooh, that is mysterious," Freya said, sending another significant look Ingrid's way. I was going to nudge her about Janet again when there was a loud *pop!* from the television, followed by an even louder grunt.

Freya whipped her head toward the TV, almost in relief. "Oh, look. It's starting."

I nodded, even though I was burning with curiosity, and turned to the television. Serena had served one of her trademark 120-mph bombs, but Janet had managed to get it back in play. Now the two were whacking the ball back and forth—two hard-core athletes, and they gave it everything they had. The ball was hurtling across the net, ricocheting from corner to corner, as first one woman and then the other chased down one seemingly ungettable shot after another. Finally, in a move that was half genius, half desperate, Serena walloped a backhand directly into Janet's body. Janet had rushed the net and barely had time to get her racket in front of her. The ball smashed into it and bounced out of the court nearly into the stands, while Serena let loose her trademark "Come on!"

"A twenty-six shot rally on the very first point," the announcer said in an awestruck voice. "If this is any indication of how the match is going to be, we're in for an afternoon of great tennis."

"'Great' is obviously a subjective term," Mardi

muttered. "Pass the Pimm's, please," she added, holding out her already-empty glass.

The announcer's words proved prophetic. For the next three hours, the two women belted bombs at each other. The third and final set went on for an hour and seventeen minutes, until Serena finally made a mistake and Janet fell to the ground in exhaustion and exultation.

"Yes!" someone screamed, and after a second, I realized it was me. I was on my feet and jumping up and down.

"What the Hell?" Mardi said, startling out of her seat. From the bleary-eyed expression on her face, she looked like she'd fallen asleep. Given how many Pimm's Cups she'd downed in the past three hours, I wouldn't have been surprised.

"She won, she won!" I yelled. "Janet won!"

"Okay, okay, settle down," Mardi said, sitting back in her chair. "It's just a tennis game, for crying out loud." She yawned and stretched. "Damn, Freya, those Pimm's Cups are strong. Knocked me right out."

"It's a *match*," I said, "and not just *any* match. It's the *French Open*, and Janet Steele just won it. She's on her way to being the first woman since Steffi Graf to win the Grand Slam!"

"Steffi who?" Mardi said.

I rolled my eyes.

"Hey," Ingrid said, "who wants some tea? I could use a little caffeine after all that alcohol."

"Yes, please!" Mardi said.

"Shhh! They're about to start the trophy presentation."

Serena accepted her runner-up trophy first. She was gracious in defeat, but you could tell she was pissed. That's what I love about Serena. She always keeps it classy, but she doesn't pretend she's happy about losing. "I'll see you at Wimbledon," she finished up, and though she was ostensibly speaking to the audience, it was pretty clear she was really calling out Janet.

"Ladies and gentleman," the announcer boomed, "your French Open women's champion, Janet Steele!"

Thunderous applause shook the stadium as Janet bounded onstage. Though she'd played a grueling three-hour-plus tennis match, she looked like she'd just stepped out of the salon. She'd pulled her long dark hair out of its braid during the commercial break, and it fell in cascading waves around the tight white jacket she'd zipped over the top part of her tennis dress to hide the sweat stains. Her smile was blinding, her skin flawless, and only the tiniest shine on the top of her lip gave any sign of all the effort she'd expended.

"Janet, you first won this tournament an amazing eighteen years ago," the announcer said, pausing to acknowledge the crowd's applause. "At the time, people were talking about you being one of the great champions of all time. But instead of defending your title, you left the game and disappeared for nearly two decades. But now you're back and playing the best tennis of your life. You won three slams last year, and you're halfway to a Grand Slam this year. Tell us what's going through your mind."

Janet waited for the applause to die down. It took nearly a minute, and she milked every second of it with that hundred-million-dollar smile.

"Oh, my God, it's amazing," she said when it was finally quiet enough for her to talk. Her Australian accent was sharp and sporty and not at all posh, which humanized her perfect looks. "I never thought I'd be standing here again after all these years. When I retired back in '97, I thought it was for good. But life has a way of surprising you, and I guess tennis wasn't done with me."

"Looking forward to Wimbledon next month, what kind of shape do you think you'll be in by then?"

Janet smiled and did a little twirl, letting her skirt flip up in the back, "I think I'm in pretty great shape right now." She laughed. The crowd roared with approval, and it was another minute before she could talk again.

"But seriously," she said, "I do have to watch my schedule now. I can't play week in and week out like I did when I was seventeen or eighteen. That's why I've decided to play a limited schedule between now and the US Open."

"But you'll play Wimbledon, of course?" the announcer asked.

In answer, Janet gave the camera her best "say what?" smirk. The audience went wild.

When the applause finally died down, she said, "I'll play Wimbledon definitely, but other than that, I'm going to spend most of the summer relaxing and training at a little house I bought on the East End of Long Island. My daughters are there, and I want to spend more time with them."

There was the sound of something hitting the floor. I realized it was my glass. Fortunately, it was empty, and the carpet kept it from breaking.

"Did she just say—" Mardi began.

"Shhh! She's still talking!" I shushed.

Actually, the announcer was talking. There was a stunned look on his face as he echoed Mardi's question. "Did you say—daughters?"

Janet's smile was beaming. "That's right. I have two gorgeous teenage daughters whom I haven't seen in far too long." She turned from the announcer and looked directly into the camera.

"Molly and Mardi Overbrook, Mummy's on her way. We're going to spend the summer together in the East End."

Just then, Ingrid came around the counter with a tray of tea.

"I made iced instead of hot," she said. "I hope that's—"

She broke off as she saw the stunned looks on all of our faces.

"Did I miss something?"

✳ 4 ✳

WOMANIZER, WOMANIZER

Mardi-Overbrook-Journal.docx

𝓜olly and I looked at each other in silence for what seemed like an eternity. Then we were both on our feet screaming.

"Our *mother*?" Molly screamed at Freya. "Janet Steele is OUR MOTHER?"

"Did you know?" I screamed at Ingrid. "Have you been hiding it from us all these years?"

Ingrid looked desperately at Freya, who suddenly found the top of her left thigh really interesting.

"WILL SOMEBODY PLEASE SAY SOMETHING?" Molly and I screamed at the same time.

Somebody did: Janet Steele.

"I'm really looking forward to getting to know my girls better this summer."

Suddenly, I felt a vibration in my pocket. I pulled my phone out and saw that my feeds were blowing up:

OMG UR MOM!!!!

JANET STEELE???? SRSLY????

DID U KNOW? Y DIDN'T U SAY SMTHNG?

AMAZEBALLS!!!! A-MAZE-BALLS!!!!

Molly had her phone out too, and judging from the way she kept scrolling down—and down, and down, and down—she was being bombarded with tweets, texts, IMs, and notifications from Instagram, Tumblr, Vine, Facebook, and Witchipoo, the by-invitation-only site for teenage witches, vampires, and other magical creatures.

Freya cleared her throat. "Well, I guess the secret's out."

"Freya, wait," Ingrid said. "It's not our place. Troy told us he would talk to the girls when the time was right."

"Daddy *knew*?" Molly said.

I looked over at my twin. Molly has a genius IQ, but sometimes she can be a little spacey.

"Yes, Molly," I said. "Dad knew who he had sex with eighteen years ago."

Molly rolled her eyes. "I *know* that, dummy. But she could've gotten pregnant and not told him."

I rolled my eyes back at her. "And then what? She mailed us to Dad after we were born?"

"Actually," Ingrid said, "she couldn't have kept it

secret. When one of our kind reproduces, we just . . . know."

"What, like a sixth sense or something?" I asked.

"In our case it's more like a sixteenth sense," Freya answered. "But yeah."

Molly was shaking her head, dumbfounded. "So Daddy knew that Janet Steele was our mom all this time and kept it from us?"

"Your dad had his reasons. Being the offspring of the god of thunder comes with a little baggage, you know."

Suddenly, my phone and Molly's rang at the same time.

"Speak of the devil," Molly said, holding her phone up.

A picture of Troy Overbrook—a.k.a. the god of thunder, a.k.a. Thor, a.k.a. our deep-in-the-doghouse dad—shone out from the screen. Molly had snapped the picture at an Italian restaurant one night when we'd gotten Dad a little drunk and dared him to stuff thirty breadsticks in his mouth.

The same picture was lit up on my screen as well. Even with his pale lips distended around what looked like a bundle of firewood, you could still see what a lady-killer he was.

Poor Janet, I thought. *She never stood a chance.*

"He must've conferenced us," I said. "Are you ready for this, sis?"

Molly smiled grimly. "The real question is: is Daddy ready?"

We both pressed our talk buttons at the same time.

"Girls!" Dad said jovially, as though he was calling to wish us happy birthday.

"Um, no," I said.

"Girls—"

"I think she means 'Hel no,'" Molly said.

"Girls—"

"As in, 'Hel no, you don't get to be all "girls!" right now.'"

"Girls—"

"As in, 'Hel no, you've got some *explaining* to do, Troy Overbrook.'"

"Girls—"

"Because if this is true, then it's the lowest, meanest, dirtiest trick you've ever pulled!" I went on. "And on your own *daughters* too."

"GIRLS!"

Dad's voice was so loud it hurt my ear, and I had to jerk the phone away from my head.

"Great Odin," I heard him sigh. "I feel like I've just been double-teamed!"

"Well, you deserve it," Molly said. "I can't believe you kept this from us!"

Dad didn't say anything for a moment. You could practically hear him thinking. "This really isn't the kind of thing you talk about on the phone," he said finally. "Especially not a cell phone. But I'm in a helicopter right now. It's taking me to the seaplane. I'll be in North Hampton soon. Can you wait till then?"

"No!" Molly said sharply.

"But I guess we'll have to," I added glumly. I have to admit, I was impressed that he'd chartered a helicopter and a seaplane to travel a hundred miles. Short of whipping out his hammer and flying—which we had no proof he could actually do—it really was the fastest way for him to get here.

"Okay, then. I'll see you shortly. And, girls," he added, "don't take this out on your aunts, please. They had nothing to do with this."

"Fat chance," Molly said even as the line went dead.

"Right?" I agreed. I turned to Freya and Ingrid. "Spill."

✳ 5 ✳

TELL IT LIKE IT IS

From the Diary of Molly Overbrook

*I*ngrid and Freya stared at each other for so long that I found myself wondering if they were just using telepathy to silently work out a plan. Witches were crafty like that. Then I realized they were just stalling.

"You guys—" I began.

"Okay, okay," Freya cut me off.

"Freya," Ingrid snapped in her worried-mother voice, "it's not our place."

"Troy's on his way here anyway. The secret's out. And it's not like we can tell them much anyway." Freya turned to us. "We don't know that much about Janet either."

"He basically told us nothing, just that she left when we were little," I said, "so I think maybe you know a *little* more than we do."

"So it's true?" Mardi said. "Janet Steele really is . . . our mother?"

Mardi paused before she said *our mother*, like having a mother was something she'd never considered before. And I felt the same way. We were curious, of course, but we'd lived our whole lives without her. Dad once called her a "giantess" (which made sense, now that I knew how tall she was), and Trent Gardiner had suggested to Mardi that our mother was one of the three Rhinemaidens, the guardians of the Rhinegold made famous in Wagner's *Ring* cycle. But when your long-gone mother is described as a fairy tale, it makes it harder to believe in her, not easier, and Mardi and I had long since concluded that we'd never know her. For years, I'd been telling myself that I didn't have any feelings for this woman whom I'd never met, but now, as I looked expectantly at Ingrid and Freya, I knew I'd been kidding myself. What can I say? Even goddesses need a mom.

"Well?" I prompted.

Finally, Ingrid sighed and slumped in defeat. "It's true. Janet Steele is your mother."

Mardi's whoop made the wineglasses rattle on their wire rack. We jumped up and threw our arms around each other and danced around the living room, heedless of Ingrid's beautiful antiques.

"I don't know if I'd get so excited," Freya said when we'd finally quieted down. "There's a reason Troy didn't want Janet in your life, after all."

"Wait, it was Troy who kept us from our mother?" I asked.

"He always said she abandoned us," Mardi threw in. "He was lying about that too?"

Ingrid frowned at Freya. "See, this is why I said we should wait till Troy gets here." She turned to us. "As Freya mentioned, Janet was a bit of a wild girl."

"She was so young when she had us," I said. "It makes sense that she was still figuring things out." I grinned. "So she was more than Dad could handle, huh?"

"In a matter of speaking," Freya said, shrugging.

"I thought we were done with the vague thing," Mardi said. "What did Mom do that was so bad that Dad had to cut her out of our lives?"

"See, that's the thing, Mardi," Ingrid said. "We don't know."

Ingrid is good at a lot of things, like gardening and baking and helping a couple conceive by intricately knotting together two pieces of their hair, but lying is not one of them. I stared her down until she had to look away. She only lasted about five seconds.

"Seriously?" I said. "'We don't know'? You expect us to believe that?"

"It's true," Freya insisted about as convincingly as Ingrid. "Troy never told us. But he made it seem pretty serious. Something to do with—"

She stopped short.

"To do with what?" I insisted.

"Don't torture us!" Mardi said.

Freya sighed helplessly.

"It had something to do with you girls."

"Well, duh," Mardi said sarcastically. "Care to be more specific?"

Now it was Ingrid's turn to sigh. "You were never supposed to be born."

"What?" Mardi and I both exclaimed.

Ingrid made a face like she'd rather be eating worms or walking on hot coals than talking to us about this.

"Normally when you're a god at Thor's level, you get to decide when and if you're going to have children. But Janet tricked him somehow. I don't think even he knows how she did it. If he does, he never told us."

I couldn't believe what I was hearing.

"Are you saying that our own *dad* didn't want us?"

"No, of course not, honey," Freya said. "Your dad loves you very much. You were just . . . unplanned, that's all."

Mardi looked at me. "Can you *believe* this? We're the result of some magical version of a condom breaking."

A little smirk flickered over her face, and despite myself, I chuckled.

"We're Mommy and Daddy's cosmic accidents," I said, getting up to go and grabbing my sweater.

"Don't say that!" Ingrid protested. "You two are practically miracles!"

"Yeah, well, these two *miracles* are gonna go confront their father and find out what's really going on. C'mon, Mardi."

"Way ahead of you," Mardi said, reaching for her leather jacket and her keys, and together we stormed out of the house.

Mardi followed me outside to her car, a vintage 1972 Ferrari convertible whose top was always down (Mardi had cast a rain-repelling hex over the vehicle, which shielded it from unexpected rainstorms). I opened the door and folded myself into the low-slung passenger's seat while Mardi hopped over the closed driver's side door like one of the Dukes of Hazzard and slid her feet beneath the steering wheel. A moment later, the car's old-fashioned engine growled to life and we were peeling out of Ingrid's driveway, a shower of pebbles spraying across her lawn.

"Mardi, come on!" I pleaded. "Just because you're mad at Ingrid doesn't mean you have to ruin her front yard."

Mardi grinned over at me. "Oh, don't be such a Goody Two-shoes. This is just the way I drive."

She shifted—up or down, I have no idea; driving is something I prefer to leave to chauffeurs—and the car squealed onto the asphalt. My head slammed back into the headrest as Mardi accelerated. Fortunately her weather hex deflected most of the wind as well, so all my hair did was bounce a little in the breeze. Believe me when I tell you that there's no crisis so dire that you have to turn an eighty-dollar blowout into a rat's nest.

"What is it with gods and secrets?" I screamed, since

the engine in my sister's vintage automobile didn't come with a muffler. "I mean, what's the point in being *immortal* if you have to hide everything like a common crook?"

"I know," Mardi shouted back. "Sometimes I feel like we're on a cosmic reality show, and somewhere just out of view there's a director giving instructions for everyone to mess with the Overbrook girls—who, apparently, shouldn't even exist anyway."

I shuddered. "What do you think Ingrid meant by that?"

"Who knows? Maybe nothing—she is the goddess of the hearth, after all. She takes things like sex and birth *way* too seriously."

"True. But whatever went down when we were born had to have been pretty serious. I mean, Troy can be a little authoritarian sometimes, but there's no way he would have kept our mother from us unless she'd done something terrible."

Mardi nodded. "Do you think she's really mortal? Or do you think maybe she's like us?"

"She has to be mortal, right? I mean, if nothing else, there's the tennis thing. The Council's super strict when it comes to supernatural beings using their powers to make money. No sports, no gambling, no spell casting during business deals—nothing that would draw attention to our kind and risk another Inquisition or witch hunt. But . . . how could a mortal trick Thor into getting her pregnant?"

Mardi shrugged. "It wouldn't be the first time humans have tricked our kind. Immortality doesn't seem to make the gods any smarter than humans, after all. Just longer-living. But, hey, now that I think about it, Trent said once that she was a Rhinemaiden. Aren't they immortal?"

"I don't think so. I think they're specially selected humans, like the Romans' vestal virgins."

"But why use mortals to guard something so precious?" Mardi countered. "Wouldn't you want the most powerful god you could get?"

"Gods can't do everything, or we'd have done away with humans centuries ago. Maybe guarding the Rhinegold is one of those tasks only humans can do."

"Gods, I hate this!" Mardi said, slamming her fist on the steering wheel and sounding the horn, which sent a flock of seagulls squawking into the sky. "Troy better have some answers, or he's going to discover just what it means to have the goddess of rage as his daughter."

"You know it," I said, grabbing her hand. Mardi squeezed my fingers tightly and flashed me a look of determination, then pressed the accelerator all the way to the floor.

✳ 6 ✳

MY HUMPS

Mardi-Overbrook-Journal.docx

I squealed into the lot by the dock at a good sixty miles an hour and fishtailed into a parking space. It was a move I couldn't have pulled off in a hundred years if I'd actually been *trying* to do it, but the truth is I was so distracted by all the thoughts running through my head that I wasn't really paying attention. Fortunately I have what we like to call "witch's insurance," which is to say: Troy had only let me have a car on the condition that he be allowed to put a safety shield on it, which made it almost impossible for me to get into an accident.

I glanced over at Molly, who was gripping the edges of her seat.

"Sorry 'bout that, Moll," I said with a big smile.

"This is why I ride in limos with professional drivers,"

Molly said, slowly relaxing in her seat. She folded the visor down, checked her hair in the mirror—it was perfect as usual, thanks to the hex, of course—then climbed out of the car. We walked across the parking lot toward the pier where the seaplanes docked.

"It's just past five," I said, glancing at my watch. "Dad called around four-thirty, so he should be here any minute."

We scanned the sky to the west, and sure enough, within a few seconds, a tiny speck appeared. It grew rapidly larger, taking on the familiar shape of the seaplane from Manhattan, with its fat yellow pontoons hanging below the wings like a pair of bananas.

"Also?" Molly said. "Can we talk about how Dad always takes the seaplane when he makes us take a car or the train?"

"I know, totally unfair," I agreed. "Although I'd go crazy out here without my car. I don't know how you can stand it."

"I manage to get around just fine," Molly said. "Besides, North Hampton is about half the size of Central Park. You can get around on a bicycle."

I couldn't help but laugh.

"What? I totally rode Ingrid's bike all over town last summer!" Molly protested. "But thank Odin we're goddesses and don't have to work out. Spandex and *headbands* don't appeal to me *at all*." She paused for a moment. Then: "Speaking of working up a sweat . . ."

I knew just what she was talking about, but I

pretended not to. When it was clear I wasn't going to say anything, she prompted, "You've been living in Fair Haven for almost two weeks now. Have you and Trent . . . ?"

I sighed heavily.

"What?" Molly said, turning away from the plane, which was only a mile or two away. "Really? You haven't slept with him? Interesting . . . "

"I mean, I really like him, you know, especially since the end of last summer, after we figured out Trent was the real Trystan Gardiner, and Tris was just—"

"Do NOT remind me," Molly cut me off. "The fact that I made out with that troll is enough to make me heave—even if he did look like a member of One Direction when we were doing the making out."

"Trent doesn't look like a member of One Direction! He's much more Bastille or MGMT, hello."

"Oh, don't be such a snob." Molly laughed. "Looking like Harry Styles isn't exactly the worst thing in the world."

"Okay, first of all, if he looks like anyone from 1D, it's Louis. And second, I'm not a snob. I just don't listen to exactly the same thing as every other seventeen-year-old girl in the world!"

"Sure. Like MGMT or Bastille are *so* radical. Like no one's ever heard of them except Mardi Overbrook and six other super-cool people."

I opened my mouth to protest but thought better of it. This was hardly the time or place to get into a stupid sister fight—not when our dad was about sixty seconds away from landing and explaining the origin of, well, *us*. But more important, I knew that Molly wasn't actually upset about whether Trent looked more like a boy bander or an indie rocker. What upset her was that she'd been duped by an evil dude who came close to stealing our Rhinegold and driving a permanent wedge between us. Ever since we'd managed to chase off Alberich, Molly had been extremely touchy on the subject of boys. In fact, she had deliberately not gone out on a date in *one whole year*. For the average teenage girl, that's like the Siberia of romance. No, it's worse than that. It's the North Korea of romance. But for a girl like my twin sister, who (if I do say so myself) is not only gorgeous but rich, smart, and, oh yeah, *a goddess*, it must be even worse. Seriously, I don't think a day goes by that Molly isn't hit on by some moonstruck Romeo, but she's turned down every single one of them since she discovered that the last boy she'd said yes to was actually a dark elf, and practically a troll. And not an Internet one at that. Like, a *real* troll.

"So," I said, figuring I only had to keep the conversation going for another minute or two before Dad's plane landed, "did you hear that Sal's son is coming to stay on the East End for the summer?"

Sal McLaughlin owned the North Inn, the übercool dive bar/celebrity hot spot where Freya tended bar.

"I might've heard something about that," Molly said in a casual kind of way.

"His name's Rocco," I continued. "Freya told me Sal's ex-wife was Italian, as in Italian-from-Italy. I figured there couldn't be too many Rocco McLaughlins out there, so I looked him up online."

"And?" Molly said, still trying to sound like she wasn't interested, but I could tell her curiosity was piqued.

I held up my phone, where I'd already pulled up Rocco's picture, after first swiping past about two hundred more IMs and alerts about Janet Steele. Seriously, if this kept up, I was going to have to get a new number. A new name even.

"He goes by Rocky," I said. "He just finished his freshman year at Dartmouth."

"Smarty-pants, huh," Molly said, taking a quick glance at my phone. A moment later, however, her eyes strayed back, and this time they stayed. "Huh," she said again, but this time with a totally different inflection.

Based on his looks, Rocky McLaughlin had inherited long inky-black locks and a smooth olive complexion from his Italian mother. From his Irish dad, he'd gotten a pair of piercing pale blue eyes and thin but wide and very pink lips. He had a lean, angular face with high cheekbones and a strong chin with a pronounced dimple. I quickly swiped to the next one, which showed him in just a pair of board shorts, so Molly could see his perfect chest and rippling abs.

"Huh," Molly repeated, except this time she didn't try to hide the fact that she was intrigued. "Well, he doesn't suck to look at, does he?"

"Not. At. All." I had a boyfriend, but there was no harm in looking, was there?

Molly glanced at my phone one more time. "We might have to return to this subject later," she said in her faux-aloof voice. She nodded toward the sky. "Dad's plane is landing. We'd better focus."

"Right," I said, tucking my phone into my pocket. We were at the shore end of the dock, and we started walking out toward the water.

"Looks like a pretty empty flight," Molly said.

"Yeah," I agreed. "Just Dad and the flight attendant and—oh, my gods!"

A dark shape appeared in the water just under Dad's plane, which was only a few feet above the surface of the Sound. It must've been twice as big as a city bus, and as Molly and I watched, horrified, it rose up out of the water like a submarine, torrents of water streaming off its curved shell.

"Is that a . . . *whale*?" Molly screamed.

I was pretty sure it *was* a whale—a humpback whale—but before I could answer, the tip of one of the pontoons on the bottom of Dad's plane caught on its massive steel-gray back. If there was any doubt that the whale's appearance wasn't a coincidence, it disappeared when the leviathan lifted its massive tail out of the water and used it to slap the plane out of the air. The plane slammed propeller-first into the whale's back, then rolled nose over tail, collapsing like a crushed can as it went. As it neared the front of the plane, the whale rolled to its side, and a collosal pectoral fin came out of the water, smashing the plane—and its occupants—in a dozen different directions.

I was about to scream, but I was distracted by a large smooth mound near the front of the whale, a brownish-gray circle with a darker circle inside it. It was only when it blinked that I realized it was the whale's eye. The whale rolled completely over and the eye was gone, but even so, I couldn't shake the thought that the eye had been staring at me. The pectoral fin, which must've been a dozen feet long, slapped the surface of the bay, sending a plume of water up into the air.

Through the mist, I could see things flying everywhere—pieces of the fuselage, seats, suitcases, and, worst of all, several spindly shapes that could have only been people. Before I knew it, I was running down the dock.

"Mardi!" Molly screamed, running beside me. "What are you doing?"

"We've got to save them!" I yelled back.

"But the water's freezing! We need to cast some kind of spell."

This was true. Though it was a balmy seventy-five degrees on land, the cool water of the Sound barely tipped the scales at fifty degrees. At that temperature, hypothermia could set in before we reached anyone— and while our souls are immortal, our bodies are made of pretty much the same flesh and blood as everyone else's.

In other words, there was a very real chance that we could die trying to save our father. But we had to do something.

"There's no time for magic!" I screamed even as I kicked my shoes off. "It's Dad!"

I guess on some level Molly felt this too. After all, she was running down the dock every bit as fast as I was, and she'd already lost her shoes. As I launched myself off the dock, I saw a flash of white out of the corner of my eye, and realized she was right behind me.

Then the freezing water closed over me, and all thoughts of Molly or Dad or anything else vanished from my brain. The only thing I wanted to do was get out. I began kicking desperately, frantically, trying to propel myself back out of the water.

But as soon as my head cleared the air, I saw pieces of the airplane fuselage all around me, and remembered why we were there. The water was freezing, but I told myself to ignore it. Dad was in here somewhere. I had to find him.

Just then, Molly's head broke the surface. Her dark hair was plastered across her face and her lips had already gone blue and quivery. There was no hiding the look of determination in her eyes.

"I saw someone that way," she said, pointing to her left. "And I think there's someone over there too." She pointed right, over my shoulder. And then, arcing to her left, she was under again.

I twisted to the right and kicked myself under. The

cold water squeezed me like a giant hand, as if it was trying to crush my bones, but I put it out of my mind, swimming as hard and fast as I could. As I went down, the pressure only grew more intense; my lungs were on fire even as my skin was turning to ice.

And then I saw it. A hand, waving in the current.

For one ghastly second, I thought it had been severed from its body, but then my eyes adjusted to the gloom and I saw the rest of the body dangling below it. I realized the hand wasn't waving in the current—it was actually trying to swim. I squinted, trying to make out the face.

It was Dad!

I kicked harder, all thoughts of exhaustion suddenly gone. In three strokes, I was there. Dad's fingers curled around mine in a vise grip, but even as they did, I noticed his other arm, his left, hanging limply at his side, along with both of his legs. But he was awake and even smiling, albeit grimly. With a nod of his chin, he indicated where we had to go:

Up!

I began frog kicking, doing my best not to hit Dad in the face. His hand clung to mine. The thought of our dad, the god of thunder, in a wheelchair was almost too much to bear.

I told myself not to think such thoughts—not now, when we were still twenty feet below the surface of the water and my lungs were burning and my legs were aching and Dad was hanging off me like a two-hundred-pound anchor. *Just kick, Mardi,* I told myself. *Kick. Kick. KICK!*

Suddenly, my head burst above the waves, and a second later, Dad's broke through. For a moment, all we could do was breathe, inhaling big ragged breaths of air. Then, faintly, I heard voices.

"There's someone there!"

I looked over my shoulder and saw a man on the dock pointing to me. Then a second man appeared, holding a life preserver. As he tossed it to me, I saw that it was dangling a line.

"Catch!"

The man's aim was good. The preserver landed less than a foot from me, and I grabbed onto it with the hand that wasn't holding Dad. As soon as I had it, I felt the rope tug as the two men began hauling us to shore. Only then did I turn my attention to Dad.

"Are you okay? Dad, can you hear me?"

His eyes had closed, but after a long moment, they fluttered open. He smiled at me weakly.

"I saw you girls on the dock," he said, and though his voice was faint, you could hear the mischief in it.

"Dad, a whale came up underneath your plane! That was what crashed it. A *whale.* That—I mean, that has to be magic, right? Was someone trying to kill you?"

Dad's eyes closed again but not before I could see a flicker of recognition in them.

"Who would try to kill you, Dad? Why?"

"Later," Dad replied, without opening his eyes.

But then they sprang open. "Molly!" he exclaimed. "Where's your sister?"

My head whipped back and forth as I scanned the dark water, but all I saw were pieces of the plane's fuselage scattered over the rippling waves like abandoned beach toys. No matter where I looked, there was no sign of Molly.

* 7 *

DIVER DOWN

From the Diary of Molly Overbrook

As the water closed over my head, I kicked in the opposite direction from Mardi toward the dark shape I'd glimpsed a moment ago. I prayed it was Dad. I prayed he was okay.

Did Mardi tell you about the whale's eye? We talked about it later—how we were sure it was staring at us. There's something especially creepy about an eye the size of your head staring you down. You get the feeling that it's looking right into your brain, reading your thoughts, daring you to do something stupid, like jump in the water and try to save your dad. If it had been anyone else, I don't think I would've had the guts. But it was Dad. We had to do it.

It seemed to take forever before I saw the dark shape I'd seen before: it was falling quickly. I thought bodies were supposed to float? Something about the air in the lungs and the stomach? But then, as I got closer, I saw why it was falling so fast: some kind of cable had coiled around one of the legs, and hanging off the opposite end was the twisted metal framework of a chair.

It wasn't Dad. It was a young woman, only five or six years older than me. Probably the flight attendant, judging from the plain button-down shirt and khakis she was wearing. Her eyes were closed and she wasn't moving, but she couldn't have been in the water for even a minute.

There's still time, I told myself. *I can save her.*

I kicked over to her and grabbed at the cable. It was stiff and heavy, and no matter how much I pulled and twisted, I couldn't get it to unwind from her leg, and all the while I felt it pulling us even farther from the surface.

Damn it! I screamed mentally. *Let go!*

But the cable refused to budge, and so, steeling myself, I grabbed the woman and pulled her to my chest and began kicking for the surface. I could feel the chair hanging off her leg, pulling me down, and for a while, it didn't seem like we were moving. But then momentum finally built, and we began to inch toward the surface. I swam harder and pushed through the water with my free hand.

I looked down at the woman's face. Her eyes were closed but her mouth was gently open, and her loose jaw waved slightly in the current. *Hold on,* I willed her. *We're almost there.*

But that wasn't really true. The surface was still ten feet away, but the chair was so heavy and my legs so tired that we were hardly moving at all. It took every ounce of resolve not to let her go and drag myself to the surface. I kicked, and kicked, and kicked—

—and suddenly I broke through the surface. A strange gasping screaming sound burst from my lungs as I tried to catch my breath. The flight attendant's head sagged backward in the water, and I had to hold it up to keep her from slipping under again. Then I realized it wasn't just her head. It was her whole body. It was both of us, being dragged back down by the weight of that chair.

I tried to kick with my legs, but there was nothing left. They barely moved in the water below me. I was slipping under too. In desperation, I started flailing around with my free arm. My hand smacked against something, and I grabbed it and hung on for dear life. Whatever it was, it floated, and it was enough to keep me and the flight attendant above water. I figured it had to be part of the plane.

In fact, I soon realized it was a big part. Like, half the fuselage. We'd actually come up inside it, I saw now. It tented over us like a giant eggshell.

At first, I was relieved because its buoyancy was holding us up. But very quickly I realized that it was also shielding us from the shore, whichever way it was, and whatever searchers might've joined Mardi and me. I would have to dive under and pull the flight attendant along with me if I wanted someone to find us. And I knew, just knew, I didn't have the strength for that.

"Help!" I yelled, my voice echoing back at me off the warped shell of the plane. "Help! We're over here!"

But I heard nothing in reply.

I looked down at the flight attendant. Her lips and skin had a blue pallor, either because of the cold or because she hadn't taken a breath in a good two minutes. I had taken a mandatory CPR class at school, but I couldn't even do that because of our situation. All I could do was stare helplessly into her face and watch her die.

"No!" I yelled.

And then it came to me: Joanna! Ingrid and Freya's mother. Something had happened to her about ten years ago that caused her to lose her earthly body, but her spirit still hovered over the East End, protecting it and lending aid to her family. She had even once saved a boy who drowned. I'd been there. I watched him come back to life with my own two eyes.

"Joanna Beauchamp!" I called. "Great goddess Skadi! I don't know if you're my grandmother or my aunt or my sister, but whatever you are, I call on you in the name of our family! Do not let this mortal die! Please! I beg you!"

When Ingrid and Freya had called on their mother that day, there had been a bolt of lightning that pierced the water, and a moment later, the drowned boy had awakened. I braced myself for the electrical current— we had been on a boat last time, and I didn't know if I should expect a shock. I didn't know if I could even survive it.

But as it turned out, I didn't need to brace myself for anything because nothing happened.

"Joanna!" I pleaded with the empty sky. "Please! Save her! She shouldn't have to die because someone was trying to kill Thor!"

Still nothing happened. Nothing except the swirl of the freezing water, numbing my limbs.

I don't know how much later it was before someone found us. Ten minutes? An hour? I couldn't tell you. I barely remember someone prying my fingers off the fuselage, uncurling my arm from the flight attendant's body and hauling us into a dinghy.

"It's okay," someone said to me. "We've got her now."

But I knew they didn't have her. She was dead. She had died in my arms.

* 8 *

MODERN GIRLS AND OLD-FASHIONED MEN

Mardi-Overbrook-Journal.docx

So who's the Norse god of the sea anyway? Who's our version of Poseidon, or what's the Roman guy's name, Neptune?"

"Well, there's Norman, of course. Ingrid and Freya's father. But he's in Niflheim now."

"The Land of the Dead."

Dad nodded. "And then there's Aegir," he said, chuckling, then quickly switching to a groan. "I have to stop laughing. The ribs are still tender."

Dad's ribs were the least of the problem. It turned out the crash had, like, *shattered* his pelvis. It was in six or seven pieces, which was why his legs had just hung there when I pulled him out of the ocean two days prior. For a mortal, such a wound would have been catastrophic—he probably would've never walked normally again, and it was a miracle his spinal cord hadn't been injured. Even for a god trapped in Midgard, it was still serious. Because of the risk of internal bleeding, Molly and I had had no choice but to let the ambulance take him to the hospital, where the doctors had done a whole series of X-rays. In addition to his broken pelvis, there were fractures in his left arm and left femur. I guess that was the side the plane had come down on. On top of all that, he also had a pretty serious concussion.

Left to nature, the injuries could have easily taken a year to heal, maybe more, and like I said, there was no guarantee that he would have fully recovered. Ingrid had been forced to whip up a fairly strong magical potion, dragging out her mother's ancient spell books to find one that she thought would work, then hopping on the Internet to get all the things she needed. (Apparently, there are places out in the world that'll FedEx the wings of a hundred Atlas moths—Ingrid only needed the dust, but she had to scrape it off herself—and a vial of venom from the Egyptian cobra, which, FYI, is the snake Cleopatra used to commit suicide.) It took almost two days to gather everything and make the potion.

Dad spent most of that time looped out of his mind on morphine, his entire middle from his sternum to his thighs encased in a plaster cast. Ouch. If Dad had been in his immortal Aesir body, the potion would have healed him completely, but because he was in a mortal body (his seventh, it turned out), the potion could only speed up the process so that what would have taken a year to heal would probably end up taking about a month. Freya had to bewitch the doctor to cut the cast off him, and after that, she and Ingrid administered a forgetting spell to every single person who worked in the hospital so they'd have no memory of how serious Dad's injuries were. That kind of thing is of course totally against Council rules, but it was that or have forty people talking about how Troy Overbrook broke his pelvis at the end of May and was back on the tennis courts by July. The Council likes that kind of talk even less than they like it when magic is used on mortals, so the aunts figured it was worth risking censure.

Finally, we brought Dad back to Ingrid's to finish his recuperation. Like I said, he was probably still going to be down for three or four more weeks, and because Ingrid's potion basically made his metabolism run ten times faster than normal, he was exhausted all the time. Exhausted but starving—Ingrid and her housekeeper were kept busy making him coconut-oil-goji-berry-bee-pollen-whey-powder-flaxseed-wheat-grass-kefir smoothies. (Kefir, by the way, is fermented goat's milk, and the smoothies tasted pretty much exactly like a barn smells.) But Dad, who's much more of a steak-with-a-side-of-steak kind of guy, couldn't seem to get enough of them. He was sipping on one while he rested in Jo's bedroom, which had only that winter been equipped with a full-sized bed. Molly had helped her decorate, so the room was suffused with what can only be described as an *excessive* amount of pink satin and white lace, but it made for some good jokes at Dad's expense. (I have to admit that I took a sadistic pleasure in making Dad squirm. It's rare that you get to turn the tables on your parent when he's a mere mortal, but when your dad is the god of thunder, you have to take every chance you get.)

As you can imagine, all the magic and smoothie making had kept us pretty busy, but once Dad was well on his way to recovery, I couldn't put off my questions any longer. I started with the whale because, well, *a whale tried to kill my dad*. I had to know if he thought it was on purpose. If he had any idea who was behind it.

"Does Aegir rule the sea animals?" I asked.

Another chuckle from Dad, followed by another groan. "What, like Aquaman?" He paused to take a sip of his greenish-grayish stink drink. "I don't really know. I assume he has some kind of influence, but if you're thinking Aegir sent that whale to kill me, you can set your mind at ease. Aegir and I go way back. We once threw a party that was the kind of party people wrote epic poems about."

"Kind of like Truman Capote's masked ball? Or Diddy's end-of-summer white party in East Hampton?"

"Ha!" Dad said, then grabbed his ribs. "No, it was more like the Norse version of a rave. There was this cauldron—you wouldn't believe what Tyr and I had to go through to get it. All I can tell you is that we pissed off a couple of giants." A faraway look came over Dad's face as he remembered the good old days when the gods took whatever they wanted and settled their disputes with swords. "It was the size of a hot tub. Much beer was made in it. Much beer was drunk from it. As I recall, Odin even ended up swimming in it." He shook his head at the memory. "Parents—even gods—should know better than to get naked in front of their kids."

Having never met my grandfather, I was forced to imagine Anthony Hopkins from the Thor movies swimming in a hot tub full of beer. It was an amusing image, although I wondered if Dad was maybe stretching the truth a little.

"Trent used to throw parties with you?" I asked. Sometimes I forgot that my seventeen-year-old boyfriend was also the two-thousand-year-old Norse god of war, and that he'd run around having adventures with my dad for centuries upon centuries before I was even born.

"Why do you think I don't trust him alone with you?" Dad said with a grimace that was only half ironic.

I blushed. "Let's not talk about Trent right now. We were talking about Aegir. You're one hundred percent sure he wouldn't try to kill you?"

Dad nodded, then took another sip of his smoothie.

"Positively. Aside from the fact that we're united in our mutual hatred of Loki, Aegir's been stuck in Utgard since the destruction of the bridge."

I fingered the tattoo on my neck, which commemorated the lost rainbow bridge.

"Is Aegir a giant?"

Dad nodded. "Although technically we're all the same species, you know. Every one of us, even the giants. Whatever the celestial version of DNA is, we all have the same kind. There's no more difference between us than there is between a Norwegian and a Russian or a Nigerian."

"But in all the drawings I've ever seen, giants are, like, twelve feet tall. How can we be related to them?"

Dad nodded again. "Some were a lot taller than that. But look at a Saint Bernard and a Chihuahua. Their DNA is virtually identical. Besides, it's not appearances that divide people—skin color, hair texture, height, things like that. It's the *ideas* people have about appearances. Prejudice isn't just a problem here in Midgard— it's rampant throughout the nine worlds, including Asgard."

"What do you mean?"

"When my father led the Aesir in their revolt against the Jotun, he and Frigg, your grandmother, chose a new form for us, one that more closely resembled the humans of Midgard, because they had already developed a special relationship with them. A little shorter, a little less hair on the shoulders and the top of the feet. As the centuries went on, they started to talk as though we'd always looked the way we do now—as though the Aesir and Vanir really were different species from the

Jotun and the elves and dwarfs. But take my word for it, there's giant blood in your veins, my sweet."

"If Odin led a revolt against the Jotun, how were you friends with Aegir?"

"In the same way the United States and England are allies. Once time passes and tempers cool, you come to realize you have more similarities than differences. Oh, some Jotun definitely held a grudge, as did some Aesir for that matter. Like any other society, it comes down to individuals. Aegir was definitely one of the good giants. I counted some Jotun as my closest friends back in the old days." A far-off look came into his eyes. "Some were very close indeed," he said longingly.

I thought about the stories I'd heard concerning our mother—that she was a giant too. And even though Janet Steele looked human, I couldn't help but wonder if that's who he was thinking about.

"We, um . . ."

I stopped short. Now that I was so close to getting real information about my mother, I found it hard to bring up the subject. Part of the problem was that Molly should have been there with me. It seemed strange—wrong—that I would learn something about our origin without her.

But ever since we'd pulled Molly out of the water, still clutching the lifeless body of that flight attendant, she'd avoided the entire family. She visited the hospital while Dad was there, but she sat apart from us in the waiting room and refused to talk to anyone, and if you actually tried to touch her, she sent out waves of negative energy so intense that cell phones and TVs would go on the fritz, randomly dialing numbers or changing channels. We were afraid that she might short out somebody's life support machine or something, so we had no choice but to leave her alone.

It hadn't gotten better since we'd brought Dad home. Molly had moved out of her guest bedroom and into Ingrid's gardening studio in the backyard. We only saw her when she came in to get food or take a bath. Still, I figured if she was taking the time to wash and comb her hair that things couldn't be too bad, and she just needed time. But this was an important conversation. My sister should have been there with us.

Dad must have sensed the struggle that was going on in me. He put his hand on mine and squeezed, as if he was the one comforting me. "Mardi? Did you want to ask me something?"

I looked at the open door, as if Molly might appear there, but the only thing that came through was the sound of the television downstairs, where Henry and Jo were playing the latest version of Zelda. I turned back to Dad.

"So Janet Steele—she's our mom, right?" I tried not to hold my breath, and watched Dad intently.

He nodded and tried not to squirm.

"And I was just going to ask if . . . I mean, there are legends. That Thor's children were born of a giantess. And so I was wondering if Janet Steele . . . ?"

Somehow I couldn't bring myself to voice the question *Is our mom a giantess?* It just sounded too weird.

To my surprise, Dad laughed again and kept on laughing despite the obvious pain it caused him.

"Janet? A giantess?" He reached for his drink and took a long pull. "By Odin, that *is* funny. I mean, she is six foot one, so I can see you might think that. But no, she's as human as they come. A special kind of human, but still human."

My ears immediately perked up when Dad said *special kind of human*, and I felt my heart start to thud in my chest.

"What do you mean, special?" I said, barely able to control my voice.

To my surprise, Dad frowned.

"I'm sorry, this brings up one of the less noble aspects of our history. But I think you're old enough to hear about it now." He took another swig of his smelly smoothie, then continued:

"When the bridge was first destroyed, and those of us who were in Midgard realized we were trapped here for all of eternity, some people didn't take it so well. There have always been some of us who took the whole god thing a little too seriously, basically treating humans like slaves or pets. I guess some people were inspired by the vampires and their human familiars and they basically claimed entire families as their indentured servants—generation after generation raised to do nothing but serve the gods. Janet is descended from one of these families. Her ancestors were forced to serve Loki for several hundred years, until the Council formally abolished the practice after Salem."

As if he'd heard us talking, Fury, Molly's canine familiar, appeared in the doorway. Poor thing: Molly had been so distraught that she hadn't even taken her out to the gardening shed with her. Fury had been wandering the house for two days looking forlorn—forlorn and ridiculous, what with her shaved hindquarters contrasting with the glossy mane that fringed her face.

"Loki!" I couldn't help but exclaim, patting my lap to invite Fury up. She stared at me blankly, then wandered away, her buffed nails clicking on the bare floorboards. "Does that mean our mother is . . . evil?"

Another laugh from Dad. "Calm yourself, daughter. Janet's got a temper on her, but I think it has more to do with being raised in the Australian outback by a bunch of rough-and-tumble cowboys and opal miners. She'd heard stories of her family's history from her grandmother, but had no idea whether they were true or just something the old woman had made up to amuse her."

"Did she know who you were?"

Dad didn't say anything for a moment. His gaze went far away, and I could imagine him conjuring a mental image of when he first met our mother. Judging from the look on his face, however, it was far from the fairytale romance I would have hoped for.

Finally, he nodded. "I wasn't aware of it at first, but later on, I realized she'd known who I was all along."

Suddenly, I remembered Ingrid's comment from the other day, about how Molly and I were never supposed to have been born.

"Did she trick you? Into having kids, I mean."

Another long pause followed by another nod.

"In the old days, when Loki and some of the refugees from the nine worlds still had human familiars, the humans would try to seduce their gods in order to have children by them. As you and your sister and Jo all demonstrate, the offspring of a mortal and an immortal usually take after the immortal parent, and these children, who loved their human parent every bit as much as they loved their celestial one, would often cast longevity spells on their mortal parent to keep him or her alive. Such spells are incredibly difficult to cast—as I recall, one of the ingredients is a dragon scale, and another is the powdered fingernails of one of the undead guardians of Niflheim, which is the only one of the nine worlds those of us trapped in Midgard can still access."

"From the seam under Fair Haven, Trent's family's house, right?"

"That's right," Dad said. "Anyway, your mother had heard these stories, and I guess she got it into her head that she wanted to have a god's child. Specifically, this god's child."

"Hey, give her credit for good taste, right?"

Dad shrugged, but you could tell he was pleased. Modesty is not one of the godly virtues, and Thor was the godliest of them all when it came to loving himself.

Then he turned to me, a nostalgic smile on his face. "She was so beautiful, she didn't need that love potion she gave me."

"She charmed you?"

"Maybe." He winked. Dad was so bad. Growing up, Molly and I had met more Victoria's Secret models, pop princesses, and grade-B starlets than Leonardo DiCaprio and Drake put together.

"You really think she had access to magic?"

"Oh, yeah."

"How do you know?" I said defiantly.

"Well, honestly, because of you. You and Molly."

I stifled a gasp.

"You mean it's true? That we weren't supposed to be born!"

"It's a little more complicated than that."

"Dad!" I almost yelled. "Don't drag this out! I'm dying here."

He smiled and patted me on the knee. "You and your sister were always destined to be born. It's just that we always thought your mother would, in fact, be a Jotun. And . . ." Again his voice fell off.

"Dad! What?"

He grimaced. "It's just, well, we thought you were going to be, well . . . *boys*."

For a moment, I didn't say anything. In the huge silence that followed this surreal announcement, all you could hear was the beeps and whirrs of Jo and Henry's video game coming faintly up the stairs.

"Boys?" I said finally. Then again: "*Boys?*"

Before my dad could answer, the doorbell rang. Simultaneously, I felt a buzz in my pocket. I pulled out my phone and saw a text from Trent.

Ringing ur doorbell. U home?

I don't know why, but I jumped up.

"Mardi?"

"I'll be back!" I said quickly. "I just have to . . ." I didn't finish my sentence, just ran downstairs to answer the door, running right past Jo and Henry, who didn't look up from their game.

As I pulled open the door, I was all ready to confront Trent, a.k.a. Tyr, my dad's old party buddy, to find out if he'd known anything about how his girlfriend and her sister were supposed to have been born male, but the look on his face stopped me in my tracks. His jaw hung open slackly, and his eyes were wide with confusion.

"Trent?" I said, my own confusion overshadowed by concern for him. "What's wrong?"

He shook his head in bewilderment. "We just got thrown out."

"*What?*" I exclaimed. "From Fair Haven?" The house had been in the Gardiner family for hundreds of years.

He nodded dumbly.

"Your, um, mother bought our house, and she just kicked us out."

✳ 9 ✳

GONNA FLY NOW

From the Diary of Molly Overbrook

$\mathcal{H}$ere, Moll, drink this," Freya said to me, pushing a frothy brown concoction down the bar. "Looks like you need it."

I sniffed at the effervescing foam, inhaling whiffs of chai, cinnamon, honey, and something I couldn't place.

"Is that . . . nutmeg?"

"Close. It's called *shahi jeera*, also known as black cumin. An Indian spice. I infuse it in the rum. It's very centering."

I glanced at the clock. It was three in the afternoon, but I could use some "centering," and although I was usually a vodka girl, rum would do. I bent the tall straw toward me and sipped. The drink had a dark, tealike taste, and I could feel it as it slid all the way down my throat and then—magically, no doubt—spread out through my limbs, making me feel as if I was a bag whose air was being sucked out by a vacuum.

"Wow, that really is"—there was no other word for it—"centering." I took another sip, bigger this time. "Would you call that taste 'umami'?"

Freya laughed. "If you're a foodie, I guess. I prefer something like 'earthy.' Now, go slow," she admonished as I took another sip. "It's got two shots of 120-proof rum in there. It'll knock even a goddess on her butt if she's not careful."

I took another drink. After all, I was already sitting down.

For the next few minutes, Freya continued measuring out her powders, seeds, leaves, and tinctures for the evening shift while I nursed my drink. At first, the surface of my skin felt flushed even as my intestines seemed to be flowing with icy water. But then my skin cooled and my insides warmed up, as if I was an oven turned on full blast, but sitting outside on an iceberg. At one point, I exhaled a long sigh and was surprised when smoke didn't come out of my mouth.

"So," Freya said from down at the other end of the bar. "Want to talk about it?"

"I don't know how to describe it," I said glumly.

"I get it," Freya said. "He's your dad. It's scary to see him like this. I mean, whether he's Thor or Troy Overbrook, you've grown up thinking of him as this invincible figure, and now all of a sudden he looks almost human."

"What?" I asked, trying not to look too guilty. "No, I'm not worried about Dad, although that was really freaky what happened to him."

"Well, we still have to figure out where that whale came from. It's not Loki, since he's made his peace with us. And this has outer worlds magic written all over it. But if it's not your dad that's bothering you, then what is it?"

I shrugged. It felt silly to say it out loud. But I did anyway. "It's that flight attendant. The one who died in my arms."

Freya nodded sympathetically. "I'm so sorry. You know it wasn't your fault."

I shook my head. "It's hard to explain. It's not her death that's bothering me. It's . . . it's that I suddenly realized that I would never die."

For the first time, I was face-to-face with my immortality, and it was overwhelming. It had never bothered me before, but it did now. Our friends, our lovers would one day pass, but we would go on. I felt sickened. "Does it ever get any easier, watching them die?"

In true Freya fashion, she didn't even try to soften the blow. "No," she said bluntly. "But that's a good thing. If it got easier, it would mean that you were detaching yourself. Numbing your feelings. Life is precious. It should be celebrated while it's here and mourned after it's gone."

I was starting to think that Freya was less in aunt mode than in wise-bartender mode, dishing out the secrets of life with each drink. I could appreciate what she was saying, but it was still a lot for the middle of the afternoon. At the same time, I didn't want to leave. Freya and Ingrid were two of the few examples Mardi and I had to show us what it meant to be immortal—goddesses locked out of Asgard, our eternal home, witches here in Midgard, but restricted in the use of our powers, which, in our case, we barely knew the extent of.

I took another sip of my drink.

"I tried to save her," I said.

"You were amazing," Freya said. "You dove into fifty-degree water and dragged a grown woman—and the forty-pound chair she was attached to—up to the surface. I can't tell you how proud we are of you."

"But that's not all I did."

Freya looked up from her apothecary bottles. "You mean magic?"

"Not exactly. Not mine anyway. I called on Joanna."

Freya's eyes went wide. "You called my mom?"

Since this is a diary and I'm doing my best to tell it like it is, I have to admit that I didn't like the way Freya said *my* and left out me and Mardi. I mean, I know Joanna isn't our mom, but still. It was almost like she was saying Joanna was her property, not ours. Her family. Not ours.

"I remembered what you guys did on the boat last summer, with that little boy. I thought maybe she could do the same for that woman."

"Okay." Freya laughed a little, nervously. "Honestly, I'm a bit taken aback."

"I didn't know what else to do," I said, my voice as uneasy as Freya's.

"Honey, you can't just go calling on the goddess Skadi to pull a soul from Niflheim every time a mortal kicks the bucket. For one thing, death is a natural thing. It's part of the cycle—that soul has other things to do, in other realms, and it's not our job to get in the way. For another, Helda, Skadi's sister, is seriously territorial. Believe me when I tell you she does *not* give up her subjects easily."

I nodded glumly.

"I know that," I said, and I could hear the petulance in my voice. "But even so . . ."

"What?" Freya's voice wasn't hostile, but it wasn't nearly as sympathetic as it had been before.

"It shouldn't matter why I called on her. I'm a goddess, for Pete's sake. I'm the newest member of this family. This was the first time I've ever had to confront something like this, and Joanna should have been there for me like she was for you and Ingrid."

For a moment, Freya didn't say anything. Then she shook her head angrily. She began grabbing up her various bottles and beakers and vials and stowing them for the evening shift.

"Look, I know you're new at this. This is your very first incarnation, and in many ways, you're just a typical seventeen-year-old girl. But it's time to face up to who you are and what that means. You're a goddess, Molly, and your father is one of the most powerful gods of them all—one of the most loved, but also one of the most hated. And that means that from time to time you're going to get caught up in plots to kill him, imprison him, or otherwise get him out of the picture so that evil beings can do the evil things they like to do. And the plain truth is that sometimes humans get caught in the cross fire when the gods go after each other, and however sad it may seem, it's not our duty—or even our right—to save every individual life that gets snuffed out too early. Our job is to protect Midgard as a whole."

"Wow," I said, pushing Freya's drink away—a hollow gesture, since it was pretty much empty. "Thanks for the tough love, *Aunt* Freya." I stood up to leave.

"You can call it whatever you want," Freya said, still angrily putting things away. "Sometimes there's no point in sugarcoating the truth."

"It's not like I asked for the dose of reality. You were the one who slipped me the drink and started asking questions. Whatever," I said, ignoring her opened mouth. "I'm taking off. You can save your charms for your customers."

I stalked out of the bar. I'd have slammed the door behind me, but it had a spring-loaded hinge that kept it from banging, so I had to content myself with turning around and flashing Freya a dirty look instead. Then I pivoted on my heel and stormed out—

—and crashed right into the chest of a some guy heading into the bar.

"Whoa, there," he said, and I felt his hands on my arms, steadying me.

Stupid mortal, I thought, shrugging him off. I guess in my anger I must have magicked it up a little because he went flying back about ten feet and would've landed flat on his back if he hadn't been wearing a huge overstuffed backpack. Only then did I recognize who it was.

Rocco McLaughlin. Rocky. Let's just say that he was even cuter IRL than he was in his pictures. *Way* cuter.

"Holy crap," I said, running to him to help him. "I didn't see you. I'm sorry."

Rocky shook his head a little dazedly, and a fan of bangs swept off his face, revealing a pair of glowing blue eyes. He looked at the door, ten feet away, and then at me.

"Ever thought about playing football? That was some tackle."

"I'm so sorry," I said again, dusting off his shoulders, which weren't actually dusty. I offered him a hand, but he waved it away and stood up on his own. He patted himself clean, and then held a hand out to shake mine. His handshake was strong (and a little gritty). Most guys give girls these weak handshakes as though if they actually squeezed, their fingers might break. I guess Rocky knew better.

"I'm Rocky McLaughlin," he said, "and you are officially the first person I've met during my summer in purgatory, besides my cabdriver, I guess."

"McLaughlin, McLaughlin . . ." I repeated, as if I didn't know who he was. "Like Sal McLaughlin, the owner of the North Inn?" I jerked a finger at the sign behind me, as if I'd only just realized I was standing in front of it.

Rocky frowned at the mention of his dad's name, which surprised me.

"I'm his son," he said in a flat voice. "Although in name only."

"Oh, right!" I said, pretending to remember. "He's mentioned you a couple of times?" I added in a questioning voice, as if I wasn't sure.

"Really?" Rocky said doubtfully. "Because that'd be a couple more times than he's called me in the past eighteen years."

I must've made some kind of grimace because a guilty look flashed over Rocky's face.

"Sorry to dump on you. Sal and my mom were married for a hot minute in the late nineties. Just long enough to make me, and then they went their separate ways. I grew up with her. Sal left when I was a baby. And I'm pretty sure he would have preferred to remain ignorant."

"Oh, Sal's a great guy!" I protested. "I'm sure you two will get along." I pointed at his bag. "Judging from the size of that backpack, I take it you're staying for a while?"

"The whole summer." His voice didn't sound happy at all.

"C'mon, lighten up." I waved my hand, gesturing at the lush greenery, the scattered beach houses and the wide, cloudless blue sky, which felt like an extension of the ocean, just out of view behind the rolling dunes. "A summer at the beach. It can't be so bad."

"No, I guess you're right," Rocky said, though he didn't sound too convinced. "Anyway, I guess I should go in and tell him I'm here." He started toward the front door of the Inn.

An image of Freya popped into my head, standing behind the bar, whipping up her love potions. She was probably still annoyed from our conversation, and if there's one thing I know about Freya, it's how she likes to work off steam.

"The Inn doesn't open till five," I said quickly, stepping in front of Rocky to bar his path. "And Sal doesn't usually come in on weekdays till eight or nine, if at all."

Rocky peered around me, trying to get a glimpse through the window set in the door.

"But doesn't he live, like, upstairs or something?" Even as Rocky said that, he was looking at the roof of the one-story building for an imaginary second floor. "Around back maybe?"

"Um, no, this isn't a Victorian novel. The innkeeper doesn't live with his wife, six children, and three pigs in a barn out back." I laughed to take the sting out of my words. "Sal lives in a very comfortable beach house about a mile, um, yonder," I said, pointing in the distance. I knew where Sal lived, but only by sight.

Rocky looked doubtful, as if I might be trying to trick him. "1762 Dune Road," he said, looking down at his phone again.

"Yup, that's the Inn," I said, pointing to the battered brass numbers nailed to the shingles.

He sighed heavily and shifted the straps of his pack, which suddenly seemed to be biting into his shoulders.

"You wouldn't happen to know his home address?"

As he asked, it popped into my head: 409 Pfenning Road.

"Sorry, no idea," I said. "But if you want, I can walk you there. Like I said, it's only about a mile."

I wasn't sure, but I thought I saw a flicker of a smile cross his face.

"Okay," he said simply.

It was the nicest word I'd heard all day.

"You're lucky I'm wearing flats today, or you'd be on your own," I said as we started out, holding up a leg to show off my espadrilles. "So what made you decide to spend the summer on the East End anyway?"

Rocky sighed again.

"I didn't. Sal did."

There was a hint of warning in his voice—more than a hint—but I chose to ignore it. We had a mile to go, after all. And you know, nothing ventured, nothing gained.

"He thought it was time for some father-son bonding?"

"I guess so."

We trudged on another dozen steps in silence. I was beginning to think that talking was going to be even more painful than not talking.

"I wanted to stay at college this summer," Rocky said finally, "but Sal said he couldn't afford it plus tuition in the fall, so all things considered, I figured I'd better come here."

"Why not stay with your mom?"

We walked another dozen steps before Rocky answered.

"My mom died in March."

"Oh," I said hollowly. "I had no idea." In my head, I yelled at Mardi, who was the one who'd looked Rocky up on social media: *How could you miss that, sis?*

"Cancer," Rocky continued. "I knew she was sick, but she said it wasn't serious. Otherwise I'd never have gone to college in the first place. I would've spent her last months with her. In the end, when she finally told me what was going on, she said she'd kept it from me because she knew I'd lose my scholarship if I deferred for a year, and she was afraid I wouldn't be able to afford college without it. She was right about that anyway. Even after I sold the house, there was barely enough to pay off her medical bills."

"Gods," I said. "That's terrible. I'm so sorry."

"'Gods,'" he repeated with a little bit of a grin. "What are you, some kind of pagan?"

"Oh, you know, just covering all the bases." I laughed. "I'm really sorry about your mom," I said again.

"Yeah, some guys spend spring break in Ft. Lauderdale or the Caribbean. I spent it at my mother's bedside, watching her die. And you want to know the kicker?"

At this point, I was pretty sure I didn't, but since I'd opened the floodgates, I couldn't exactly refuse him.

"I lost my scholarship anyway. It was dependent on my GPA, and after I found out my mom was terminal, I kind of lost all interest in studying. Go figure."

"That really sucks. I'm sorry."

Rocky stopped suddenly, turning to me with a confounded stare. "I didn't mean to dump all that on you."

"It's okay," I said. "You can dump on Molly all you want." Ew. Did I really just say that?

He didn't say anything for a moment. Then: "Molly. Is that your name?"

With a start, I realized I hadn't properly introduced myself. "Molly Overbrook: offensive tackle, shoulder to cry on, and all-around tour guide, at your service."

"I read about you didn't I?" he said. "The girl who pulled the flight attendant out of the water? It was on BuzzFeed."

"That was me," I said. "I tried to save her . . ."

"It's not your fault she died. What you did was pretty freaking brave."

"It didn't *feel* brave," I said. "It felt like I didn't do enough. It felt like—" I cut myself off. There was no way to explain to this mortal I'd just met that it felt like the goddess Skadi, who just happened to be my grandmother/aunt/sister-in-law/cousin ten times re-moved, had turned her back on me when I needed her most.

"Man, it's hot," Rocky said after a minute. "And this bag is heavy. Hold up a sec." He stopped walking and dropped his bag to the ground. There were wide lines of sweat where the straps had cut across his shoulders, and when he turned, I could see his whole back was soaked. And with a single smooth motion, he stripped off the soaked T-shirt, revealing a six-pack and smooth hard chest plastered with sweat. His jeans hung well be-low his hips, exposing about two inches of boxer shorts.

It took all my strength to tear my eyes away, and while I tried not to stare, Rocky hoisted his backpack again, then tied his wet shirt on one of the many straps hanging from it.

"That's a little better," he said. "Onward, fearless leader."

We started walking again.

"So," he said after a moment. "Is it true what that woman said?"

My heart jumped in my chest.

"Is what true?" I said, trying to keep my voice light.

"Janet Steele? The tennis star? She's your mother?"

I gasped and smacked his upper arm, not too hard, but hard enough to leave a bit of a red mark. It was tense beneath its light film of sweat.

"You knew who I was the whole time!"

Rocky's face colored. "Well, not exactly."

"What do you mean, 'not exactly'?"

"When Sal told me I had to stay here this summer, I did a little looking around on social media to see who'd tagged things in the East End, and North Hampton specifically. You and your sister stood out."

"Are you saying that you didn't know if I was Molly or Mardi?" I asked.

He nodded sheepishly.

"But we're so different!"

"Um, you have pretty much the same face."

"That is SO not true! I can't believe you couldn't be bothered to remember which one of us doesn't get strange tattoos in highly visible places and wear torn clothes that haven't been in style since before she was born. I'm almost starting to regret my decision to walk you to Sal's."

Rocky chuckled. "I don't think Mardi's look is so out there—although she does look like she'd be a lot to handle."

"And you think I'm more, what? *Manageable?*"

"If I was ever stupid enough to think that, you have thoroughly disabused me of any such a notion."

"'Disabused'? Trying to show off your college vocabulary?"

The words came out harsher than I'd intended, and I found myself wondering if we were flirting or actually fighting. But the next thing out of Rocky's mouth told me exactly which side of the line we were on.

"What I'm *trying* to say is, I'm glad you're the sister I ran into first."

"You're—oh." I couldn't keep the smile off my face, so I turned and looked over my right shoulder, as if I found the dunes fascinating. I was trying to think what my next line should be. Like "I'm glad you ran into me too" or "Do you have a girlfriend at college?" or "Want to play strip poker?" Before I could make up my mind, however, the sounds of a roaring engine and screeching wheels made themselves heard over the faint wash of the surf.

"Wow," Rocky said. "Someone seriously needs to get a muffler. And learn to slow down."

I nodded but didn't say anything. It's not like I'm an expert on car engine noises or anything, but I was pretty sure whose car I was hearing. The roaring and screeching grew exponentially louder as the still-unseen car raced toward us.

"Sounds like he's coming right this way," Rocky said. "We'd better get off the road."

It's not a he, I wanted to say as Rocky took my hand and led me onto the sandy shoulder of the road. For one moment, I thought about squeezing tightly and pulling him into the dunes and hiding. Then Mardi's Ferrari shot over the crest of the nearest dune. It didn't actually leave the ground or anything, but it might as well have, it was going so fast.

"Holy flying Ferraris, Batman!" Rocky laughed, pulling me back a few feet farther. He opened his mouth to say something else, but whatever it was got lost in the squeal of brakes. I don't know how Mardi managed to stop the car going a thousand miles an hour in ten feet, but she did, right in front of me and Rocky.

The first thing I saw was Trent because the passenger side of the car was closest to us. Second was Mardi, looking at us with a half-amused, half-regretful expression as her eyes flitted between my face and Rocky's, and then down to our hands. That's when we both realized we were still holding hands, and we stepped apart simultaneously.

"Man, I am so sorry to have to do this," Mardi said, "but get in, Molly. We have to deal with something."

"I can't. I'm showing Rocky where Sal lives."

"Up two more dunes, take the first right. You'll see an old junkyard with a beaten-down old trailer in the middle of it. It's not a junkyard. It's Sal's house. 409 Pfenning Road. Now get in, Molls. This is serious."

I turned to Rocky. "You want us to give you a lift?"

Rocky smiled sympathetically. "There's not really a backseat in that thing. And your sister seems like she's in a hurry. I'll see you at the Inn sometime? Or the beach?"

"Beers or bikinis," I said as flirtatiously as I could. "Two of my favorite things." Rocky actually blushed.

I hopped over the edge of the car and squeezed myself into what Rocky had correctly identified as "not really a backseat," even if it was covered with creamy leather.

"Hey!" Trent protested. "You're getting sand all over me!"

"And this is the warrior who's supposed to save us at Ragnarok?" I smirked to Mardi. "We're all doomed." I turned to Rocky as Mardi gunned it.

"Watch out for Freya," I called. "She's incorrigible."

✳ *10* ✳

HOMEWARD BOUND

Mardi-Overbrook-Journal.docx

$\mathscr{I}$ glanced at Molly in the rearview as I sped toward Fair Haven. She was looking out the side of the car with a little smile on her face and her fingers were rubbing together slightly, as if she was remembering the feel of Rocky's hand in hers. I have to say, it was nice to see that smile after days of scowls. I thought about saying it out loud, but figured that would just make her frown again. Instead, I said:

"So that's Rocky McLaughlin, huh?"

Molly met my gaze in the mirror. Her eyes were guarded.

"I guess so."

When we were younger, Beyoncé released *I Am . . . Sasha Fierce.* Molly set her alarm for midnight, when the album went on sale on iTunes, so she could download it to her phone, and by the time everyone in the house woke up the next morning, she'd memorized the lyrics to every single song on the album. She listened to it for three days straight, once going so far as to cast a spell on this poor woman on the subway who tapped Molly on the shoulder and asked her to turn it down because the music was blasting out of her earbuds (Molly turned the woman's gum to glue, which sealed her lips shut for the duration of her subway ride). When she finally took her headphones out to shower, I asked her if she liked the new Beyoncé album and she said, "I guess so."

What I mean is, Rocky didn't know what was about to hit him.

But as fascinating as that was, we didn't have time to talk about it.

I found Molly's eyes in the mirror again. "You're probably wondering why I picked you up."

"Little bit," Molly said.

"You remember how Janet Steele"—I couldn't bring myself to say *our mom*—"said she'd bought a beach house on the East End?"

For the first time since she'd gotten in the car, Molly's expression showed a little bit of interest.

"Yeah. What about it?"

"Well, turns out the house is Fair Haven."

"What?" Molly turned to Trent. "What is she talking about?"

"It's true," Trent said. "Your mo—Janet Steele bought Fair Haven. And she kicked us all out."

"But how? You can't just buy someone's house out from under them, can you?"

"I was kind of wondering the same thing," I said.

"I'm a little vague on the whole thing myself," Trent said. "I guess sometime in the nineteenth century my father transferred ownership of the house to a corporation to dissociate it from the Gardiner family. We'd leave for sixty or seventy years at a time, living in London or Paris or New York, then come back, pretending to be our own grandsons and granddaughters. That way no one would notice that we never aged."

I nodded. Troy had told us about similar schemes he'd used over the centuries. One day, Molly and I would have to do the same thing.

"So anyway," Trent continued, "that first corporation was eventually sold to another corporation, and that corporation was sold to another corporation, and so on and so forth. The whole thing was still supposed to be owned by Gardiner Industries, but after the 2008 stock market crash, the board of directors spun off a few assets to raise some cash."

"Ugh, did you just say 'spun off a few assets'?" I groaned.

"Seriously," Molly agreed from the backseat. "That kind of banker bro talk is just . . . yuck."

"Whatever," Trent said, grinning. "I'm sorry I can't always be all, 'Dude, that dress is radical!' all the time."

"Did you really just say 'Dude, that dress is radical!'?" Molly teased.

"Cowabunga, dude," I chimed in. "Let's go nosh some 'za and kick it at your crib."

Trent rolled his eyes upward. "Odin help me!" He sighed. "Speaking of my *crib*," he persisted, "it turns out the board didn't realize one of the companies they'd sold was the one that owns Fair Haven. But superstar athlete Janet Steele did, and she swooped in and snatched it up—for a song, I have to tell you. She bought the whole place for less than what my stepmother spent on renovations."

"Oh, your stepmother!" I said. "She must be having a fit!"

"Wait a minute," Molly spoke over me. "Are you saying that Janet bought your home on purpose? Like she actually wanted to kick you out?"

"What?" Trent said guiltily. "N-no. I'm sure it was just a coincidence."

"Gods, you're a terrible liar," I said, chucking him under the cheek. "Good thing you're so cute. It's okay," I continued when he started to protest. "Dad told me everything."

"Told you what?" Molly said.

"One sec," I said to Molly, then turned to Trent. "Did you know?"

Trent did something complicated with his face, which I think was meant to be his I'm-so-guilty-I-can't-even-pretend-to-play-innocent expression. "What's the best answer to this question? You tell me what to say, and I'll say it."

"The correct answer is, how in the Hel could you keep something like this from me? We've been dating for a whole year! You should've told me!" I fumed.

"Told you *what*?" Molly practically yelled. "If someone doesn't tell me what in Frigg's name is going on RIGHT NOW," Molly screamed from the backseat, "I'm going to cast a decomposition hex on this Ferrari and you're going to wake up in the morning to a pile of rust!"

I caught Molly's eyes in the rearview mirror.

"Sorry, sorry," I said. "I'm still trying to process all this too."

As quickly as I could, I filled her in on what Dad had told me about the tradition of human familiars among some of the Aesir and Vanir trapped in Midgard, and how some of the familiars would try to trick the gods into having children with them. She absorbed it with an increasingly dumbfounded expression on her face, and when I'd finished, all she said was:

"So Mom's definitely human?"

She didn't look at me when she asked it. She looked at Trent, though it was clear she wasn't looking at a seventeen-year-old boy but at Tyr, Norse god of war.

He held up his hands. "As far as I know, Janet Steele is a perfectly average human being."

In the backseat, Molly looked disappointed.

"Our mother's human," she said in a dejected voice.

"Don't be sad, Molls," I said. "Look at Ingrid and Matt. Humans and witches can get along just fine."

"I know," she said, but if anything, her voice was even sadder. "But we're only just meeting her, and before you know it"—she found my eyes in the mirror—"*we're going to have to watch her die.*"

I held Molly's gaze for a long moment without speaking. I could see it wasn't just our mother's future death she was upset about—it was the flight attendant whose life she hadn't been able to save. I racked my brain for something soothing to say but nothing came, and it was Trent who spoke first.

"Why don't you concentrate on getting to know her first?" He pointed at the sharp outline of Fair Haven, which had just appeared above the horizon. "We're almost there."

No one spoke for the last couple of minutes of the drive. The Ferrari shot over the bridge to Gardiners Island and tore deep ruts in the meticulously combed gravel of their mile-long looping driveway. Trent glanced back at them, then flashed me a look, but didn't say anything.

I pulled up to the front courtyard of the two-hundred-year-old mansion, which wouldn't have looked out of place on the Scottish highlands or in French wine country. The pink bricks glowed softly, and the hundreds of white-framed windowpanes reflected the bright light of the afternoon sun. Ivy grew over the east wing, which was the oldest part of the house, and dozens of rhododendrons bloomed in a dizzying array of purple blossoms.

I tried to remember if rhododendrons bloomed this early in the season or if they were magically enhanced, but horticulture was never my thing.

"It looks so strange," Trent said. "Now that it's not mine anymore."

"It's our mother's," Molly snapped. She pried herself loose from the tiny compartment and jumped out of the car without waiting to see if I was following. She made it almost all the way to the door before she suddenly pivoted on her heel.

"Mardi!" she stage-whispered. "Can you believe we're about to meet *our mother*?"

All I could do was point.

Molly whirled back toward the house. The door had opened just as she'd turned, and there she was:

Janet Steele.

Our mom.

I don't know why, but I'd envisioned her in a tennis dress. I mean, I know why—she's a tennis star, duh— but I also knew that tennis stars are allowed to wear regular clothes when they're not playing, which was what Janet was wearing: a sleeveless sundress with a crisscrossed Greek bodice that loosened into a full skirt flowing softly around her legs. But even so. I'd pictured her in a tennis dress, and it was only when she appeared in civvies that it hit me.

This was our mom!

Molly's brain seemed to be free of such inane

ramblings, however. After a single eternal second during which she stared at Janet, she just ran to her and threw her arms around her.

"Oh, my gods! Mom!" I heard her muffled voice.

Janet's very long, very toned arms folded around Molly's back, and almost regally, she bent her head forward and kissed the top of her head. Since she was so tall, it looked like a normal-heighted woman kissing a little girl.

"My daughter," she whispered, yet I seemed to hear her clearly. "My beautiful Molly."

As she said all this, however, her eyes were still on me. They were piercingly blue and, despite the tenderness of her voice, they bored into me almost aggressively.

"Will you not come to your own mother, Mardi?" I heard her say, although I was so entranced by her stare that I didn't even notice her lips move. Before I knew it, I was out of the car, racing across the gravel to throw my arms around her too.

"Mom!" I cried as she pressed me against her with arms that felt powerful enough to crush bone. "Mom, it's really you!" In answer, I felt the same lips that had kissed my sister press gently against the top of my head.

"Actually, call me Mum" was all she said.

I don't know how long we stood like that, but finally Janet—Mum, I guess I should call her—stood back.

"This calls for champagne."

It was surreal, to say the least. We never had a mother our entire lives and now here she was.

Molly and I looked at each other. In the plus category for having a mum: good hugs and champagne. In the minus: so far nothing. But then:

Mum's gaze hardened as she stared over our heads. I turned and saw she was looking at Trent.

"You should not have brought the Aesir," she said in a voice cold enough to freeze water.

I found myself wondering if Trent was onto something, if "Mum" had a beef with all the gods, and not just Dad. I tried to catch Trent's eye, but he was busy returning Mum's stare. His gaze was cool and guarded. Not quite hostile, but when it comes to ocular interactions between your mum and your boyfriend, I'm pretty sure "not quite hostile" doesn't cut it.

"It's okay; Trent's my boyfriend," I said.

Mum smirked. "Isn't he a little old for you?" I know she didn't mean that he was eighteen.

"Hello, Janet," Trent said now. "It's been a long time."

"Hello, Tyr," Mum answered. "Yes, it has."

They stared at each other defiantly. I guess they knew each other after all.

Mum started to usher us inside, and it was clear Trent was not welcome. I wanted to defend him, but I was too excited to finally meet my mother. I hoped he'd understand.

"It's kind of hot out here," he said.

"As I said before, Aesir, you are not welcome here," she replied.

"This used to be my house, you know," Trent said. "And we mean to take it back."

"The deed is done. Now get off my property before I call the police on you." She looked down at me. "That would be Ingrid's husband, Matthew Noble, wouldn't it? I doubt he'd be too happy arresting his niece's boyfriend, but I'm sure he'd do it. And I'm sorry to be rude to the Aesir, but I really need to talk to you girls alone for now."

Something happened to Trent then. I'm not sure what it was, but even though nothing seemed to change in his outward appearance, he still got bigger somehow. Not bigger, but more substantial, as if his body was sucking in a little more daylight, so that his skin seemed to glow a little, even as he was shrouded in shadow. When he spoke, his voice was deeper than I'd ever heard it, and for the first time, I truly believed my boyfriend was in fact the god of war.

"You overstep your boundaries, mortal. The Council has always treated you with leniency because you are the mother of Magdi and Mooi, the prophesied goddesses of rage and strength. But you can push us too far, and then—"

"It's cool, Trent. Come on, please?" I cut him off before he said something he couldn't take back. "Drive my car to Ingrid's. We'll get a cab to take us home."

"Nonsense," Janet said. "I'll have my driver take you,

of course." She winked at Molly. "I won a Maybach in Monaco last year. It's like riding in a cloud."

"Trent," I said because he was still doing that glowing/shadow thing. "*Go. Please.*"

After another long, tense moment, the glow subsided, and Trent was just Trent again.

"I'm not happy about this," he said, sliding over into the driver's seat and starting the car. He pumped the gas, making the Ferrari's engine scream.

"I know it's not ideal, but please don't take it out on the car." My last words were cut off as Trent dropped the car into first without pressing the clutch down all the way, producing a hideous noise from the transmission. Gravel spurted from beneath the tires as the Ferrari lurched into motion.

Trent may be a god, but he sure never mastered the art of driving stick.

* *11* *

IT'S A FAMILY AFFAIR

From the Diary of Molly Overbrook

It was all I could do to bite my tongue during the whole exchange between Mum and Trent. How dare he speak to her that way. Through hard work and guts and determination, she'd turned herself into the world's best tennis player *and* managed to seduce a god and get a couple of children out of him. Everything Trent had—everything Trent *was*—had been handed to him on a magical silver platter. He needed to climb down off his high horse and admit that a human had outwitted him and his family.

I knew Mardi loved him, but I was upset.

He was rude to our mother.

Our mother. We had a mother. And she was here.

Mum put one arm around my shoulder and one around Mardi's and walked us through the grand central hallway of Fair Haven, beneath the coffered ceiling and enormous spiral staircase, to the rear terrace, which opened onto the estate's formal gardens and the more rustic orchards and coastland of Gardiners Island. As we sat down on a set of white-enameled Venetian grotto chairs, a small man appeared, who looked sort of familiar. Still, it wasn't until Mum said his name that I realized who it was.

"Girls, this is Ivan," Mum announced. "He's my butler-slash-chauffeur-slash-henchman-slash-hitting partner-slash-I-couldn't-get-anything-done-without-him. Ivan, would you bring us a bottle of Jacob's Creek sparkling white wine." She looked down at Mardi and me, a twinkle in her eye. "Have to represent for Australia, you know."

To be promised champagne and then offered sparkling white wine is a bit of a, well, letdown, and it was a struggle to keep the smile on my face, and I could see that Mardi was struggling as well.

But then Mum burst out laughing. "Oh, you girls are terrible actresses. Ivan, break out the Krug for my princesses."

Now I couldn't keep the smile off my face. Krug was so expensive that even a wine snob like our father never bought it, or at least not for family dinners.

"Very good, Ms. Steele," Ivan replied, and bowed. No, really: he bowed, and not like a little nod of the head. He bent all the way over at the waist until he was practically kissing his knees before scurrying away.

"Sit, sit," Mum said, pulling out chairs. "Just look at that view. Isn't it gorgeous?"

It was. Up close there were clipped hedges and multi-colored flowerbeds planted in patterns as intricate as Tibetan mandalas, while farther away windswept hills covered in densely green grass and gnarled fruit trees gave way to golden dunes, and the silvery blueness of Long Island Sound. In the misty distance, across twenty-five miles of water, Rhode Island was just visible, looking like a world in another dimension.

Faster than seemed possible, Ivan reappeared with three Baccarat flutes balanced on a silver tray held on one open palm, in the other a silver ice bucket on a three-foot pedestal that must've weighed fifty pounds. He handled everything as deftly as an acrobat, setting the ice bucket down soundlessly, pouring the champagne into the flutes while they were still balanced on the tray resting on his palm, then setting a glass down in front of each of us.

"Will that be all, Ms. Steele?"

"Thank you, Ivan," Mum said. "That will be all, for now." Mum's tone of voice could only be described as imperious. She may have been "new money," but she knew how to act to the manor born. Another bow from Ivan, and he was gone.

Mum raised her glass in a toast, and we raised ours.

"To the new gods of Midgard."

To what? I exchanged a glance with Molly, but it was clear she didn't know what Mum was talking about either. We clinked glasses anyway, and sipped at the Krug.

(I don't want to get anyone jealous, because they only make a few bottles each year, and most of them end up in Russia or the Persian Gulf, but: Krug. Is. Amazing.)

"Why new?" Mardi asked after savoring the Krug.

Mum sort of frowned and smiled at the same time. "Don't you know?"

"No."

Mum laughed. "I guess you wouldn't, even though you two are the first." She paused dramatically, fixing first Mardi in the eye, then me. Then, once again summoning that imperious tone, she proclaimed: "You, my daughters, will be the new gods of Midgard and will propagate an entirely new race of divine beings."

I held her gaze for as long as I could, which was about two seconds, then turned nervously to Mardi, whose expression was somewhere between "Say what?" and "Is she crazy?"

"Whoa there," I said, turning back to Mum. "I know we've just met, and Mardi said she wanted to wait a little before we got into the birds and the bees, but the simple truth is I'm still carrying my V card, and after what happened with Alberich last summer, I'm in no hurry to give it up, let alone start, um, propagating 'an entirely new race of divine beings.'"

Mum's expression didn't change. In fact, her face was totally motionless. Still, I could tell she was disappointed. Disappointed and, well, irritated. I mean, the only thing that happened was that her nostrils flared, but somehow even that tiny gesture was enough to make me blanch a little. It was like, if she sniffed through those flared nostrils, she would suck up me and Mardi through those pink cavities and we'd disappear into her body again. During the French Open match against Serena, I'd seen her shoot that look across the net a couple of times, which Serena, being Serena, shot right back. Since I didn't have Serena's guns, I found myself looking away pretty fast.

But then Mum laughed, and the tense moment was over as fast as it had come.

"I heard about your misadventure with Alberich. The dark elves can be nasty creatures, and he's the worst of them."

"Yeah, Dad was saying something about that too," said Mardi.

"When did you talk to him about this?" I asked, looking over at her. Dad usually only discussed god stuff when both of us were present.

"Um, earlier today," Mardi said, obviously uncomfortable. "We were talking about, um, things," she said, glancing at Mum nervously, and I realized she meant the attack a few days ago, which she obviously didn't want to bring up in front of Mum. "Anyway, I knew I should've waited for you, but you were off, I don't know, sulking—"

"I wasn't sulking!" I cut her off. "I was upset. You'd be upset too, if that happened to you."

I glanced over at Mum as I said this, but she didn't say anything. Just watched both of us keenly, as if she already knew what had happened and was completely not bothered by it.

"Sorry," Mardi said. "Sulking was totally the wrong word. Anyway, I got to talking with Dad, and he told me that all the gods are pretty much the same."

"I wouldn't go that far," Mum snorted. "We are all but pale copies of the great Jotun, whether it's a lowly human like me or a beautiful elf like Ivan."

"Wait," I said incredulously. "Ivan's an . . . elf?"

Mum smiled proudly, as though someone had complimented her on a thoroughbred horse. "Only three in all of Midgard, and just one works for a mortal."

"Wow," Mardi said. "No offense, but how do you rate your own elf?"

Mum's smile grew bigger. "Why, because I'm the mother of the Mimir, after all. My descendants will eradicate the Aesir and Vanir from Midgard, paving the way for the hegemony of the Mimir."

Mardi and I stared at each other for a moment.

"Um, hegemony?" I said finally, although I was pretty sure I knew what the word meant.

"Rule," Mum said simply, confirming my assumption.

"And, um, *eradicate*?" Mardi said.

Mum shrugged. "If you prefer a simpler term: kill."

Mardi set her $250 Baccarat flute down so heavily that about $100 worth of champagne splashed on the table.

"Whoa," she said. "Shit just got real."

. . .

No one said anything for what seemed like forever. The only sound was the dripping of Mardi's Krug onto Fair Haven's fieldstone patio and, in the distance, the faint wash of the surf.

Finally, Mum clapped her hands and Ivan appeared as if by magic. (Which, given the circumstances, may very well have been magic.)

"Ivan, Mardi's glass needs refilling."

"Of course, Ms. Steele." Ivan grabbed the bottle from the ice bucket and tilted it over one towel-draped arm, expertly filling Mardi's flute with the maximum amount of liquid and the minimum amount of fizz. The whole operation took maybe thirty seconds, but it was long enough for me to regain some sense of equilibrium.

"M-Mum," I said, stuttering slightly as I realized it was the first time I'd said the word, or at least addressed it to my actual mother. "Are you saying that me and Mardi are supposed to . . . to . . . kill all the old gods here in Midgard? Ingrid and Freya and Trent and, and *Thor*?"

Mum's eyes flitted back and forth between us for a moment. Then, without warning, she threw back her head and laughed.

"Oh, my gods, the look on your face is priceless!" she said when she could talk again. "No, I'm not saying you have to kill your own *father*! That would be unseemly!"

"But didn't you just say we were supposed to kill the older generation of gods?"

"I said the *Mimir* would do it. That doesn't mean it has to be you two! It could be your daughters, or your daughters' daughters!" She smiled brightly as if she'd told us that we'd just run over the last wild panda but it was okay because there were still some in zoos.

"Look, I can see you're a little upset about this, but really, it's nothing you have to think about now. The war is hundreds of years down the road. Maybe thousands. Who knows, maybe by then you'll be so tired of Thor's shenanigans that you'll *want* him dead."

Mardi looked at me with an "are you hearing what I'm hearing?" expression on her face. She was holding her freshly filled flute in her hand like she wanted to break it or throw it or something. And I knew why she was upset and all, but still. This was our mother, whom Thor had hidden from us our whole lives. We'd only just met her, and I wasn't ready to give up on her just yet. So I shot Mardi my best "calm down!" stare, and I don't know if it worked, but at least she put down her glass before she broke it (not to mention wasted all that irreplaceable Krug again). Still, her face was as pink as a breast cancer ribbon, and I spoke up before she could say something she'd regret.

"Are you sure about this?" I said to Mum. "Why can't we just share the space since we're family?"

"Family?" Mum said. "Did you feel like family two days ago, when you called on Skadi for help and she ignored you?"

"Wait, what?" Mardi said, turning to me. "What's she talking about?"

I ignored her. "How did you know I called on Joanna?"

"You think just because I'm human I don't know about magic? But then why wouldn't you think that? You were raised by Thor. He thinks humans are just playthings. All they're good for is pouring his drinks and cleaning his house and sharing his bed. Your call was a noble thing, Mooi. Noble and pure. I felt it all the way on the other side of the world."

"So you know magic?" Mardi said to Mum. "And you called on Joanna to save that flight attendant?" she said to me. "Oh, Moll, why didn't you tell me? I thought you were just upset about the fact that she died, but now I see there was a whole other dimension to it."

"Indeed there was," Mum said. "Mooi was learning that the Aesir care only about themselves."

"But that's not true!" Mardi protested. "Joanna and Freya and Ingrid have saved countless human lives. I've seen it with my own eyes."

"For every life they save, they let a hundred others slip away," Mum said coldly.

"But it would be impossible to save every human life! I mean, you're mortal, after all. You're not meant to live forever."

Mum shook her head back in forth in disappointment. And even though we'd only met her half an hour ago, it was still impossible not to feel a sense of shame.

I mean, she wasn't even shaking her head at me, and I still felt bad, as if I'd let her down.

"Oh, Magdi. Such lies they've filled your head with. You think immortality is something only the gods deserve? What nonsense! Life is not a gift that can be taken back. It belongs to all sentient creatures—forever."

As Mum said this, I felt a warmth fill my body (and it wasn't just the champagne). If I was hearing her right, she was saying that just because she was human she didn't have to die. That I wouldn't have to face the prospect of losing her forty or fifty years down the line, and then have to spend eternity without a mother.

As if she'd sensed my thoughts somehow, Mum whirled toward me, her expression full of tenderness. "Listen to me, my darlings," she said, looking straight at me. "No doubt you know that Gardiners Island sits on a seam between Midgard and Niflheim. But millennia ago, this seam didn't exist, because the nine worlds were all one. Everything existed on the same plane, separated by nothing more than a river or an ocean or a wall or a bit of space.

"But when Odin led the Aesir in his treasonous revolt against the Jotun, he tore the worlds apart and flung them into different dimensions. He wanted to protect the Aesir and Vanir against some future uprising in which the giants and the dark and light elves and humans might unite against Odin and become a tiny band of rebels. This sundering split Midgard from Hel, the great city of Niflheim, which is where the soul goes after its human body has served its purpose, to be born again in a new body free of the weaknesses of this frail shell."

"But, I mean, it's *Hel*," Mardi said. "It doesn't sound like a very pleasant place to spend eternity."

"Indeed it's not, Magdi," Mum said, "but that's your grandfather's doing. Hel is a part of Niflheim, which you know as the land of ice. The sun never shines, and the only plants that grow are pale trees covered in poisonous spikes instead of leaves, and a kind of black moss filled with acid. But once upon a time, before Odin cast it to the farthest edge of the universe, Niflheim was a paradise and Hel was its most beautiful region. Imagine some tropical island, but take away the flies and the snakes and the crocodiles. Every day was like this— high spring, with flowers blooming and birds singing and the fruit of the trees falling at your feet to delight your senses and nourish your body. It was only after Odin split the worlds that it became such a terrible place, which is why it lent its name to the Christian Hell."

"I don't want you to end up there!" I said then. "It's not fair!"

Mum smiled at me. "Don't you worry about me, Mooi. I can take care of myself. But the real question is, why should *anyone* end up there?"

She said *anyone*, but I knew she was talking about the flight attendant who had died in my arms. And she was right: she didn't deserve to be in Hel.

"But what can we do about it?" I said helplessly.

"Why, everything, of course!" Mum said. "Once the Mimir vanquish the Aesir, the barriers holding the nine worlds apart from each other will be destroyed, and they'll finally be reunited. Death as we know it will cease to exist—and it will all be thanks to you!"

12

SAY MY NAME

Mardi-Overbrook-Journal.docx

Once again, another awkward silence took over the patio. One minute, our newfound mum was telling us that it was our job to kill our father and grandparents and aunts and uncles and cousins, the next she was telling us that we were going to save the world.

It was all a bit much, really. Clearly, Mum was insane.

I stood up, a bit unsteadily. The Krug was light on the tongue, but it packed a wallop. "I've got to go."

"Go?" Mum said. "Go where?"

"Home."

"But this is your home now, Magdi!"

"First of all," I said, "I go by Mardi. Not Magdi, which sounds like a food supplement or a website for comic nerds. Secondly, this is *supposed* to be Trent's home and I *was* staying here with him. But since you kicked him out, I guess I'll crash at Ingrid's with Molly, not Mooi—she's not a cow—I mean, until Trent and I can figure something out." I turned to Molly. "You ready?"

Molly looked at me over the lip of her empty champagne flute. I could see that she was a little tipsy too but not so tipsy that she didn't know what was going on. "I . . . think . . . I'm . . . going . . . to . . . *stay*," she said finally, as if she hadn't made up her mind until the last word came out of her mouth.

"You're welcome here as long as you want, Mooi," Mum said, bestowing one of her million-dollar smiles on my sister. "And, Magdi, you are welcome here anytime you wish to return."

The way she said that made me pause. *Anytime you wish to return,* she said. Not *you're welcome here* like she'd said to Molly. It was like she'd already written me off, and it was on me to make it better. We couldn't have been there for an hour, making ours what must have been the shortest mother-daughter relationship in history.

But I didn't know how to express any of that out loud, so all I said was:

"Mardi. *Mardi.*"

Mum smiled without showing her teeth, and I had the sense that she was snarling behind her pursed lips. "Changing a few letters does not change your destiny. Remember, I didn't pick this fate out for you. I'm merely destiny's conduit."

"Well, I guess that makes me destiny's child," I

said, "and as an independent woman and a survivor, I, uh . . ." Whatever I was going for got lost in the haze of bubbles that filled my brain. "I'm outta here," I finished lamely.

"Of course," Mum said, the edges of her voice mild but concealing a heart of steel. "I'll have Ivan bring the car around."

"No thanks, I think I'll walk. I need to clear my head."

"Whatever you want, my darling."

Her *my darling* could've cracked a piece of granite in two.

"I, uh . . ." Again my voice faded away. "I'll see you around," I said to both of them, and turned for the door.

As I walked through Fair Haven's wide, empty hallway—Trent had told me that Mum had been "kind" enough to allow the Gardiners to move their furniture out before she took possession, but she hadn't replaced it with anything of her own—I couldn't help but notice how the house seemed indifferent to its change of ownership. Well, Gardiners Island was a magical place, and Fair Haven was where that magic was most heavily concentrated. In a way, the people who lived in Fair Haven belonged to it more than the house—or the island, or the magical portal between worlds—belonged to them. But even so. I had woken up in an upstairs guest bedroom just this morning, a bedroom that had a connecting door to Trent's bedroom (although he had yet to walk through it, or push it open and invite me to the other side). This might not have been the Gardiners' house, but the Gardiners belonged here. And yet they'd been banished by a mortal. A mortal who just happened to be my mother.

It took about ten minutes to walk off the island. The bridge to Gardiners Island wasn't far from the dock where Dad's plane had crashed. I stared at the water, peering for some sign of the accident, but North Hampton is a fastidious kind of place (I've always suspected that Joanna added something to her protection spells to make people more civic-minded, though Ingrid and Freya both deny this), and there was nothing left on the cold gray water to indicate something had happened here. An iridescent sheen was swirling around the dock pilings that might have been oil or gasoline, but also might have been good old-fashioned tide scum.

Nor was there any sign of the whale that had crashed the plane. Matt had told us that it wasn't all that uncommon for humpback whales to feed near the East End, though they usually stayed a few miles offshore. The Sound is pretty deep near North Hampton, however, and it was possible—just barely—that a whale could have strayed in, attracted by food maybe, or the sounds of ships or music, which could sometimes confuse them and lure them off course. Ingrid and Freya had searched through Joanna's spell books for magical detection spells, and late on the evening after the crash, after the docks had cleared, they'd cast the spells over the water. But though they tried three or four different spells, they didn't discover anything incriminating.

If someone *had* sent a whale to kill our father, he or she had used a plain old Midgardian whale and convinced it to attack Dad's plane without the aid of magic. Either that, or the person had managed to scrub any traces of magic from the water and the dock before Ingrid and Freya got there—which suggested that Dad's would-be murderer was living in our midst.

It was hard to say which possibility was more disturbing, and the thought of some evil sorcerer suddenly popping up and deciding to go after Thor's daughter in lieu of the god of thunder sent a chill down my spine. I hurried past the dark pier and the yacht club, from which came the faint sound of late '90s Destiny's Child. I thought it was someone getting the party started a little early, but when I peeked in, I saw it was actually a lone employee, dancing to "Say My Name" while he mopped the floors in preparation for the evening dinner crowd. The guy was lip-synching as he worked, using the handle of the mop as a microphone, and the sight brought a smile to my lips until I remembered the way Mum had refused to say *my* name—kept calling me Magdi, even though no one, not even Dad, ever uses that name. I'd asked Dad why he'd even bothered giving Molly and me Norse names, but all he'd done was roll his eyes and point upward, by which I assumed he meant Asgard. "I didn't have a choice," he'd said.

"Someone is very particular about the names of his grandchildren."

I left quickly, walking past the yacht club and into town proper. North Hampton doesn't have more than a couple thousand year-round residents, but the summer population swells to about five thousand, most of them well-heeled, though not usually as rich as your typical Hamptonite, or as flashy. As a consequence, Main Street is like a cross between a nineteenth-century New England village and something like Beacon Hill in Boston, where they have the same Burberry and Gucci and Louis Vuitton boutiques they have on Rodeo Drive or in the Meatpacking District in Manhattan, but they're housed in quaint old wooden buildings with cedar shingles on the walls as well as the roofs, and slatted shutters that aren't just decorative, but can be closed when a squall or a nor'easter blows in off the Atlantic Ocean. In between the boutiques are the usual assortment of artisanal ice cream and fair trade coffee shops as well as a few shops unique to the area, like a smoky boutique that sells nothing but pipes made from whale bones covered in scrimshaw (Dr. Mésomier put a truth hex on this journal, so you know I'm not making that up—as if I even would) and another store that only sells these ridiculous raincoats made out of some kind of shapeless, colorless waxed cotton that weigh about a hundred pounds but keeps you so dry that you'd think it was magic.

And then there was the Cheesemonger, the store

where Molly had taken a job last summer, mostly because it was run by this cute boy named Marshall, who unfortunately turned out to be Alberich in yet another of his disguises. Last I'd heard, the space was being taken over by Ocean Vines, the fancy wine shop that sold fifty-dollar bottles of Margaux and Montrachet (as opposed to Bob's Booze on the highway, which sells five-dollar airplane-sized bottles of whiskey and rum for people who want a drink on the go). But as I walked past the storefront, I was surprised to see that the CHEESE-MONGER sign was still up, and inside was none other than Sal McLaughlin standing behind the counter, with a crisp white apron pulled over a worn denim shirt rolled up at the sleeves. It was so hard for me to imagine Sal anywhere other than at the North Inn that I had to walk in and see what was going on.

There were three people in the store, and I browsed the shelves of twelve-dollar crackers made of "ancient grains" and jars of things that shouldn't have been pickled but somehow were, including clementines, fiddlehead ferns, and—ugh—snails. I got so caught up in the strange combinations of mouthwatering and disgusting foods that I didn't notice the last customer leave until the bells rang over the door and Sal called out:

"Mardi? Is that you?"

I put down a jar of "postmodern lasagna" made from layers of tripe (the lining of a cow's stomach), pureed breadfruit, and aspic infused with basil oil, and turned toward the counter. Sal was already coming out onto the floor, and he gave me a huge bear hug. Sal is a big man in his late fifties, a good six foot two or six foot three and probably around 250 pounds, a healthy combination of muscles and fat, and I disappeared in his grip, my cheek pressed up against his beard.

"My God, look at you. Where have you been all summer?" he said when he let me go. "Is it possible that you're even more beautiful than you were last year?"

From just about any other man this would have come across as pervy, but Sal was so comfortable in his skin that he made everyone else comfortable too—he hadn't worked behind bars for nearly forty years for nothing.

I waved my hand around the store. "What's going on, Sal? You branching out?"

"Believe me, I'm as surprised as you are. You remember that boy who worked here last summer, Marshall Brighton? Well, we all thought his parents owned the store and he was just working for them. But get this— there were no parents. I mean, I'm sure he had parents somewhere, but he owned the store on his own."

Given the fact that Marshall, a.k.a. Alberich, was around during the dawn of the universe, it wouldn't surprise me to learn that he did not, in fact, have any parents, but I just nodded.

"So anyway, he skipped out at the end of last summer, which is when the Flinzers next door at Ocean Vines decided to move in. But then last October, before they'd even begun renovating, Andy Flinzer checked himself into rehab. Turns out he'd been sampling his own merchandise a little too liberally, if you know what I mean. He's out now, and doing well, knock wood"—here Sal knocked on my head—"but he and Janice have decided to call off the expansion. They don't want any extra stress while Andy's still so new into his recovery."

"Wow, that's crazy. But I still don't get what you're doing here."

"Oh," Sal said, bopping his own forehead. "Didn't I mention? I own the building. I've got three buildings here in town. No wait, four. Five!" he corrected himself. "No wonder my accountant gets so frustrated with me. Anyway, when the Brighton boy took off, he left behind loads of merchandise. The cheese all went bad, of course—you cannot *imagine* the smell when I came in here in March—but there were all these other things, crackers and pickles and, uh, whatever this is." He picked up a jar of something that looked a lot like eyes, grimaced, and set it down hurriedly. "And so anyway, when I found out Rocky was coming, I thought, Why not keep this around for him to run? He's too young to work in the bar and it was too late in the spring to get a tenant in here, so this way I could pay him and it wouldn't look like charity. Rocky's my son, by the way."

"I know," I said. "I met him this morning actually. I guess his cab dropped him at the bar instead of your house, and Molly was walking him there."

"One sec," Sal said because a couple had just walked in. He scooted back behind the counter and whipped up a couple of heroes—thinly sliced speck, shaved Parmesan, and arugula on one, mozzarella and sun-dried tomato pesto on the other. While he was making the sandwiches, the couple also picked up a box of crackers and a jar of pickles—regular pickles—then ordered three different cheeses. Their total came to a whopping seventy-five dollars for what basically amounted to an afternoon snack.

"So how'd he look?" Sal asked as he came back around the counter, his normally smooth brow furrowing with concern. "His mother and I split just after his first birthday, and I've hardly seen him since. Poor Sophia died in March, and I get the sense that he's a little angry at the world."

I shrugged. "I only talked to him for a second, but he seemed okay. You should ask Molly, though. She spent more time with him."

"Actually," Sal said, "I was going to ask Molly if she wanted her old job back. This place is proving busier than I thought, and it's ridiculously lucrative too. I really can't figure out why that boy ran away from such a gold mine."

If only you knew how close you were to the truth, I thought.

"I'll mention it to Molly, but I'm not sure what she'll say. I don't know if you've heard about our own family drama?"

"You mean your father and that freaky accident? How is he doing, by the way?"

"Oh, he's fine; thanks for asking. Ingrid whipped up one of her potions, and he's practically as good as new. But I was referring to our mother." As quickly as I could, I filled him in on the story of Janet Steele and her move to Fair Haven.

"Kicking out the Gardiners!" Sal exclaimed, but you could see he was amused. "I can't say I feel too badly for them. My father always said they were Johnny-come-latelys to the East End—the McLaughlins have been here for four hundred years to their three hundred—but I'm sure they'll land on their feet. People like them always do." He frowned then. "Too bad you girls are all caught up in that, though. I was really hoping to get someone in here with Rocky. I don't want him to feel like he's in solitary confinement."

I shrugged. "I'll talk to Molly, but I dunno. I think she only took the job last year because she kind of liked Marshall, and when he took off, she felt a little burned."

"Well, if she doesn't want it, maybe you do?"

"Maybe," I said noncommittally, although I had a hard time picturing myself in an apron stained with pesto and ketchup. "I'll let you know."

And, after submitting to another bear hug, I headed off to Ingrid's.

＊ 13 ＊

WALKING ON THE MOON

From the Diary of Molly Overbrook

𝒯hat night—my first in Fair Haven—I had the dream again.

The ruined mansion. The ice-cold swampy yard. The strobing light in the east wing.

The outline of a female figure, appearing and reappearing with each pulse of the light.

In my dream, I pushed my way toward it across the puddle-filled lawn. Even as I struggled through the mud, I remembered that the east wing was the oldest part of the house, which housed the kitchen and servants' quarters. I'd heard from Trent (and Alberich when he pretended to be Trent) that despite its age, it was by far the sturdiest part of the house: its posts were entire tree trunks, and it had stood through dozens of hurricanes and even one earthquake, and even in the dream I realized how strange it was that this part of the house was in far worse shape than the rest of the mansion. It was almost as if the main part of the mansion had fallen to ruin through natural means, but this part was a complete ruin.

As I grew closer, the outline of the woman grew more distinct. I could see that she was slender, and her hair was long and flowing, but what I couldn't tell was if she was Mum or not. I thought of calling out, but something kept me silent. It wasn't that dream thing where you open your mouth and nothing comes out. My lips were sealed—I didn't want to call out to her. No, that wasn't quite it. I didn't want her to answer.

I didn't want it to be Mum.

By the time I made it to the house, I was covered in mud, grass, leaves. My bare feet were so cold they were numb, but not so numb that they didn't hurt. At least it was easy to get inside—the front door was long gone. But once inside, I had to tread carefully. The hallway floor was destroyed. It looked like someone had taken a hammer—like, say, Thor's hammer—and smashed it to bits. Whatever had happened, it had been done so long ago that trees had had time to grow up through the basement. They reached all the way through the second story and the attic and the holes in the roof, and the light that pushed around their leafless, tangled branches was the only thing that helped me see. I picked my way from one solid foothold to the next, slipping and sliding on my numb, wet feet, until I reached the door to the ballroom. The ballroom was on the east side of the main house. The new wing should be right on the other side.

The ballroom was also where the seam to Niflheim was hidden.

But this is a dream, I told myself. Nothing can actually hurt you here.

But somehow that didn't make me feel better. It was like knowing that I was dreaming somehow made it *more* real. Made me feel more vulnerable rather than safer. But I didn't see that I had a choice. The hallway beyond the ballroom doors had been completely ripped away. There was nothing but shadows disappearing down who knew how far. No way was I going down there.

The ballroom still had its doors, but when I grabbed the one on the right, it turned out it was only leaning against the frame. It was made of solid wood, though, and must've weighed a hundred pounds, and it seemed to be wedged in place, so I had to jerk on it several times before it came away, and then I had to jump back before it fell on me. It clattered and slid across the broken floor before disappearing down a hole. It was a good couple of seconds before I heard it hit bottom—not a crash, but a splash.

I shuddered as I turned back to the . . . well, I was going to say I *turned back to the ballroom*, but the space beyond the opened door wasn't a ballroom anymore. It was more of a . . . a cave, I guess, or a tunnel, really.

In place of the expansive parquetry floors and intricate marquetry walls, there was just dirt and rocks. No, not rocks, I realized. Ice. Great big chunks of dirty, jagged ice, as if they'd been frozen somewhere else, then broken off and dumped here. I remembered what I'd heard about Niflheim. That it orbited a tiny, cold white star and was covered in glaciers the size of continents. Could the seam have been opened somehow? Could Niflheim be pushing into our world? Or was it sucking our world into its own dimension?

My question was answered as soon as I stepped across the threshold. I don't know how, but I knew, somehow, that I was no longer in Midgard. Or no longer just in Midgard. The air felt different. Not smelled different. *Felt* different. Felt like it was made out of thick bolts of velvet that had been soaked in gasoline. Breathing it wasn't hard, exactly, but I could feel it in my lungs. It sat heavy in my chest, like a lungful of dead bees.

As strange as that was, however, what was even weirder was the weight of the room. The gravity, I guess. It was lighter. Like I felt myself weighing less. It seemed like I had to push my foot down to make it touch the ground, or else it was just going to float away. But I stamped my bare foot onto the ground and pushed my way into the room. It took a good, hard push, as if I was walking through water, but as soon as I was all the way in the room, I saw the light. The pulsing green light I'd seen from the lawn. It was at the far end of the tunnel that the ballroom had been turned into, but there was just enough of a curve to the tunnel that I still couldn't see the source. Even so, it was much brighter than it had been outside.

I took a step toward it. The gravity was so light that I half felt like I was going to float off the ground. I threw my hands out to either side of the tunnel, steadying myself on the slippery ice. Suddenly, an old song popped into my head. It was one of Freya's favorites, and she played it all the time at the North Inn, especially when she was closing up.

"Giant steps are what you take, walking on the moon. I hope my legs don't break, walking on the moon . . ."

It wasn't enough to make me feel safe, but it was enough to make me smile. I pushed forward.

But immediately stopped. Something had passed in front of the light up ahead, blocking most of it. It took me a moment to spot the shadow on the wall. The woman's shadow.

Waving at me.

And . . . speaking to me.

"Mooi," it called in a voice I knew I'd heard before, though I couldn't quite place it. "Mooi, is that you?"

It could have been Mum. And yet I wasn't sure—and I felt that if it were Mum, I'd recognize her voice.

"Mooi," it called again. "Mooi? Are you there?"

With a start, I opened my eyes, to the sound of a faint knock on the door.

"Mooi," a voice called. This time, it was really Mum's voice. No one else's. "Are you in there?"

"C-come in," I called, sitting up groggily. The feel of 800-thread-count sheets, lightly scented with lavender, was quickly bringing me back to reality.

The door opened, and there was Mum. She was dressed in a pair of loose gray pants, flats, and a light pink sweater. A Balenciaga purse was slung over one shoulder, a cup of coffee in her hand.

"Are you going somewhere?" I asked.

Mum gave me a regretful smile as she walked across the room and sat on the side of the bed. "This is for you," she said, handing me the coffee. "Hazelnut latte with soy milk."

"How did you know?" I said, taking the cup thankfully.

"Seriously?" Mum laughed. "You've only tweeted about it a thousand times."

"Guilty," I said, taking a sip. "Gods, that's amazing. Did you run into town for this?"

Mum shook her head. "Ivan's a genius in the kitchen."

"Is there anything he can't do?" I asked, laughing. By now I was fully awake. The sun was shining through pale yellow curtains, revealing the polished wood floors and mint-condition French country antiques. My dream felt no more real to me than a bad sci-fi movie I'd scanned past on cable. "So," I said, "loose pants, light sweater, sensible shoes. If I didn't know better, I'd say you were getting on an airplane."

Mum nodded. "England."

"England!" I repeated. And then it came to me. "Oh, my gods, Wimbledon! I completely forgot it comes right after the French Open." I was filled with a strange mixture of excitement and regret. This was the third leg of the Grand Slam, after all, and probably Mum's toughest challenge. "I can't believe you have to take off so fast, though," I said, sounding more like a little girl than I'd intended.

I guess I had stayed at Fair Haven because I was curious about our mother; Daddy and Ingrid didn't much like the idea, but they couldn't stop me either. After all, Janet Steele was our mother. More than curiosity, though, something had drawn me to the house. My dream, I guess.

Mum patted my head. "Believe me, I hate it too. But all of this"—Mum waved a hand at the house—"doesn't pay for itself."

"And there's that Grand Slam to think about too."

"Let's not get ahead of ourselves. One match at a time. I hate to leave you here all by yourself, but, hey, you'll have the whole mansion as your crib, and of course the staff will get you anything you want. Except for those lattes, I'm afraid. I have to take Ivan with me."

An idea popped into my head.

"Maybe I could go?" Once again my voice sounded as eager as a five-year-old's, and I tried to play it down. "I mean, these lattes are pretty addictive."

Mum smiled gently. "I thought about it. But it's the

kind of thing I really should clear with your dad, and given his accident, and the fact that I've only just reappeared, I think we should take it slow."

I resolved to bring it up with Dad when we visited him at Ingrid's as we usually did every few days.

I knew she was right, though I didn't want to say it out loud. I wished Mardi had been here to witness Mum being so reasonable. These weren't the ravings of a snubbed human bent on deicide, but the sound reasoning of a mature co-parent.

"How long will you be gone?" I asked, though I knew the tournament lasted two weeks.

"You never know," Mum said. "I could lose in the first round and be back tomorrow night."

I couldn't help it. I laughed out loud. "We both know it'll be you and Serena in the final. And that you're going to beat her."

"Promise you'll watch me on TV?"

"You know it."

"Come here!"

I threw my arms around her, even though I was still clutching my cup of coffee. Mum's long strong arms wrapped around me, and one of her hands stroked my hair.

"I'm going to miss you," I said. "I mean, I know we've only just met but . . ."

"But I'm your mum," Mum whispered in my ear, "and you're my daughter, and I'm going to miss you too."

She stood up and walked toward the door. Before she went out, though, she stopped. "Oh, I almost forgot." She reached into her purse, pulled out something shiny, and tossed it to me. I snatched it out of the air.

"Nice reflexes," Mum said.

I looked down at my hand. It was a key fob to a car. The logo was a sharply pointed trident. It took me a moment to place it.

"Is this for a *Maserati*?"

Mum smiled mischievously. "Don't think I'm trying to buy your affection or anything. The car's mine. But there's no need for it to languish in the garage while I'm gone. It's a convertible," she added just before she left. "Wear sunscreen."

And then she was gone.

An hour later—one shower, one bagel, and one practice drive on the road that ran around Gardiners Island—I was flying down North Road, which, as the name suggested, ran along the northern edge of the East End, right on the Long Island Sound. I know I've said I prefer a chauffeur, but I do know how to drive, and the Maserati handled like a dream. You could steer it with a single finger. And it was the best accessory ever. It set off my outfit perfectly.

Speaking of which: my initial plan had been to go to Ingrid and Matt's to pick up my clothes, but when I got out of the shower and glanced at the dresser, I saw a little note atop it.

I thought it would be easier if Ivan fetched your things.—Mum

I pulled open one drawer after another and discovered that they were full of all my summer clothes, plus a few items I didn't recognize, but which went perfectly with everything I'd brought. How Ivan had gotten them in there was a whole other question. I was a pretty sound sleeper, but I had a hard time imagining he'd been able to unload four suitcases without waking me. Well, he was an elf. I supposed he was rather light on his feet.

I pulled on a pair of white denim shorts and a sleeveless printed blouse I didn't recognize. I glanced at the label. Tom Ford. My mother had the best taste in the world. Then I made my way downstairs, where an already sliced bagel sat in the toaster, waiting for me, then to the garage. As I walked down the hallway, it occurred to me that this was the part of the mansion where I'd seen the light in my dream, but everything was so new and clean and bright that it was hard to hold on to the image. Even the garage had the pristine feel of a laboratory, with polished concrete floors and just the faintest tinge of gasoline. There were six bays, but only one of them was filled. A bright yellow

Maserati, the top already down, sat in the center of the vast space like an exhibit in a museum. It was as shiny as Katy Perry and curvy as Beyoncé, but even so, it exuded a tough, commanding energy. Just looking at it made me feel powerful.

And okay, I know I shouldn't have liked Mum's Maserati as much as I did, but Oh. My. God. What a car. Like seriously, why does Mardi drive that vintage hoopty when she could cruise around in a whip like this? I mean, it's not just that the engine made about a tenth as much noise as Mardi's did, even as it was about twice as fast: it also had a better stereo, a navigation screen that included a DVD player and seats that spooned you so close you felt like an underwear model was standing behind you and kissing the back of your neck. And they'd somehow designed the windshield so that even when the top was down the wind whipped over your head rather than messing up your hair—all without the need of an anti-weather spell.

The car seemed to know where I was going better than I did. North Road to Cross Fork Lane, Cross Fork to Pfenning Road. Pfenning to 409. Sal's house.

Sal and Rocky's.

He came out before I even made it to the porch. He was wearing a pair of low-slung drawstring shorts and a faded T-shirt with a cartoon cat on it.

"Is that Garfield?" I asked as I got out of the car and started toward the front door.

Rocky paused on the narrow porch, looking down at his shirt. "Seriously? This is Azrael. From the Smurfs," he added when my face must've given away that I had no idea who he was talking about. He nodded at the car. "Is that a Lamborghini?"

"A man's got to be secure in his masculinity to admit to watching the Smurfs. The car's a Maserati."

"You say potato, I say *ensalada de papas*." He said the last part in a thick Spanish accent.

"Potato salad?" By now I was at the foot of the steps. I climbed the first and then the second, till I was standing a step below him. There wasn't really room for two people on the top, unless they squeezed together.

Rocky shrugged sheepishly. "*Papa* didn't have quite the ring to it I wanted."

I decided to go for it. I mounted the last step. Rocky had to step back to accommodate me, but we were still only a couple of inches apart. I tapped the cat on his chest.

"And what'd you call him? Azrael?"

Rocky looked down toward my finger, though I'm not sure his eyes made it past my boobs. When he looked up, there was a small, happy grin on his face. His cheeks were dusted with stubble.

"I grew up without a dad. Papa Smurf was my role model."

"Just don't grow the beard, okay? I know it's all the rage right now, but—"

I was going to say that it sucks to kiss a beard, but it seemed a bit premature. I'm pretty sure my blush gave me away, though, because Rocky started blushing too.

"So, do you want to invite me in or something? This porch is architecturally fascinating, but I think I've seen the highlights."

Rocky looked out toward Mum's car. "You drive up in a Maserati and you want to hang out in my dad's trailer? Really?"

"Good point," I said, although from what I could see through the screen door, the interior of the trailer had been completely redone, so that it looked more like something you'd see photographed in *Hamptons* magazine rather than, I don't know, *White Trash Living*, or whatever.

"Oh, and why don't you drive?" I said, tossing the keys up in the air. "I know you want to."

✷ 14 ✷

TONIGHT'S THE NIGHT

Mardi-Overbrook-Journal.docx

$\mathcal{M}$olly's move to Fair Haven was helpful on one front: Ingrid was able to move Trent off the couch and out to the gardener's shed. She'd denied my request that he sleep in my room when he first moved in, saying that, goddess or no goddess, I was still a teenager. I could sneak around like one. But under her roof, we played by her rules.

"Good lord, Ingrid, she's seventeen," Freya teased her. "Back in our day, she would have been married and had a couple of kids by now."

"Yes, and back in our day, Tyr would have signaled his intentions by clubbing her on the head and dragging her into his hut. Times have changed."

"They certainly have," Freya said drily. "It's not 1950 anymore. Or 1750, for that matter."

"I don't get it," I protested. "You were fine with me staying with him at Fair Haven. And Dad doesn't care where I sleep." I didn't mention that we hadn't actually shared a bedroom at Trent's house, let alone a bed. I guess it would be a little weird since Dad was staying at Ingrid's too, but he was a progressive kind of guy.

"That was your father's decision, not mine. But this is my house and my rules."

"Oh, *Mother*," Jo chimed. "You're such a *prude*." And she took her iPad and stalked up to her room.

"That girl is growing up way too fast," Ingrid said, shaking her head.

But she refused to give in, and so after one of her delicious home-cooked meals and a couple of games of family-friendly Scrabble (no four-letter words allowed, even after I pointed out that they were in the official Scrabble dictionary, so no surprise when the librarian won) Trent headed out to the shed. When he kissed me good night, though, it was on my forehead. I tilted my head up, but all I got was a second kiss on the tip of my nose.

I wasn't surprised that Ingrid didn't let us sleep together, but what surprised me was that Trent didn't put up any kind of resistance at all. In fact, he seemed almost relieved to be able to move out of the house, and so, the next morning, after Ingrid had gone to the library and Matt had driven off in his sheriff's car and Dad was dozing after downing three of Ingrid's buttermilk waffles slathered in homemade raspberry compote, and Graciella, the housekeeper, had arrived to supervise Jo and Henry, I found Trent and announced:

"We're going for a drive."

Trent looked at me with a wary expression. But he followed me out to the car. I, too, was silent, not saying a word until we were through town and out on the highway. I punched it then and felt the satisfying jolt of the engine in the place where my legs met my abdomen.

I knew what I wanted to say to him, but I didn't know how. The thing is, ever since I'd been back, things hadn't been the same between us. It's like we were starting over again. I thought he was my boyfriend, but he hadn't really acted like one. It was so strange because when we were apart, we did nothing but text and talk on the phone and look forward to being together.

"What's wrong?" I asked. "You know what I mean."

"Nothing's wrong," Trent said, running his fingers through his hair and looking everywhere but at me. "Everything's great. I love that we're together again."

"Really? Because you don't act that way. You act like you're nervous to be around me."

Trent unclasped his hands. "Maybe it's because you're totally ambushing me!"

"Uh-uh. Don't make this about me. You've been like this all summer, and it's just gotten worse." I turned to him, despite the fact that I was driving sixty-five in two-way traffic. "Do you not like me anymore?"

"Uh, Mardi," Trent said, nodding at the road, "you want to, uh . . . ?" He nodded at the road again.

In fact, I'd beefed up the protection spells on the car in anticipation of this converstation, and it was practically steering itself, but Trent didn't need to know that. I stepped on the gas, and though I couldn't see the speedometer, I could feel the car's thrust in my gut.

"Answer the question," I demanded, my stomach falling.

Trent looked back and forth between the road and me for several seconds. His eyes were squinted, nervous, though it seemed to me they were more nervous about talking to me than about the possibility of an accident.

"Fine," he said finally. "Just pull over, okay? It's way too soon for me to be starting over again in another body."

The next turnout was for the beach, and I screeched into it. It was a weekday, and early too, so the small parking lot was nearly empty, as was the beach beyond. There was a stiff breeze, and when I killed the engine, the three-foot waves could be heard crashing heavily against the shore.

"Walk with me," Trent said, kicking off his flip-flops and getting out of the car.

This felt like a stalling tactic, but I decided to go along with him. I toed off my sandals and followed him out of the car, where he stood with his hand extended. I curled mine into his gratefully, and he squeezed back, and we made our way out onto the nearly deserted beach. The sand was cool beneath my bare feet, still damp from the tide. The wind almost brought up goose pimples on my legs, but with a moment of concentration, I was able to make them fade away.

"First of all," Trent said, "I like you. I like you a lot."

"I like you too," I said.

Trent shook his head and sighed. "Has anyone ever told you about the Reawakening?" he said finally.

The word rang a bell, but I couldn't remember what it meant.

"It has something to do with our reincarnation, doesn't it? When our Midgardian bodies are destroyed and we're born in new ones?"

"It does," Trent said, "but it doesn't refer to our bodies. It refers to our memories. Our memories and our magic."

"I'm not sure I understand."

"When we're born into a new body, we're not born with all our memories or abilities. We're not infants with the minds of two-thousand-year-old gods. We're not four-year-olds with the ability to blink our eyes and kill our classmates because they spilled our chocolate milk on our finger painting. Those things come later. The magic comes gradually, starting from the time we're born and accelerating during our teenage years before finally finishing up when we're about thirty. But the memories hold off until, ah, juvenescence is almost over."

"'Juvenescence'?" I repeated. "You mean *puberty*?"

Trent's hand squeezed a little in mine, though it felt more like a spasm than something he'd done on purpose.

"So wait," I continued. "Are you saying that this is happening to you now?"

I saw Trent nod out of the corner of my eye. "It started right around the time we met last year. Slowly. Like, really vivid dreams and stuff. But it's kept up the whole time."

"Well, that explains why you speak Norse in your sleep," I said, scratching at the tattoo of the rainbow bridge that coiled around my neck. "But whatever. Keep going with this Reawakening."

"There's not much more to say," Trent said. "I mean, there's two thousand years more, but you don't need to hear the blow-by-blow, do you?"

"I don't get it. So you're just now getting some memories that I thought you already had. What's the big deal?"

Trent sighed heavily and kicked at a seashell in the wet sand, sending it flying.

"It's not 'some memories.' It's century upon century upon century of memories. I'm the god of war, Mardi. I was born in Asgard. I was there when Odin divided the nine worlds and scattered them across the universe. I've been to every one of them, dozens, hundreds, of times. I've—" He broke off, catching his breath.

"I get it!" I said, cutting him off. "You're *old*. You've

done things. But so what? We're both immortal. Age doesn't mean anything to us."

"We're both immortal," Trent said. "But you're only seventeen."

"So what are you saying? I'm too young for you?"

Trent shrugged miserably. "Maybe I'm saying I'm too old for you."

That sounded like a cop-out to me, but I didn't call him on it because I was just starting to figure out what was happening. I stopped walking and turned to him.

"Trent Gardiner! *Are you breaking up with me?*"

Trent turned toward me, catching my other hand in his. But even though he was holding me tightly, I felt him slipping away.

"No. Never. We're meant to be together, Mardi. I feel it."

"But?"

"But maybe not right now. Maybe not for a decade or a century."

I stared at him for what felt like an eternity, dumbfounded. Then I shook his hands off and stepped back.

"I can't believe I'm hearing this!"

"Mardi, please. Don't be angry."

"I'm the goddess of rage, Trent."

"It's not forever. It's just until we're on the same level."

"'The same level'? Condescend much?"

I turned and started running up the beach. But even

as I was running, I was thinking, *Come after me. Catch me. Tell me you were kidding. Tell me you take it all back.*

"Mardi, please!" Trent called. But he didn't come after me.

I kept running.

✳ 15 ✳

HEY, GOOD LOOKIN'

From the Diary of Molly Overbrook

The next day, I showed up at Rocky's at seven in the morning. I know, what self-respecting girl shows up *anywhere* at seven in the morning? But it was the first day of Wimbledon, and as defending champ, Mum was scheduled for the first match of the day—it was noon over in London, but the five-hour difference meant that I had to be up at the crack of dawn if I wanted to see her kick some tennis ass.

Of course, I could've just watched it at Fair Haven. Even though all eighteen TVs that had been in the mansion had left with the Gardiners, there was always the screening room with reclining stadium-style seating. But the more time I'd spent driving around with Rocky yesterday, the less I wanted to go back to Gardiners Island.

The bright, burnished mansion I'd woken up in re-ceded further and further and further in my memory, and the haunted house of my dreams loomed larger and larger. I know that was just my mind playing tricks on me, but even if you took the house for what it was, it was still drearily empty. Not just of people (although where the servants Mum spoke of were hiding I could never tell) but of furniture or any other sign of human habitation. Mum had been kind enough to let the Gar-diners pack up their belongings when she kicked them out, but she hadn't had the time to do any redecorating herself, so aside from my bedroom, the mansion was freakishly empty. The hallways echoed with the sound of my footsteps, and their doors opened onto one empty room after another, with nothing to show that anyone had ever lived here besides the faded outlines of paint-ings that had hung on the walls for generations, and similar patches on the floorboards where the carpets had lain. It was hard to shake the impression that the mansion was somehow letting go of its hold on Mid-gard, as if it was preparing to slide into Niflheim, and the nightmare I'd dreamed about.

Besides all that, there was the fact that Rocky's house—or, well, Sal's—was neutral ground. No matter how empty Fair Haven was, it still felt like Trent's house to me, and even though I knew Mum had acquired it fair and square, I still felt a little guilty walking through its grand, derelict rooms knowing Trent and the rest of the Gardiners were forbidden from doing the same.

• • •

Once again, Rocky met me on the porch. He was wearing another pair of floppy shorts, another holey T-shirt,
both relatively unwrinkled, but his thick dark hair
looked like he'd just rolled out of bed.

"How do you look so wide awake?" he said in a bleary
voice. "I haven't been up this early since, I don't know,
seventh grade."

I'm a goddess, I almost said. *I don't actually need to
sleep.* But all I said aloud was "I'm a morning person.
I've already read fifty pages of *Madame Bovary*, done
Pilates, and touched up my nails."

"Why do I get the feeling that none of that is true,
and that you're dying for a coffee as much as I am?"

"Coffee!" I screamed. "Oh, gods, yes!" I'd tried to figure out the espresso machine at Fair Haven, but it had
more buttons than an airplane cockpit, and the most
I'd been able to do was get it to beep angrily and shoot
out jets of steam.

Rocky held the door open for me, and I squeezed
past him, inhaling a faint, pleasant whiff of clean but
unshowered boy, which quickly gave way to the aroma
of brewing coffee.

"That smells heavenly."

"Sal does run an upscale bar, after all. He's not going
to serve Folgers."

"Anything with caffeine sounds appealing right
now."

"Coming right up," Rocky said, shuffling on his bare feet toward the kitchen at the far end of the room.

I looked around the space. It was definitely a bachelor pad, but it was still nothing like I expected. The entire interior of the trailer had been gutted, so the room was one long tube, kind of like a train carriage but even longer and wider and taller. The far end held the kitchen, with gleaming Sub-Zero and Viking appliances, while the middle held a long narrow dining table made out of bleached, battered planks with eight chic mismatched chairs running down the sides, while the near end served as the living area, with a pair of low modern sectionals upholstered pale green flanking a TV that looked like a pool table on its side.

"That is one big TV."

"Sal's single, and he likes his sports. That TV's the wife he doesn't have."

"Well, let's turn his wife on," I said, plopping down on one of the sectionals. "Mum should be walking out on Centre Court right about now."

"Just lemme finish with the coffees," Rocky said. "Hot or iced?"

"Oh, iced! What a good idea!"

"Milk and sugar?"

"As Prince Charming said to Snow White, 'I like my coffee like I like my women: pale and sweet.'"

Rocky laughed so hard he almost spilled the milk he was pouring into a pair of tall glasses. He stirred in some sugar, then hurried down to my end of the trailer.

"Okay, okay," he said, setting the glasses on the coffee table. "Let's see if I can remember how to work this thing." He picked up an iPad. "Sal's got everything networked. Guys and their gadgets," he scoffed, and his voice was a little harsher than it had to be.

"So how's that been, anyway?" I said while he fiddled with the iPad. I had pointedly ignored the subject of family during our time together yesterday.

"Oh, fine, I guess," Rocky said distractedly, his fingers swiping and stabbing over the tablet's screen. "Sal's trying really, really hard. Like when he asked me what I wanted for dinner last night and I said, 'Anything,' and he said, 'If you could have anything in the world for dinner, what would it be?' and I said, 'Filet mignon, I guess,' which is funny because I don't actually like filet mignon. I mean, I don't hate it or anything, but if I'm going to have a steak, I like a good T-bone and—finally!"

The TV glowed to life. It was already tuned to ESPN. There was Mum, still dressed in her warm-up jacket, swatting balls lightly across the court.

"Wow. She is not a small woman, is she?"

"She's listed at six foot two, but when you stand next to her, she feels even bigger. So: filet mignon?"

"Oh, right. So anyway, yeah, Sal doesn't even, like, get the fact that I'm joking; he just called up some place called Michael's and asked them if they delivered."

"Michael's? They're in East Hampton. That's forty-five minutes away."

"Which must be why it took an hour and a half for our dinner to get here, and it was pretty much ice cold by the time it arrived."

"But it was a nice gesture, no? Like you said, he's trying."

"I guess." Rocky shrugged. "I just wish—no, that's not fair."

"What?"

Rocky sighed. "I was just going to say, I wish he'd tried this hard when Mom was alive."

"Ouch," I said. "You're right. Not fair."

Rocky shrugged again. "A lot of things aren't fair. But whatever, let's not be morbid. We've got some tennis to watch. Here's to a speedy victory by Janet Steele."

We clinked glasses and settled in for the match. Mum was playing someone named Svetlana Turkena—or something. I could look it up, but it would take more time than the match did.

"Do we have an official stat on this?" one of the announcers said over nineteen minutes later. "Is this the fastest match in history? Janet Steele just demolished her opponent."

"That poor girl," Rocky said, nodding at Mum's opponent, who was clearly holding back tears as she packed up her rackets and tried to get off court before she started bawling.

"If it makes you feel better, she got paid something like thirty thousand dollars for losing this match."

"I suppose money does soften the blow."

I glanced at my watch. It was past 7:30. Somehow

when I'd suggested that we watch the match today, I'd pictured us hanging out together all morning and into the afternoon, drinking coffee, snacking on chips and popcorn, maybe ordering some burgers from North Inn. At some point around the early afternoon, I was going to suggest casually that we head to the beach for a swim, which would have naturally transitioned to the two of us lying next to each other on towels, at which point I was pretty sure my body in a bikini would push things to their natural next step. I don't mean to sound conceited, but I am a goddess. But 7:30 is a little early to start macking on someone.

Rocky seemed to be similarly at a loss.

"So, uh, did you have breakfast?"

"I haven't actually."

"I think we've got eggs?" He said it with a question mark, although I couldn't tell if he wasn't sure if Sal had eggs, or if he wanted to make them. I decided to put him to the test.

"I would love eggs!" I said with forced brightness. "Poached, please!"

Rocky laughed in my face. "I can do scrambled or burned."

"Scrambled, please."

"Fine. But you have to do the toast."

We got up and made our way to the kitchen.

"Such gallantry," I said. "Do you always make your dates sing for their supper?"

Rocky winked back at me. "Oh, so this is a date?"

I blushed. I couldn't believe I'd let that slip out.

"Hey, I'm not the one who was on social media looking up hot prospects in the East End."

"Really?" Rocky smirked. "That's how you want to play this?"

"What're you talking about, McLaughlin?" I said, grabbing a loaf of bread and twisting it open.

"I'm just saying I don't think I was the only person who was looking around Instagram for, um, what was the term? 'Hot prospects'?"

He handed me his phone, which was open to his social media feed. The header read *Who's been checking me out?* and the first name on the list: *Molly Overbrook.*

"What the Hell," I said, grabbing his phone. I glanced at the time stamp, saw that it was from four days ago, right before Dad's accident.

"Why, that little sneak!" I said.

"What?" Rocky said, opening the fridge and grabbing a carton of eggs.

"Mardi was using my profile when she looked you up!"

Rocky laughed skeptically. "Sure she was."

"Seriously? You don't think I know how to do private viewing?"

"Well, maybe you wanted me to know you'd been checking me out."

"Um, excuse me," I said, taking a step back. I waved my hand down my body like a game-show girl showing off a refrigerator. "Does this look like I have to work that hard?"

Rocky turned pink. But then he recovered enough to say, "Well, even if it was your sister who looked up my profile, you still knew who I was when you met me the other day."

"Yeah? Well, you knew who I was too!" I almost yelled.

"So I guess that makes us even, doesn't it!" Rocky shot back.

"I guess it does!"

"So I guess I'm going to kiss you now!"

"I guess you damn well better!"

Turns out 7:30 in the morning isn't too early for macking at all. Or making out for that matter.

* 16 *

WRECKING BALL

Mardi-Overbrook-Journal.docx

Two miserable days after Trent dumped me on the beach, while I was hanging out with Ingrid's kids, my phone rang. It was a local number, but it wasn't in my phone book.

"No!" Henry screamed at Jo. "First you have to play the *jacks*, then you have to play the queens, and THEN you play the kings. EVERYBODY knows that."

"Whatever," Jo said, slapping down a handful of cards. "I think you're just making the rules up as you go along!"

"Hey!" I yelled. "Keep it down! I've got a phone call!" And a headache, I added silently.

"Hello?" I said guardedly.

"Mardi!" a deep male voice all but yelled into the phone. "Oh, thank God!"

"Sal?" I said. I was pretty sure it was him. "What's the matter?"

"One moment, ma'am," Sal said, although I didn't think he was talking to me. Then, louder: "Herring crème fraîche is the matter!"

"Um . . . sorry?"

"Ma'am, I said I'll be with you in a moment!" Sal repeated in a sharper tone of voice. "Mardi, please, you've got to help me out. I just got an order for six quarts of herring crème fraîche down at the Cheesemonger!"

"Um, okay." I racked my brain for the significance of this factoid. I had vague memories of a sandwich called the Debbie Harry. Molly told me it was one of Marshall's, a.k.a. Alberich's, more inspired creations. Hickory smoked salmon, fermented dill pesto, and herring crème fraîche served on a sourdough and onion brioche. Sounds gross, but somehow it was really good.

"I think it's for the Debbie Harry."

"In my world, Debbie Harry is still the twenty-eight-year-old ex–Playboy Bunny who sang 'Atomic' and 'Heart of Glass.' She is not—thank you!" he interrupted himself in a sarcastic tone. "Please come again! She is not a sandwich. Nevertheless, the East End seems to be full of people who don't know anything about her music career and everything about her reincarnation as one of the most disgusting combinations of flavors I can possibly imagine."

"It's kind of an acquired taste," I admitted. "But what's all this got to do with me?"

"Oh, nothing," Sal said testily. "Except that you said you'd make them for me."

"I . . . huh?"

"The other day? When you wandered into the Cheesemonger? I said I was thinking of asking Molly to work here for the summer, and you said that you wanted to do it?"

"Oh, right!" I'd totally forgotten about it, what with everything that had gone down in the past couple of days. The Gardiners getting kicked out of their house and Molly moving into it and Trent dumping me on the beach, and then just disappearing. Ingrid said something about "Europe," as if that somehow narrowed it down. Trent went all the way to Europe to get away from me? So depressing.

"So I take it Molly turned you down?" I said now.

"Not exactly. She's been too busy letting my son squire her all around the East End in a bright yellow Maserati."

"Rocky has a Maserati?"

"I drive a 1974 Toyota Land Cruiser, Mardi. Do you think my son has a Maserati?"

I didn't bother pointing out that he also owned five buildings in one of the most expensive square miles of real estate east of Rodeo Drive, and that the Land Cruiser, like the refurbished trailer house he lived in, was a total WASP affectation.

"You mean it's Molly's? But where would Molly . . . oh, of course. Janet."

"Who's Janet?"

"Steele? The tennis player. Our mother—never mind. Anyway, I'm sorry Molly's kidnapped Rocky, but I'm not sure—"

"You have to help me out," Sal cut me off. "I can't keep running back and forth between the Inn and the sandwich shop. I'm losing business at both places. Freya's ready to quit, and you know I can't lose her—she's the best bartender on the East Coast."

"I'm only seventeen; I can't help out in the bar."

"The Cheesemonger, Mardi. I need you in the sandwich shop."

"But I don't know the menu or the merchandise or—"

"You knew about the Debbie Harry. Please, Mardi. I'm begging. I'm begging a kid to save my ass."

An hour later, I was parking in front of the Cheesemonger, when Sal came out of the store in a filthy apron.

"No, no, no," he said. "You can't park right in front of the store. That's for customers."

"Seriously, Sal? I'm doing you a favor here."

"And I'm paying you for it! Now move the car."

I thought about remarking that my dad made in the high eight figures last year, plus he was, you know, a god. But all I did was pull the Ferrari around back, to the small municipal lot there.

"Okay, then," Sal said as I walked in the back door. "So, it turns out that Billy and Bruce's B&B, you know, the one next to the yacht club, has a standing order for a dozen sandwiches every day at eleven-thirty. Just get those ready, and they'll send over their, um, houseboy to pick them up at eleven-fifteen. Then you should go ahead and get ready for the eleven-thirty train from the city. It usually lets off a hungry crowd. I'd just make another dozen assorted sandwiches—making sure you've got at least two veggie, two vegan, and two gluten-free. You know this crowd—they have more dietary restrictions than Catholics during Lent. That'll pretty much wipe out your prepared stocks, so you should probably make some more prep for the afternoon crowd. We've got smoked salmon, cured trout, smoked and herbed turkey, Parma ham, Iberian ham, Smithfield ham, prosciutto, and all the various things that go into the dips and spreads and dressings in the walk-in. Marshall left really detailed instructions on how to make everything—the kid may have been a flake, but he was a wizard in the kitchen. Oh, and I haven't had a chance to get the linen service back in here, so you'll have to wear this for now." And he pulled the stained apron off his sweaty body and draped it unceremoniously over my neck. "Your employee discount is fifty percent," he added, "so feel free to chow down."

And with that, he trotted toward the back door.

"Um, Sal?"

He turned back to me with an impatient look.

"I thought you said Rocky was going to be working here too."

Sal looked at me as though I was speaking Norse.

"Rocky? I told you. He's running around with your sister. They're probably at the beach right now."

And with that, he was gone.

"Holy crap," I said out loud. "What just happened?"

* 17 *

SAIL AWAY SWEET SISTER

From the Diary of Molly Overbrook

So much happened over the course of the next two weeks that I almost forgot about the fact that I hadn't spoken to Mardi once that whole time.

I suppose I could just as easily say that I didn't speak to Dad, Ingrid, Freya, Matt, Jo, or even Henry, but let's face it: as important as all those people were to me, none of them came close to Mardi. Not even Dad, who was still recovering.

Mardi was my twin. She was the most important person in my life. I'd never gone more than two days without seeing her. I'd never gone a single day without talking to her. In fact, I don't think I'd ever gone six hours without talking to her. That's how I knew this fight was serious, even if I didn't know what it was about.

Because really, what had happened to get her so upset? Mum had repeated some stuff about some old prophecy or something. If I had a dollar for every time someone in our family spouted off about how such-and-such had been foretold or so-and-so was the promised one . . . well, I'm already rich, but I'd be even richer.

Like most old religions, we had prophecies up the wazoo, and the vast majority of them were so vague that you never really knew if they'd actually come true, or if people were just making stuff up. And even if this was one of the real ones, well, what could we do about it? If the fates had decreed that we were supposed to be the end of the old gods, the old gods could hardly blame *us*, could they? And besides, like Mum said, who knew when it would all come to pass? It could be decades. Centuries. Millennia. Couldn't we all just chill and have some fun till then?

Who knew, maybe Mardi was having the time of her life while she was apart from me—I have to say, those two weeks were some of the best of my life.

First of all, Mum was on TV every other day. And she was kicking some serious ass. She won her first three matches 6–0, which if you don't know anything about tennis, that's a total beatdown, and it's pretty much unheard of for it to happen three times in a row. After the third match, Rocky said, "Damn. It's like she's got a magic racket or something." I glanced at him sharply, but he didn't notice. Of course I was wondering the same thing. I mean, she barely broke a sweat when she played—and it was almost ninety degrees on the court. She'd said she was human, and Ingrid and Freya and Dad had confirmed that, but they'd also hinted that it would have taken magic for her to get pregnant by Dad without his consent, or knowledge, for that matter. And if she could pull off something like that, why couldn't she get a nice little hex on her racket, as Rocky had unwittingly suggested, or maybe just on her right arm. It was exactly the kind of thing the Council was likely to miss. They were much more concerned with events like elections or business ventures, or things that left people dead. Tennis was a little under the radar for them.

But then, Mum had been at it for a while now, at two different periods, and she certainly hadn't played down her success, either on or off the court. And as the ex-girlfriend of Thor, she was likely to fall under more scrutiny than most people. No, the more I thought about it, the more unlikely it seemed that she was using magic to win matches. My mother was simply a kick-ass tennis player.

And even better than watching her cruise toward the Wimbledon final was the way she ended each of her on-court interviews: "I just want to say hi to my daughter Molly, who's watching back home in North Hampton. Mum loves you, and she'll be home soon."

And you know, that was great. Really great, except I felt a tiny pang that she didn't mention Mardi. So great that the first time she said it, I actually felt myself tearing up. I didn't realize how much I had missed having a mother. But although the emotions she was bringing up were totally real, Mum was three thousand miles away, and she was still kind of unreal to me.

I mean, I was living in her house and I was driving her car, but I'd only met her once, spent maybe a grand total of four hours talking to her, and it was hard to think of her in the same way I thought of Dad. So mostly I was biding my time, waiting for her to come back to the East End, to figure out if she really was as awesome as she seemed.

But much closer at hand was Rocky. And, well, Rocky really *was* awesome. Like if you ever took one of those quizzes in *Teen Vogue* or *Girls' Life* about the perfect boyfriend, Rocky seemed to have been created right from my answers. He was athletic but not a jock; he was smart but not a nerd; he liked R&B but not gangster rap; he was a great kisser but he didn't pressure me to go too fast. In fact, when we were making out, he was usually the one to break things off first.

I also got the feeling he was always thinking about his mom. It had only been a few months since she'd died, after all. There were times when we'd be doing something—popping popcorn maybe (Rocky liked to make it the old-fashioned way, in a pot on the stove), or flipping past some dumb reality show on TV—and he'd fall silent with this faraway look on his face. I asked him about it a couple times, but he'd always give me this half-happy, half-sad smile and say, "It's nothing."

I hadn't exactly earned the right to his heart's secrets after only a few days of hanging out, and I wasn't even sure I felt ready to carry them, let alone reciprocate them. I mean, it's not like I was going to tell him I was a goddess anytime soon. But it was nice knowing the guy I was hanging out with had some depth to him. The abs didn't hurt either.

And let's not forget: we were both all alone. I mean, Rocky had Sal, and I had Mardi and Dad and Freya and Ingrid and Matt and the kids. But Rocky didn't really know Sal, who was always busy with the North Inn and his other businesses, and I had done a great job of driving a wedge between me and the family by moving into Fair Haven. Not that it would have been hard to avoid them: Dad was laid up in bed, Ingrid had her job at the library as well as two kids to raise, and Mardi, well, Mardi seemed to just disappear, as did Trent for that matter.

I didn't check up on them on social media, but even so, I assumed they hadn't gone off somewhere together or I'd have heard—through Freya if no one else, since she was the one member of my family I still saw, usually in the evenings, after Rocky and I had spent the day watching Wimbledon or lazing on the beach or driving around the North Fork.

In fact, we ended up at the North Inn almost every

night, since neither of us wanted to cook and the chef at Fair Haven didn't know how to make anything less complicated than boeuf en daube, and the North Inn's Kobe beef burger was pretty amazing, plus Freya would give us free drinks.

And on our thirteenth day together, she handed me a box of condoms.

"Freya!" I exclaimed, quickly hiding them in my purse. I glanced around to see if Rocky had noticed, but he was back at our table, staring at his phone. "What are you doing?"

"Better safe than sorry," Freya said as she wiped down the bar. "I can smell the hormones on you two even through all the suntan lotion."

"Nothing has happened! And even if something did, it's not like I'd need these."

"He doesn't know that," Freya said. "First rule of fooling around with mortals: don't give them any reason to suspect that you're different. And secondly, you should be prepared, even though you haven't rounded third."

I blushed. "What makes you think I've never gone to third before?"

"Seriously, Mooi? I'm the goddess of love, in case you've forgotten. I don't miss details like that. If it makes you feel better, he's a virgin too."

"What? You can tell?"

"Goddess of love," Freya said again. "It's not just an honorary title, you know. Also?" Freya paused dramatically.

"Yes?" I prompted.

"He wants you to be his first."

Over at his table, Rocky looked up with a start.

I put my head down on the bar, my heart pounding, while Freya cheerfully made drinks as if she hadn't just blown my mind.

Like I said, this happened on our thirteenth night at the North Inn, which is to say, the night before the Wimbledon final. Although we'd watched the whole tournament at Sal's house, we'd made plans to watch the final at Fair Haven in the home theater. I'd left a note with the cook to prepare a full English breakfast, even though I wasn't quite sure what that was. I woke up to the fragrant smell of bacon and sausage filling the mansion, although when I went downstairs I was, as usual, unable to find any sign of the staff.

A banquet table had been set up in the screening room, laden with warming trays filled with enough food to provision an army. In addition to three different kinds of bacon (regular, Canadian, and maple-glazed) and four different kinds of sausages (bratwurst, chorizo, kielbasa, merguez), there were also scrambled eggs, baked beans, grilled mushrooms, an assortment of scones, enough toast to shingle a barn, and an unappealing black mess that was helpfully labeled "blood pudding," which almost made me not want to eat anything else on the table.

Rocky showed up promptly at seven. I handed him a Bloody Mary, fully loaded with celery stalk, toothpicked olives, and lemon and lime wedges. He made space among all the garnishes for his mouth, took a sip, smiled, and took a longer sip.

"I've gotta say, this is the earliest I've ever showed up for a date in my life."

"Date? Who said anything about a date? Anything before three is just an . . . assignation."

"Hmmm," Rocky said, pursing his lips. "Let me ponder that." But instead of pondering, he leaned in and planted his pursed lips atop mine.

It was 7:05 before he stood up again. Goddesses have an unerring sense of time.

"Nope," he said with a sly grin, "I'm pretty sure this is a date."

"I, uh, I concur," I said hoarsely, then, grabbing his hand, led him toward the screening room.

Rocky lagged behind me like a tourist seeing Venice or New York City for the first time, gawking at the vast rooms as we passed through.

"Wow," he said. "I Google-mapped this place, so I knew it was fancy. But I never realized it was this, well, fancy. Except where's all the furniture?"

"Mum took possession right before Wimbledon. I guess she hasn't had time to decorate."

"Wasn't there furniture from her old house? This place is seriously empty."

"Silly, Rocky. Rich people don't sell one house when

they buy another. They keep adding to their collection, like marbles or baseball cards."

"Okay," Rocky said dubiously. "I just hope you're not sleeping on the floor or anything."

"Wouldn't you like to know?" I teased, and though Rocky didn't answer me, his silence spoke volumes. As did mine, for that matter: the sconces in the hallway, which were off, suddenly flashed on.

"Must be the old wiring," I said before Rocky could ask.

We made it to the screening room without further incident. Once again, Rocky's jaw hit the floor. The screening room at Fair Haven had been done in high Art Deco style, like the movie palaces of the thirties. The walls were covered in heavy red velvet accented with ornate gilded trim. The gilded coffered ceiling was hung with miniature chandeliers whose flickering bulbs imitated gaslight. The plush velvet chairs came in single and love seats, with individual recliners and burled walnut trays for your snacks.

"I don't want to sound like a hick from the sticks, but—wow. I thought only rappers and movie stars had rooms like this. Actually, I never really thought they had them either."

"The truth is, any house or apartment over 10,000 square feet pretty much has to have one, even though the people who own the houses watch their reality shows and pay-per-view on flat-screen TVs just like everyone else. It's a resale thing. You have to have a catering kitchen, and a screening room, and an elevator, even though these things only get used once or twice a year."

Rocky looked at me like I'd just revealed that I could read Egyptian hieroglyphics.

"Sorry, Dad's a Realtor. This stuff is dinner conversation at our house."

Rocky laughed, and we made our way to the buffet.

"How is your dad?" Rocky said as he began heaping a plate with steaming meats and eggs. "You haven't really mentioned him." He tried to keep his tone light, but I could hear the effort in his voice, as if he didn't want to upset me, or seem prying.

"Oh, he's fine," I said as I began filling my own plate. "On the mend? I mean, as far as I know."

"You haven't been to see him?" Rocky said, even though I'd spent every waking hour with him.

"Oh, look at the time!" I said, feeling guilty about not having gone to see Dad. "The prematch chat is just about to start."

Rocky flashed me a look but didn't probe. We took our plates to one of the love seats and sat down next to each other. I could tell he wanted to pry, but decided not to. Good. I picked up the iPad on the side table and turned on the home theater system. It had already been tuned to ESPN. They were talking about my mother and her chances.

"Does it make you nervous?" Rocky asked me. "Your mom being a sports star?"

"I guess?" I said casually. "I mean, it's all so new to me. I'm used to not having a mother, you know? Like I almost forget that the woman they're talking about is actually related to me."

Rocky munched on a piece of bacon before answering. If it's possible to imagine someone eating bacon sadly, that's what Rocky was doing.

"I guess I don't really see myself as ever getting used to not having a mother."

I grabbed the remote and muted the sound.

"Oh, Rocky, I'm sorry. That was insensitive of me."

"Crap," Rocky said. "I didn't mean to sound like I was blaming you or something. You could be talking about, I don't know, bacon or something"—he held up another piece—"and I'd still end up thinking about her."

"It must be so rough," I said.

"You know what's rough? When I *don't* think about her. When I brush my teeth and rinse out the sink afterward, not because my mom will get on my case if I leave toothpaste in it, but because it's just what I do now. I know I just said I can't see myself getting used to not having a mother, but the truth is that I'm afraid that I will get used to it one day. I'll just be another one of those kids who doesn't have a mom and doesn't ever give it a moment's thought."

"I've only known you two weeks, but I already know that's not true. You'll never forget your mom. But that doesn't mean you have to feel sad every single day. She wouldn't want that. She'd want you to be happy."

"I almost hate to say it," Rocky said with a little smile, "but I have been pretty happy lately. And I don't feel like she would mind."

I knew he was talking about me, and willed myself to keep calm. The last thing I needed to do was short out the entertainment system.

Rocky nodded at the screen, where Mum and Serena were finishing their warm-ups. "Turn it up. That's what we're here for."

Before I turned the sound back on, I took his hand.

"Just so you know, I've been pretty happy too."

And that was the last thought I had about Rocky for the next three hours and twenty-seven minutes, because my attention was completely absorbed by the match. I'd barely noticed we were holding hands. I had no idea for how long. And I was so keyed up I couldn't speak—I just squeezed his hand and watched the screen. My heart was beating so hard that I might as well have been out on the court myself.

The women were screaming with each and every shot, and both of them were given fines for "audible obscenity" before the match was over. I couldn't even describe what went on during the last set, it was so intense and I was so overwhelmed. But then suddenly Mum was serving a ball and Serena lobbed it back and Mum pounced on it, firing it past Serena, and then Rocky and I were both on our feet.

"Oh, my gods, she won! She won!" I screamed hoarsely.

"She won!" Rocky screamed just as loud and just as hoarsely. "That was unbelievable!"

On screen, Mum fell down on the ragged grass and lay there for a full thirty seconds, half stunned, half exhausted. When she sat up, she had a dumbfounded smile on her face. The camera flashed to Ivan in her box. He was jumping up and down, screaming.

Rocky and I sat back in our seats as Mum slowly stood up, using her racket as a cane. She walked on heavy feet to the net and shook Serena's hand. Serena's face was stony, but then Mum said something and Serena said something back and offered a flash of her trademark smile, and they walked together to shake the umpire's hands.

"That's class," Rocky said. "I don't know if I could look someone in the eye after they beat me in a match like that, let alone smile at her."

I was still too dazed to reply.

"I can't believe it," I said. "I . . . . I just can't believe it."

Mum made her way to her player's box, where she gave Ivan a huge hug.

"That's your mom," Rocky said.

"That's my mum," I said, turning to Rocky. "That's really my mum."

Rocky turned to me. "You must be so—"

"Shhh," I said.

"Huh?"

"Just come here." I pulled him close.

Rocky resisted for a half a second, then fell against me. I put a hand around the back of his head and brought his lips to mine.

"This is a date, remember?"

"I never forgot," Rocky said, and this time his voice didn't sound hoarse as much as husky.

"It's kind of a weird date, but maybe we can give it a more normal ending."

"Are you kidding?" Rocky said after we'd made out for a couple more minutes. "This is the Best. Date. Ever."

He looked up several minutes later. First he said, "Are you sure?" and when I nodded, he smiled and gave me a little nip on my lips. "Turn the TV off," he said then. "I don't want your mom to watch this."

I was so caught up in what was about to happen that all I did was nod and wave a hand at the screen, which went black.

"Wow," Rocky said. "What are you, magic or something?"

"You're about to find out," I said, and I pulled him close again.

✳ *18* ✳

YOU'VE GOT ME
FEELING EMOTIONS

Mardi-Overbrook-Journal.docx

The two weeks after Molly moved into Fair Haven and Trent dumped me and I started working at the Cheesemonger were the worst in my entire life.

Okay, first let me admit that I've led a pretty sheltered life. My family's rich, and, you know, there's a pretty good chance I'm going to live, well, forever. So any complaining I do comes with a pretty big asterisk next to it. And I'm not so self-involved that I don't know that a breakup isn't the end of the world. There'll be other boys. Other Trents even.

Who knows, there might even be Trent again.

But screw that. Screw his *This isn't forever.* Screw

keeping perspective and putting a good face on it and making the best of a bad situation. When Trent told me on the beach that he couldn't be with me, my first thought was that he'd reached inside my chest and ripped out my heart, and my second thought was that the ground had opened up and swallowed me, and my third thought was that if I didn't put as much space between me and Trent as possible, I was going to reach inside his chest and rip out his heart and dig a hole on the beach and bury the body right there.

So I ran. And what made it all a hundred, a million times worse was that the only thing I could think of was running straight to Molly and telling her everything that had happened and crying on her shoulder and eating pint after pint of Ben & Jerry's until even my divine body felt bloated with sugar and cream. But with each step I took away from Trent, I knew I was getting farther and farther away from Molly as well. She'd made it clear: she'd rather be with a mother she didn't know than her own family. And somehow I knew that if I tried to explain any of this to Dad or Ingrid or Freya, they'd end up taking Trent's side. For the first time in my life, I was alone.

Then, one afternoon, Molly walked into the Cheesemonger.

"Mardi!" she said, obviously surprised to find me working there.

I reached out a hand, and the door swung shut. I had never done anything like this before, but I could feel the energy surging through my body.

"Door, lock!" The dead bolt slammed in the door. "Shades, down!" The shades fell with a thump, plunging the store into twilight.

"Okay, sis," I said, turning to Molly. "It's just you and me. We need to talk."

For a long moment, we stood there in semidarkness. Suddenly, the lights snapped on of their own accord. A half second later, they snapped off with a loud pop, and then I heard the motor power down on the refrigerated cases.

"Was that you?" I said.

"I guess." Molly shrugged. "It's been happening a lot lately."

"You know what else has been happening a lot lately? I know things that I didn't know I knew, or I think of something and it just happens?"

"Kind of?" Molly said, in a way that sounded like *all the time.*

"I think it has something to do with the Reawakening."

"The Reaw-what?" Molly said, then waved a hand. "Okay, wait. First things first. What are you doing working here?"

"Covering for you!"

"What do you mean, covering for me? I haven't worked here since Marshall—ugh, Alberich—was here last summer."

I explained to her about my run-in with Sal, and how he'd wanted her to work here with Rocky. "But since you and Rocky seem to have found each other without his help, he decided to ask me to work here instead."

Molly laughed. "No offense, sis, but you're not exactly the vision of a counter girl."

"I figured if you could do it, it can't be that hard."

"Touché. It was kind of fun, but that was mostly because of the flirting."

"Flirting would definitely make this more fun."

"Ha! Trent would murder someone if he even thought you were flirting with him."

I didn't say anything, but suddenly the power kicked back on again.

"Whoa!" Molly said. "Was that you?"

"I guess."

"Oh! Something happened with you and Trent, didn't it? What?"

"Nothing," I murmured.

"Bull! What happened, Molly? Oh no! Did he break up with you?"

"He said we're just on a break."

"Oh, Hel no. You *do not* Ross-and-Rachel my sister. When I see that little punk, I'm going to tear him a new one."

"Before you judge him too harshly, listen." And as briefly as I could, I explained to her about the Reawakening.

"So what?" she said in a bemused voice. "I don't care. No one dumps my sister."

"Too late," I said.

"Okay, whatever, I'll deal with him later. So you think this Reawakening thing is happening to us?"

"I guess you'd have to call it an Awakening, since this is our first time around. But yeah. I mean, how else do you explain all these strange surges of power that have been coming out of our bodies, or, I dunno, dreams and whatever."

"Dreams?" Molly said. "What kind of dreams?"

"I've been having this crazy dream about Fair Haven. Where it's all, like—"

"Ruined?" Molly interjected.

"Yeah! How did you know?"

"And the front yard is like this icy swamp, and there are trees growing through the roof, and this weird light—"

"In the east wing?"

"Yes!"

"You've been having the same dream that I've been having!"

"I have."

I should say this wasn't totally unprecedented. When Molly and I were little girls, three and four, we often had the same dreams, and even sometimes talked to each other in our sleep—from different bedrooms. But it hadn't happened in well over a decade.

"So you saw the silhouette?"

"The what?"

"This woman's silhouette. In the east wing, by the green light."

"Ew, no." I paused, then said cautiously, "Do you think it's Mum?"

"I don't know," Molly said. "Before I can get close to her, I always wake up."

"But you think it's her?"

"I don't know," Molly said again, but I could tell that she thought it was—that she was afraid it was.

"How is she?" I asked now. "How are things between you two?"

Molly frowned at me. "Wait, you don't know?"

"Don't know what?"

"That she's been in England for the past two weeks?"

"No, why would I know that? And why's she there?"

"Seriously?" Molly said. "You don't know?"

"Um, that's why I asked what she's doing there."

"Mardi, she won Wimbledon yesterday!"

"She did?" I asked incredulously. "How do I not know this?"

"I don't know. It's been everywhere. She's even going to be on *Jimmy Kimmel* tonight."

"Oh, my gods, I have got to get out of this sandwich shop! But wait. If she's been in England for the past two weeks, what have you been doing?"

And . . . snap! The lights went off again, and the refrigerator powered down.

"Molly! What—holy crap! No! You—you and Rocky?"

My voice was practically squealing. "And you didn't tell me first? Or call me right after?"

"It just kind of happened," Molly said, blushing.

"I can't believe this. And you didn't call me?"

"Are you mad?"

"At you? No. I mean, I'm still mad about Mum kicking the Gardiners out of Fair Haven, and you taking her side, but of course I want you to be happy."

"I am happy," she said.

I was jealous that she knew something I didn't, but I was glad we were talking again. I missed her.

The power began blinking on and off.

"Is that you?" I said.

"I think it's you," Molly said. "Maybe it's both of us."

I told myself to calm down, and I could see her doing the same. Eventually the lights stopped blinking and everything went dark.

"Wait, do you think we can leave the power on? I have a couple thousand dollars of food that'll go bad otherwise."

"Let's do it together," Molly said. "On three. One. Two. Three."

I willed the power on, and even as I did, I felt a kind of energy moving through me, and realized it was Molly, and the lights popped on.

"Did you feel that?" Molly said.

"That was you, wasn't it?"

"I think I've felt that before," she said. "I just never realized it."

"Maybe it's because we've been apart for the past two weeks."

"Ugh, it was terrible."

I laughed. "You don't sound like you've been having that bad of a time."

"You know what I mean. Rocky's great. But without you it just didn't feel the same."

"I know." I bumped her shoulder. We weren't the sentimental type. For most of our seventeen years, all we did was fight and compete for our father's attention. But we were sisters. Twins. We were each other's closest companion and fiercest enemy.

There was a knock on the door.

"Rocky!" we both said at the same time, and Molly ran to the door, unlocked it, threw it open.

"Hey," he said. "Am I interrupting? I was tired of waiting in the car."

"No," Molly said soothingly, patting him on the back. "We're done. You remember my sister, Mardi."

"Hey, Mardi."

"Hey, Rocky," I said. He wasn't like the preppie monsters Molly often dated, and I immediately decided I liked him.

"So did you get your coffee?" Rocky asked her. He curled his fingers into hers, pulled Molly close to him, and kissed her softly.

"Uh, yeah," Molly said, then kissed him back.

Then he kissed her back.

Then she kissed him back.

Get a room, people!

"So I guess we should be heading out to the Inn," Rocky said. "Dad texted. He said he's got some lunch for us."

"Right," Molly said. She turned to me. "So I'll see you around?" she said, and in that moment, I realized she was going to go back to Fair Haven. To Mum. Somehow I'd just assumed that she was going to come back to Ingrid's with me.

"Sure!" I said with false brightness. "We'll totally see each other around!" I could feel the power surging in me again and had to tamp it down before one of the coolers blew a motor. "Bye!"

But Molly was already out the door. A moment later, a bright yellow Maserati flew down the street, with Molly at the wheel.

"Molly? Driving? The world really is coming to an end."

∗ 19 ∗

CHANDELIER

From the Diary of Molly Overbrook

I woke up the morning after I saw Mardi to an empty bed. I'd made Rocky go back to Sal's because I wasn't sure when Mum was getting in. She might have been trying to win the Coolest Mom of All Time award, but that didn't mean she wouldn't flip her wig if she came home to find her teenage daughter in bed with a boy.

I had to smile at the thought. Here I was, the goddess of strength, worried about what my mortal mother would do if she caught me in bed with my boyfriend. But I had a lot more experience being a teenager than I did being a goddess, and like every other teenager, I had a pretty good instinct for just how far I could push it.

I hopped in the shower, washed quickly, then pulled on a pair of shorts and a tank top—the AC was cranking inside the mansion, but it looked blisteringly hot outside. Then I headed downstairs. I'd been living there for two weeks, but really, I'd been at Rocky's every day and hung out with him until I went to bed. The only substantial amount of time I'd spent there had been the day before yesterday, and, well, I hadn't been paying too much attention to my surroundings, if you know what I mean. But now as I walked through the wide empty hallways, I was struck anew by the abandoned nature of the place. Not abandoned exactly, but invaded I guess. Even though virtually every trace of the Gardiners had been removed, the place still oozed their presence—in the ghostly outlines of paintings and pictures and rugs, in the paint colors and wallpapers, which reeked of the Georgian aesthetic that Trent's mom favored. Yet swirling around that was a second, more modern presence. The gadgety appliances in the kitchen. The sectional sofa in the drawing room, which had shown up last week and remained the only piece of furniture on the ground floor, aside from a couple of chrome barstools around the kitchen island. The shiny new Maserati. Slowly but surely, Fair Haven was being dragged into the twenty-first century.

And yet, underneath both of these feelings, deeper than them, older than them, was that strange swirling cool energy that emanated from the ballroom. It was almost imperceptible. If the phone rang or I was watching TV, I forgot all about it. But when I first woke up in the morning and my mind was clear, I felt it as clearly as a draft coming in through an open window.

I made my way to the ballroom now, thinking about what Mardi had told me yesterday: that she'd been having the same dream I'd been having. Did that make it more significant? More ominous? She seemed much less bothered by it than I was, but that's Mardi: always putting a brave face on everything. Part of me thought that we'd been sharing the dream just because we missed each other, and this was our minds' way of reaching out for each other. But a bigger part of me told me that was too simple. That we wouldn't be having such a detailed dream over and over again if it wasn't trying to communicate something specific. Something about Fair Haven, and about some kind of danger that it faced, or maybe that came from it. But what?

I found myself at the door of the ballroom. I'd never paid attention to the ornately inlaid panels before, but as I examined them, I realized they corresponded exactly to what I'd seen in my dream. I even recognized one little scratch that I hadn't paid any attention to in the dream—I mean, the door was so damaged that one scratch out of hundreds was hardly noticeable—yet now it popped right out at me, as if to tell me that the doors I'd seen in my dream had really been these doors, and not just something my imagination had made up. Eerie.

Unlike the dream doors, however, these were still mounted on perfectly oiled hinges, and they swung open at a touch. The current of energy grew instantly stronger, so much so that I wondered if perhaps the pattern on the doors wasn't some kind of hex holding it in check, or disguising it from immortal beings who could sense these things. Whatever it was, the sense of . . . something trying to push its way into this room—this world—was so distinct that my skin immediately goose-pimpled, a sensation I'd read about but never actually felt before, since I'm immune to temperatures that fall within the normal range of weather. I rubbed my hands over my arms to warm them, wondering if maybe the Gardiners had been using their magic to keep this energy in check, or if it was just more noticeable with nothing else in the room. The only things left in the tennis court–sized room were its three chandeliers: two good-sized ones at either end, and one massive one in the center.

"I'm gonna swing from the chandelier," I sang. "From the cha-hand-e-lier."

"I don't know if that's such a good idea. That ceiling's older than this country. Who knows how much weight it can support."

I whirled around. Mum was standing in the doorway, dressed in light gray wrap skirt and a skintight midriff-baring top that showed off her toned abs.

"Mum!" I yelled, and ran into her arms.

I hit her so hard that anyone else would have been knocked over, but Janet Steele just threw her arms around me, picked me up, and whirled me around as if I were a five-year-old.

"Welcome back! Congratulations! I'm so glad you're home. And oh, my gods, you won Wimbledon. That match was awesome! I missed you so much!"

"Slow down, slow down," she said. "One thing at a time. First of all, let me get a good look at you." She took a step back and ran her eyes over me, then smiled proudly. "I have to hand it to myself, I gave you some good genes." She pursed her lips. "But there's something different about you."

My mind immediately flashed on my conversation with Freya at the North Inn a few days ago. How she'd been able to tell that Rocky and I were virgins just by looking at us. Could Mum do the same thing?

"Midgard to Mooi," I heard Mum's voice. "Come in, Mooi."

"Sorry, I spaced out there. What did you say?"

"I said it looks like you found the clothes I had Ivan pick out for you. Even so, there's something I've always wanted to do with my daughter."

My heart was still beating over my fears that Mum had figured out I'd had sex, and it was all I could do stammer out, "Wh-what's that?"

Mum flashed her best smile.

"Take her shopping."

I knew I shouldn't let it be so easy to buy my affections, but I couldn't help it. And hey, it's not going to be *that* easy. I have expensive taste.

"If this is your way of making up for lost time," I

said, "you're doing a fantastic job." I gave the chandelier a parting glance, then headed for the door. "Let's go buy my love."

There are a couple of nice shops in North Hampton, but Mum decided to drive us to East Hampton, where there's a Blue & Cream and BCBG and Theory and even Lilly Pulitzer. (Yes, I admit it. I like Lilly Pulitzer. Every girl should have at least one pair of short shorts that looks like it was made from the curtains in *The Sound of Music*.) We grabbed coffee and croissants at a café before we started, and by the time we finished, it was nearly three, and we went to the Clam Bar near Montauk, which is simply *the* 3:00 P.M. place on the East End. Fancy European cars (almost every one of them a convertible) lined the highway for a quarter mile in either direction because, in the classic Hamptons WASPy manner, everything has to be a little bit inconvenient or else it's déclassé or—gasp!—nouveau riche. But luck was with us as we pulled up: a Porsche was backing out of a space right in front of the restaurant.

We hopped out of the car, and even though there was a line of about fifty people, the maître d' took one look at Mum, then called over a couple of busboys.

"Pull out a table for Ms. Steele. Dune view, but make sure she can still see everyone."

I'd gone there a couple of times with Rocky, and I was a little afraid the maître d' was going to say something, but all her attention was focused on Mum—I could've been Mum's assistant for all she noticed me.

Less than a minute later, we were ensconced at a table on the far edge of the terrace, shielded from the sound and smell of the highway but still offering a view of the entire dining area. Mum had said hi to no fewer than six people as the maître d' led us to our table, but when one woman in an East Hampton Tennis Club polo asked for a picture, she just smiled and said, "I've got a starving daughter here. Look for me when I head out."

The woman looked at me with pure envy. "Your mother," she said rapturously, "is a *goddess*."

Janet laughed loudly. "I'm just a tennis player," she said. "It's Molly who's the goddess."

The maître d' asked if she could start us with anything, and Mum looked at me.

"Champagne seemed to go over well the last time I saw you," she said, "but I'm thinking today is more of a mojito kind of day. What do you say, Mooi?"

I blinked a little in surprise. Mum's joke about me being a goddess was one thing, but using my real name? She liked to push the envelope.

"Mojitos sound great."

"Two mojitos, please. Don Q Cristal if you've got it."

"Coming right up."

The maître d' walked away, and Mum turned to me. "What?"

"It's nothing," I said. "It's just that I don't quite believe I'm here. Like I'm going to wake up from this amazing dream where Janet Steele was my mother and she took me shopping and bought me mojitos with premium rum and told autograph hounds to wait until she'd fed her daughter. You're just, well, *fabulous*, aren't you?"

Mum smiled brightly. "I do my best with what nature gave me. And this is no dream. We're really here, and later you're going to use that divine metabolism of yours to sober up and drive your mother home while she sleeps it off in the passenger seat."

I had to shake my head in wonder. It was impossible to believe my mum was this cool, but she really was.

Our drinks came then, and Mum took a sip of the cool minty sweetness before speaking. "I couldn't help noticing that you put nearly five hundred miles on the odometer in the last two weeks. So tell me: what's his name?"

"Wh-what?" I stammered, caught off guard.

"You said yourself that you prefer to be driven than to drive. So I'm assuming you didn't put all those miles on the car yourself, and if you did, it wasn't for your own benefit. Plus I've seen you check your phone about twenty times."

In fact, I'd driven all over the East End with Rocky, showing him the sights, but I had no idea the miles had added up so much—or that I should have worried about them. And I had checked my phone several times that day, but Rocky hadn't texted or called even once. Nor had Mardi, for that matter.

"I, um," I started, then gave up any pretense of lying.

"His name's Rocky—Rocco. His dad owns the North Inn, where Freya works."

Mum frowned. "Rocco. That doesn't sound very Norse."

I knew what she meant by *Norse.*

"He's not a god, if that's what you're asking."

"Mooi!" Mum said, her voice soft but sharp. "A mortal!"

She said it the way some people use racial epithets, which was weird, to say the least, since she didn't know anything about Rocky, not to mention the fact that she was a mortal herself.

"I guess it runs in the family," I said, trying to joke it off.

Mum blinked her eyes in confusion. "What do you mean?"

"You and Dad?" I said. Who else could I have meant?

Mum frowned at the thought of Dad. "What your father and I had was very different," she said. "My family's connection to Aesir goes back generations. But you are a new goddess. You need to set your sights higher."

I really didn't want to get into the whole new gods thing.

"Whatever," I said. "He's just here for the summer. It's not a big deal."

Mum continued to frown for a moment longer, then suddenly smiled. "My first taste of a sulky teenager! How exciting!"

"I said it's nothing—"

"And I trust you," Mum said. "I'm sorry I overreacted. I've got seventeen years of parenting to catch up on. Truce?" she said, raising her glass.

I clinked mine against hers. "Truce," I said, and we drank on it. "So, uh, speaking of Dad," I began.

"Why, what a seamless transition," Mum joked, and we both laughed.

"Sorry," I said. "I know it's totally nosy, but, well, I'm dying to know."

"To know what?" she said, her voice so level that I couldn't tell if she was being coy or serious.

"Everything!" I blurted out. "I mean, mostly about how you met Dad and all that. You didn't just . . . seduce him, did you? You loved him, right? At least a little?"

Mum softened, and had a faraway look in her eyes, and ever so slowly a little, whimsical smile appeared on her face. She reached out and took my hand in one of hers and gave it a squeeze.

"Yes, Mooi, I did love your father. Very much. And it might surprise you to know that *he* seduced *me*."

I laughed. "Don't forget, I've spent the past seventeen years with Troy Overbrook. I've seen all his moves. So what did he do? Send you a drink at a bar, or just saunter up and use that million-dollar smile of his?"

Mum shook her head. "He bought out an entire stadium."

"He *what*?"

"It was 1996. I'd made it to the quarterfinals of the

US Open that year, which had helped get my name out there, but I was still working my way up the rankings. I was playing in a little tournament in Adelaide, Australia, of all places, just to get some practice time before the Australian Open, and when I walked out on court for my first round match, there was no one there except for the umpire and linesmen and four or five people in the players' boxes—and your father. Of course I didn't know then that he was only twenty-two years into a new body. All I knew was that there was this insanely cute boy sitting all by himself in the middle of the stands, and he only clapped when I made a point. My poor opponent was so flustered she could hardly hit the ball, and, well, she was playing me too. I ended beating her 6–0, 6–1 in forty-two minutes. Your dad told me later he spent ninety-eight thousand dollars to buy up all the tickets, plus another twenty grand or so on a private jet from New York, which comes out to almost three thousand dollars a minute. That's a pretty expensive blind date."

"And? Did you go up to him? Did he come up to you?"

"Like I told you, Mooi: I never make the first move. Thor came up to me. He said he'd seen me play at the US Open the year before and he'd decided then and there that he had to meet me."

"But couldn't he have just found you in New York?"

"Oh, that would be too easy, wouldn't it? Especially for a god. He wanted to impress me. And he said he was a little intimidated."

"Dad? I can't believe it! No offense, but he's a straight-up manwhore."

Mum laughed out loud. "Believe me, I had plenty of opportunities to find out. But I wasn't another lingerie model or wannabe starlet. I was an athlete, somebody who had to work her ass off to get anything in life. And then I guess he sensed something about me. Something different. Unique. He wanted to do his research."

"What do you mean?"

"Your father thought I might have been a Rhinemaiden."

I gasped. Alberich had said our mother was a Rhinemaiden! Maybe she wasn't human after all. Maybe she would live forever, with me and Mardi.

"Are you?" I asked eagerly.

"I can tell by the look on your face that you wish the answer was yes, but unfortunately it's no. My ten-times-removed great-grandmother was."

"But weren't the Rhinemaidens goddesses? Or some kind of nature spirit that's basically the same thing as a goddess?"

Mum shook her head. "Legends portray them that way, but they were as mortal as me and the maître d' and everyone else on this terrace—except you. But the bridge was destroyed and Odin was trapped in Asgard; the link between the maidens and the Rhinegold began to weaken. Thor was afraid that they would no longer be able to protect the gold, and so he stole it from them. The maidens died defending it, but my ancestral grandmother, Flosshilde, survived."

"Dad killed the Rhinemaidens? I can't believe it."

"I'm sorry, Mooi, but it's true."

"So what happened then? And why'd Dad spare your grandmother?"

"Why else do men spare women? Because he loved her, of course. But Odin said he had to choose, the gold or the maiden. Thor agreed to let her go only if the gold could be secured with the most powerful spells to his prophesied children, Mooi and Magdi. Odin thought he had won, since the prophecies said that Magdi and Mooi's mother was going to be a Jotun, and since Midgard was cut off from Jotunheim as well as Asgard, he assumed Thor's children would never be born. But prophecies are written in symbolic language, and it seems they misinterpreted what the ancient oracles meant by 'giantess.' And here you are."

"But wait. Did Dad know all this when he saw you?"

Mum shook her head. "He only suspected it. Apparently, I bear more than a passing likeness to my ancestral grandmother."

"And what about you? Did you know it?"

Mum smiled and shook her head. "I suspected it, but I wasn't sure." Another smile, this one rueful and nostalgic and lovelorn all at the same time. "No, all he wanted to do was finally kiss his Rhinemaiden."

I reached for my drink, and was surprised to find

it was empty. I'd hardly noticed drinking it. "So what happened when you met? You won your match, he came up to you, and . . . *what?*"

Mum sipped at her own drink, her lips curled in a demure smile around her straw.

"He shook my hand, and he said, 'My name is Troy Overbrook. I enjoyed watching you play today, Ms. Stahl.'"

"Stahl?"

"German for 'steel.'"

"Oh! He was testing you! What did you say?"

"Your father wasn't finished yet. He said, 'If you win the tournament, would it be okay if I took you out to dinner to celebrate?'"

"Oh, my gods, Dad! Such a smoothie! What did you say?"

Mum smiled wickedly.

"I said, 'My name is Steele, Mr. Overbrook, and I'm going to win this tournament, so you'd better make a reservation now.'"

I clapped my hand over mouth. "And?" I said through my fingers.

"And your father said, 'I already did.'"

* 20 *

HANGING ON
THE TELEPHONE

Mardi-Overbrook-Journal.docx

I thought Molly and I were back on track after we ran into each other in the Cheesemonger, but I guess not. I texted her the next morning when I woke up, and then again after I'd had a cup of coffee, and after I showered, I called her. The texts were unanswered, and the call went straight to voice mail, as if she'd shut her phone off. Which, if you know Molly—or, well, any teenage girl—you know it's something she'd *never* do.

Which meant my sister was ignoring me.

Part of me thought that maybe she was hanging with Rocky, but another part of me knew that Janet was getting back from England today, and that Molly was probably with her. This was all but confirmed when Rocky showed up at the Cheesemonger a half hour after I opened the shop. From the look on his face, he was as happy to be there as I was.

"Hey," I said jokingly. "What can I get you?"

Rocky shrugged unhappily. "An apron, I guess."

"What?" I pretended to be nonchalant, but inside I was thrilled. If I haven't made this clear, making sandwiches is *way* overrated. "You're here to work?"

"Sal's been wanting me to work here since I got to North Hampton, but I was hanging with Molly and I guess he let it go. But when she didn't come over this morning, he was all like, Why don't you head down to the Cheesemonger?"

"So where is Molly? I thought you two were joined at the hip by this point."

Another shrug, even more dejected. "Dunno. I texted her a couple of times this morning and tried calling her too, but it went straight to voice mail. I guess she's hanging with her mom or something?"

"Janet's back?" I said, as if I didn't know.

I could tell that Rocky had noticed I said *Janet* instead of *Mum*, just as he'd said *Sal* instead of *Dad*, but he didn't ask me about it.

"Molly thought she was getting back today, or maybe last night. She had some talk shows to do—*The View*, Seth Meyers, one of those ESPN roundtable things where people talk really fast at the top of their lungs—so she told Molly she wasn't a hundred percent sure when she'd manage to get out here. I guess she made it."

"Well, don't worry. I'm sure she'll call you in a bit. So," I continued, grabbing an apron from beneath the counter and tossing it to him, "you want to help me get Billy and Bruce's order ready?"

"I guess," Rocky said, draping the apron over his head. "If you tell me what that means."

I nodded. "If you head to the walk-in and bring out the parsley–pine nut pesto, arugula-walnut pesto, habanero–black bean tapenade, chipotle mayonnaise, red pepper hummus, gefilte fish, smoked brisket, and blood pudding, I'll get out the cured meats, cheeses, and pickled products, and we'll assembly line this production together in no time."

Rocky looked at me slack-jawed, as if waiting to see if I was joking.

"It's not as overwhelming as it sounds. Just bring out everything from the middle two shelves left of the door."

With two people working, we got the order together before their errand boy arrived.

After that, we got the sandwiches ready for the 11:30 train, then passed the rest of the day in near silence, both of us on our phones when we weren't helping customers or dealing with the occasional delivery. I resisted texting or calling Molly, but I couldn't stop myself from looking in on her various social media accounts. She wasn't posting anywhere, not even a single like on

Facebook or Instagram or one raving Tweet about the latest celebrity breakup or shoe trend. Was it possible she really had turned her phone off? Was Ragnarok upon us?

It was busy enough that we never really got bored, however, and soon enough it was five o'clock. There was one last mini-rush from the afternoon train, and then we closed.

"Don't worry" was the last thing I said to Rocky on his first day at the Cheesemonger. "I'm sure she'll call you later."

That night, after we closed up shop, I decided to head over to the North Inn. I'd heard through Ingrid that Molly and Rocky were spending a lot of time there, and so I'd avoided it out of respect. I'd figured if they hadn't invited me, they wanted some alone time, and the North Inn was the one surefire place where Molly and Rocky would get served. Who was I to stand in the way of young love? But now that I knew Molly had put Rocky (and me) on hold, I figured the Inn was fair game, and I hadn't seen Freya in a while. And I could have used a good stiff drink, preferably something magicked up enough so that even my divine body would feel it.

When I walked into the bar, Freya took one look at me, shook her head, and pointed to a barstool. I slumped into it gratefully as Freya began pulling out unlabeled bottles and lining them up on the bar.

"I'm a good aunt, aren't I?" she said as she began pouring transparent, brown, and red liquids together.

"What do you mean?" I said confusedly. "Of course you are."

"I serve you drinks even though you're underage. I give you the run of my closet, which contains the best items of clothing between here and Madison Avenue. Or, let's face it, between here and Rodeo Drive."

"You're awesome, Freya. Getting to know you has been one of the best things about this past year."

"And I'm pretty good with the advice, if I do say so myself. Not too many people know how to negotiate the fine line between being an immortal goddess and a teenager, but I don't think I've ever steered you in the wrong direction, have I?"

"Of course not. You're like a big sister–best friend– super-cool aunt all rolled into one."

Freya nodded as she poured her concoction into a cocktail shaker filled with ice, capped it, and shook it vigorously. She set the shaker aside, grabbed a chilled martini glass and a bottle of absinthe, poured a splash of the green, anise-smelling liquid into the glass and swirled it around, coating the inside of the glass, then poured the residue out and strained the liquid from the shaker into the glass. It had a beautiful golden-brown color, just touched by red, and smelled of licorice and cinnamon, and the tangy bite of some kind of sharp whiskey. My mouth immediately began to water.

I reached for the drink, but Freya pulled it away.

"Then why, dear Mardi," she said in a tone that was half hurt, half theatrical, "would you not tell me that you broke up with Trent Gardiner *two weeks ago*?"

It was still early, and there were only a half dozen people in the bar, all coupled off at individual tables, but still I winced at Freya's words. It made it seem so final.

I looked up at Freya, who was eyeing me with an expression that was half reproachful, half sorrowful.

"I'm always here for you and your sister, Mardi. Always." She pushed the drink toward me. "Now. Dish. What did that dirty SOB do?"

One hour and three drinks later, I raised my hand and waved it around.

"And why should I even care if he thinks I'm too young?" I said in a voice just this side of a shout. "No offense," I said to Freya. "You look great for your age."

"None taken," said Freya, who was busily pouring a round of shots for a group of investment bankers who were doing their best imitation of weekend rockers. She winked at the banker-rockers with a look that said, "Kids. They can't handle their alcohol."

"What's in these things anyway?" I said, holding up my empty glass. "I don't usually get drunk, but I am feeling *all right*."

"A magician never tells," Freya said, pushing the drinks toward the banker-rockers and slipping the stack of twenties they gave her into the register. She turned toward me.

"So enough about him," she said. "Here's the real question: do you want him back?"

"Oh, gods," I said, pushing my glass toward her. "That requires another drink."

"Give me your car keys, and I'll think about it."

I pulled my car keys from my pocket and handed them over. It was worth it.

"So?" Freya said as she began lining up her bottled potions and tonics. "Forget about Tyr for a moment. What is it that Mardi wants?"

Freya's use of Trent's Norse name made me think about what he had said that terrible day on the beach— how as the memories of his millennia-long past came back to him, he felt further and further away from me. And though I'd never thought about it much, I'd always felt it. Despite the fact that Trent looked and dressed and generally acted like a hot eighteen-year-old, there was always something older lurking inside of that. A kind of amused distance in his eyes when he watched me and Molly shopping or bickering or doing the "Single Ladies" dance. And now that I thought about it, I realized that detachment had always kept me from committing to him 100 percent. I gave him 90 percent maybe, 95 percent even, but there was always a part of myself I held back. A part of me knew Trent would always be different from me, and maybe that difference would never be bridged.

From out of nowhere, a thought popped into my head: *He's Aesir. You're Mimir.* You don't belong together. I could even hear it in Janet Steele's Australian accent.

I shook my head to make the words go away. Just because I didn't know what I wanted, like every other teenage girl in her first relationship, didn't mean I was ready to sign on to some cosmic war between the generations of gods. It sucked to be dumped, but I didn't actually want to kill Trent. But all I said to Freya's question was:

"Have you met Sal's son? Rocky?"

Freya smiled, but it quickly turned into a frown when she saw the look on my face.

"You mean the cute boy who's been following Molly around like a puppy dog for the past two weeks? The one Molly seems to be equally smitten by?"

"If she's so smitten with him, why didn't she return any of his texts or calls today?"

Freya pushed a fresh drink toward me. "Because she's a woman, and it's her prerogative. And how do you know this?"

"Because Sal made him work at the Cheesemonger with me today?"

"Back up. You're working at the Cheesemonger? That's why you smell ever so faintly of speck and Gruyère?"

The last sandwich I'd made that night had been the Italo Calvino: speck (an Italian ham that's somewhere between pancetta and prosciutto), Gruyère, rosemary-infused olive oil, twenty-five-year-old balsamic vinegar, served open-faced atop a chewy piece of focaccia.

"Wow. That's some nose you've got on you."

"Never mind my nose. You're not really thinking about making a play for your sister's boyfriend, are you? Are you that mad at her?"

"I would never make a play for Rocky if Molly was with him. But let's face it: this was her pattern before Alberich messed with her head last summer. She crushes on a boy, attaches herself to him at the hip for two weeks, then abruptly severs the connection and runs for the hills. I would never go against girl code or twin code, but still . . . "

"Huh," Freya said, in this way that was supposed to be blasé but was clearly just a stalling tactic. She whipped up a couple of drinks, then made her way back to me.

"How many men do you think I've been with?" she said in a casual voice.

"What?" I said, taken aback. "How should I—"

"*A lot*," Freya said sharply. "You live three thousand years in a body like this, you see plenty of action, especially when you're the goddess of love. And how many of those men do you think I met because Ingrid had dated them first?"

"Um, I don't know—"

"None! Zero, zilch, *null*. You don't go for your sister's castoffs, Mardi. It just never, ever, ever turns out well!"

"How do you know if you've never tried it?" I asked, annoyed at Freya for reading my mind.

"Seriously?" Freya said. "Our kind have started wars over this kind of thing. Promise me that you won't go after this poor boy."

"Fine," I said. "I won't go after him." *But what if he comes after me?*

"Don't think I don't know what you're thinking," Freya said. "I invented the it's-not-my-fault-if-he-makes-the-first-move excuse. Literally."

"Look, I promised not to go after him. But I can't promise to be a saint."

"Well, don't call me when this explodes in your face. And by explodes, I mean literally explodes. I don't care if Molly's dumped him or not. She is not going to look kindly on you taking sloppy seconds on her ex."

The way she said *sloppy seconds* made me look at Freya sharply. Of course she was right. I was being crazy even entertaining this. I had to stop thinking of Rocky. He was totally off-limits. To change the subject, I said, "Have you ever heard about the Mimir?"

Freya pursed her lips. "That's not what you were going to ask me about."

"What makes you say that?" I said as innocently as I could.

"Because whatever you were thinking about had something to do with love." She jerked a thumb into her chest. "Goddess of love, remember?"

"I'll say!" one of the investment bankers called out from down the bar.

"Easy, slugger," Freya called, but it seemed to break

her line of thought. "What did you ask me about? The Mimir."

I nodded.

"Definitely rings a bell," Freya said, "but I can't put my finger on it."

"It refers to the gods of Midgard. As distinct from the Aesir and Vanir."

Freya laughed. "Hate to break it to you, but the Aesir and Vanir *are* the only gods."

"Well, yeah," I said. "Right now they are. But according to Janet, prophecies have been predicting the Mimir since the beginning of time. Supposedly they're the offspring of the Aesir and humans, and they'll overthrow the Aesir and the Vanir in the same way the Aesir overthrew the giants and took control of Asgard."

For a moment, Freya continued mixing up a couple of East End Manhattans, but then she suddenly put her shaker down and turned to me.

"Hold on a sec," she said. "Janet thinks that you and Molly are these Mimir peeps?"

I nodded my head. It sounded kind of silly when I heard it aloud.

Freya quickly grabbed her shaker, poured the two Manhattans, and shooed her customers away.

"On me," she said when they tried to pay. "Okay, first of all," she continued to me, "it's not like the Jotun and the Aesir were all buddy-buddy and then the Aesir just got it in their heads to take down their friends. The Jotun were a violent, oppressive bunch, subjugating any kingdom or country they could find, killing people pretty much at random, and enslaving the rest. Including the Aesir. What Odin and the others did was no different from what the European settlers did to the Native Americans."

Freya's tone had been forceful enough that a few people had turned to look at her, but she glared at them so hard that they all quickly glanced away. One clueless fellow approached the bar with an empty glass in hand, but Freya snapped, "Can't you see I'm busy?" and he went scurrying back to his table.

"Secondly," Freya continued, turning back to me, "these Mimir that Janet told you about. I'm starting to remember the stories. But they're not the children of Aesir and humans, like you and Molly. They're the children of Aesir and Jotun. And given how much the Aesir and the Jotun hate each other, the chances of two of them hooking up are looking a lot worse than the chances of you and Tyr getting back together."

"Ouch!" I said. "It's not like I *believe* anything she told us," I continued defensively. "It's just why I haven't been all up her skirt the way Molly has. I don't think she should be telling those kinds of stories any more than you do—and especially if they're not true."

"Sorry," Freya said. "But that kind of nonsense makes me angry. I've got half a mind to head out to Fair Haven tomorrow and give Janet a piece of my mind. That said, I think you shouldn't avoid her."

"Really?"

"She's your mom. Sounds like she's got a chip on her shoulder, which, given the way our kind treated her ancestors, seems understandable. But the only thing that's going to get rid of it is if someone starts telling her the truth."

"That makes sense, I guess. Though I'm not exactly known for my tact."

"News flash, Mardi: none of the Overbrooks are. Nor are the Beauchamps, for that matter. Even Ingrid's got a temper. But like I said. She's your mom. You deserve to have a relationship with her. If it's a bit strained sometimes, well, welcome to the rest of the world. Moms are complicated." She glanced up at the sky. "Sorry, Joanna," she mouthed with a grin.

I took a moment to finish my drink. "Okay, then," I said as I put it down. "Maybe I'll give her a second chance." I slid my empty glass toward Freya and stood up. "You want to call me a cab?"

"Nah," Freya said, tossing me back my keys. "You're not drunk anymore."

"What?" I said, then realized that I did in fact feel totally sober. "How did you . . . ?" I glanced at my empty glass, which Freya was whisking away.

"Helps when the bartender's a witch." She winked, then hurried down the bar to a fresh round of customers.

* 21 *

TONIGHT'S THE NIGHT

From the Diary of Molly Overbrook

It was over a week before I spoke to Mardi again. I have to admit, I was surprised when she didn't respond to my texts or answer any of my calls. As the goddess of rage, Mardi is, not surprisingly, hot-tempered, but she's not petty or vindictive.

I was more surprised, though, that Rocky didn't reach out to me either or respond to my texts. He'd seemed totally cool about what happened on Saturday. So why freak out now? Part of me thought that maybe it was because I didn't call him on the Monday when Mum came home until late that night, when I went up to bed. But we'd been running around constantly and there hadn't been a chance. For some reason, I knew Mum wouldn't like it if I was on my phone while I was with her, and I was also learning about her life, and her time with Dad, and that was so fascinating that I barely gave my phone a thought the whole day.

And Janet Steele, I was learning, was a busy woman. By the time I rolled out of bed in the morning, she'd already been up for hours. She would have gone for a five-mile run on the beach or a two-mile swim in the ocean, or worked out in the state-of-the-art gym she'd set up in the basement. She also spent at least an hour on social media, making a point to respond personally to fifteen or twenty of her Twitter followers as well as posting a few pics on Instagram and her official Facebook page. A lot of the recent pictures featured me, which on the one hand was kind of amazing because there I was: Molly Overbrook, eating barbecued shrimp with Janet Steele (with a tamarind-sesame glaze courtesy of Ivan); Molly Overbrook, trying on bikinis with Janet Steele (a Lolli one-piece with cutouts in all the right places for her, a Stone Fox cheeky bikini with a string bow over the bottom for me); Molly Overbrook, picking out bedroom furniture with Janet Steele (an Art Deco white lacquered suite whose six-foot-tall wedding cake headboard looked like something right out of a Golden Age of Hollywood black-and-white movie, probably because it had been used in Jean Harlow's bedroom in *Dinner at Eight*).

But on the other hand, well, it was only me, and aside from selfies I snapped in the bathroom to get my makeup approved by my friends at school, I'd never really been photographed alone.

Sure, we had our ups and downs, but it was always me and Mardi because, you know, we were twins. A package deal. We were always photographed together, one punky, the other a little more princess. It was just how it had always been, and looking at pictures of myself without Mardi made me feel lonely. But when I shot her a cute little text, nothing came back. It was like my messages were going out into a black hole.

After her morning workout and fan stuff, Mum practiced tennis. Fair Haven was from "that generation of mansions," as Mum put it, that had a clay tennis court, which is a perfectly fine kind of tennis court, but it's more European than American, and besides, the clay court season was over, and it was time for hard courts, so Mum drove to the North Hampton Tennis Club to practice there. I didn't even know there was a North Hampton Tennis Club, although it made sense—there was a North Hampton Yacht Club, a North Hampton Polo Club, and a North Hampton *Water* Polo Club, so of course there would be a tennis club too. It wasn't big, only twelve courts, but even so, Mum didn't want anyone watching her practice, so she made arrangements for the club to close each day between 10:00 and 1:00 so she could practice in private, which is to say, she basically rented all twelve courts at a premium fee, because the just-before lunch slot was by far the most popular time for the North Hampton set to get their game in, since their hour on court was really just an excuse for them to spend another hour in the day spa getting a massage and pedicure and facial, followed by another two hours dining on a liquid lunch. I assumed it must be costing Mum a fortune to get the club to turn away so much business, but it turned out Mum's apparel sponsor was this cool Australian sportswear brand called Lorna Jane, which was trying to break into the American market. LJ of course had a Janet Steele line of tennis clothes, and in exchange for allowing a photographer to snap pics of Mum working out in her own line, the company picked up the bill for her practices. This is why the rich get richer: because half the time, they don't actually pay for anything.

So anyway, 10:00–1:00 tennis practice, and of course I went with Mum the first couple of times because, one, I loved tennis, and she was Janet Steele, and of course I was going to watch her at a private practice, and two, she was my mum, and I wanted to spend every minute with her to make up for lost time.

What I didn't realize I'd be doing, though, was not just watching, but *playing* tennis with her.

"Uh-uh," she said the first day we went to the club. "No daughter of Janet Steele's is going to sit on the sidelines while Mum's on the court."

I think I mentioned that I'd played tennis a little. I mean, you're a girl growing up on the Upper East Side, you're going to take tennis lessons, along with ballet, piano, conversational French, dressage, and cotillion. (Seriously. People still do that.) So yeah, I could swing a racket. But with Janet Steele?

"Uh, that's okay, Mum. I'm happy to just watch and tweet a few pictures for you."

Mum didn't say anything. All she did was toss me a racket. Since her Wilson Pro Staff rackets cost $2,000 each (they stopped making them in the 1980s, but Mum swears by them), I figured I'd better catch it before it clattered to the ground, and more on reflex than anything, my right hand shot out and snatched it from the air. My palm stung from the impact. Turned out Mum threw a racket just like she hit a tennis ball: hard.

"Nice reflexes," she said. "Let's see how you serve."

I tossed the ball up in the air a couple of times to see how the breeze affected it. Then I held the ball up.

"Ready?"

I tossed the ball in the air. I smashed the racket into it. It shot away from me, skimming a half inch over the top of the net and slicing deep into the service box. Mum actually had to jump the get the ball, and for one brief moment, I thought she might actually miss. Then the ball was whizzing back at me faster than I would have believed possible. I was still unwinding from my serve as the ball bounced off the baseline and smashed into the fence behind me.

I turned and saw that Mum had hit it so hard that the ball stuck in the chain link. When I turned back to Mum, a broad smile was plastered on her face.

"Mooi," she said proudly, "that was one hell of a serve." Her face set in a determined line. "Again."

• • •

And that's how the next ten days passed. Mum dragged me to the club every morning (although dragged makes it sound like she forced me when I wanted to go), and we played for two, three, sometimes four hours a day, then lunched on tuna niçoise salads or ostrich burgers. When word got out that Janet Steele was playing tennis with her daughter every morning at the North Hampton Tennis Club, people began to show up to watch. Since Mum had rented the place out, the club left it up to her to let the spectators in or not. At first, she said no, thinking the crowd would make me self-conscious, but when I told her I didn't mind, she gave the okay. By the end of the week, it was all over the Twitterverse and the blogosphere and the gossip mill, there were more than a hundred people in the tiny bleachers each morning. And the crazy thing was, most of them were there for me. I mean, don't get me wrong, they never would have come if Janet Steele hadn't been on the court. But everyone knew who Janet was, and how she played. I was the unknown commodity, and they all wanted to see what I could do. And it turned out what I could do is play tennis.

Even today I couldn't tell you if magic was involved. I mean, I know objectively that it had to be. I only ever played tennis in seventh and eighth grade, and here I was holding my own with the number one tennis player in the world. That couldn't just be good genes, right?

But I certainly never thought about magic when I was on the court. There were a dozen pretty simple spells I could have cast that would have improved my performance and made Mum's worse—hexes I could have cast on my racket or the balls or, say, Mum's shoes (I will admit that the idea of making each of her shoes weigh ten pounds appealed to the practical joker in me), but once I stepped on the court, all those fantasies disappeared and all I wanted was to hit a tennis ball with my mum. Never mind that she was Janet Steele. Never mind that I was the goddess of strength. I was a teenage girl with a mother, and we had this interest in common. I wanted to milk it as much as possible, as long as possible.

But each night as I made my way through my social media feeds, checking out what people had to say about me, I knew that wasn't all that was going on. I scanned through the thousands of comments, always looking for one name that never showed up. Mardi's. I knew she had to be seeing the pictures—despite the obscurity spells Joanna had cast around North Hampton, they were still showing up everywhere, from TMZ to Dlisted to Radar. I thought that if she could see how much fun Mum was, how normal she was, she would realize that we weren't sitting around scheming about killing Dad or casting Ingrid and Freya into some dark corner of Hel. But if Mardi was indeed seeing all the pictures and stories about me and Mum, she gave no indication.

And of course there was Rocky too. The couple of

weeks I'd spent with him had been like a dream, and after a day of missing him, and another day of being pissed at him, and then a third day of being pissed at myself for missing him, he started to fade away from my mind. *Screw him,* I told myself (no pun intended). *If he can't take a modern woman, it's his loss.* Of course a part of me knew I was just covering up my real feelings with anger, it was easier to be mad than to be hurt. Between Rocky this summer and Alberich last summer, I was starting to think that boys weren't worth the trouble.

Almost two weeks had gone by and I felt like a junkie desperate for a fix. I needed to see my sister—to talk to her, punch her, fight with her, make up with her, gossip with her, steal clothes from her, get makeup tips from her. (Okay, not that last thing. If I want raccoon eyes, I'll walk into a door or something. But everything else.) And so anyway, Mum must've read my mind, because on Friday afternoon, as we were munching on Caprese salads made from heirloom tomatoes, buffalo mozzarella, and olive oil infused with Thai basil, she said:

"So you know tomorrow I have to fly down to the Bahamas for the Nassau Open. It's one of the mandatory tournaments on the pro tour, and as much as I'd like to skip it and hang out here with my daughter, I'm the defending champion, and my ranking will take a big hit if I don't play."

Of course I knew the tournament was coming up and that Mum was the defending champion. I'd watched on TV last year as she beat Aga Radwanska for the title. But I wasn't expecting what came out of her mouth next.

"I'm hoping you'll come and sit in my player's box. And I'm hoping you can talk Magdi into coming too."

My heart flipped in my chest when she said that she was hoping I'd come, and then it did a backflip with a triple twist and, I don't know, a half gainer, when she said she was hoping Mardi would come too.

"Oh, it's perfect!" I said. "There's no way she could say no to an invitation like that!" Which didn't really make sense, since Mardi cared about tennis about as much as she cared about, oh, Ariana Grande, which is to say: not at all.

"My fingers are crossed," Mum said. "But even so, I think it'd be better if you asked her. Phrase it as a sister-sister thing, not a mother-daughter thing."

There was something about the way Mum said this. It seemed a little dishonest. A little sneaky. But I also suspected she was right.

"I'll do it!"

"Marvy," Mum said. She reached into her bag and tossed me the car keys. "Take the Maserati. I'll have Ivan pick me up in the Maybach."

After almost two weeks of being driven around, it was fun to be back behind the wheel, especially of a

Maserati. That seat—I mean I know it was the same shape as the one on the passenger side, but somehow, with one hand curled around the gear stick and the other dangling off the leather-clad steering wheel, the fit just seemed so much tighter.

This feeling of rightness was amplified by, like, a hundred when I pressed the ignition and the car roared into life. The sound was so full of adrenaline that I didn't even think about turning the stereo on. The engine was its own music, and I thrilled along to it for the twenty minutes it took me to drive from the tennis club to the Cheesemonger. I had a brief flash of Marshall/Alberich, but pushed it out of my mind and marched up to the door of the shop.

I stopped just before I pushed it open, however, because when I looked through the glass and past the ten-dollar stone-ground ancient-grain flatbreads and fifteen-dollar mochi cookies, I saw that Mardi wasn't working alone.

She was with Rocky McLaughlin.

There they were, in matching seersucker aprons with the Cheesemonger logo embroidered on the chest (say what you want about Alberich, he had surprisingly good taste in food and clothes for a dark elf), hanging out behind the counter. Rocky was making a sandwich for a short, portly man while Mardi sat on the counter sipping some kind of boutique soda in a bottle shaped like a brandy snifter, and both were laughing at something with a kind of private look on their faces—as though they'd developed a special code so they could crack each other up without upsetting their customers. That look told me that this arrangement wasn't a new thing. That they'd been working together for a while.

Then it happened.

Rocky turned around to get something. He leaned over Mardi, deliberately getting in her space, and she was smiling up at him. Nothing was happening, it looked innocent, but something about it seemed a little too intimate, a little too close for my comfort.

I shoved the door open hard enough that all three of the store's occupants jumped, but my voice was all sweetness and light.

"Hey! So this is where you've been keeping each other!"

Mardi's eyes shifted nervously between me and Rocky.

"Hey, Molly," she said uncertainly. "Yeah, I'm working here, just like I said I was."

"And you too!" I said, turning toward Rocky with what I could tell was an insane smile on my face. "Who would've guessed you'd end up here too, working with my sister!"

Rocky's expression was a little confused, a lot more guilty. "Uh, yeah. I mean, Sal owns the shop and everything, and he'd been wanting me to work here. Keeps me off the streets and all that," he said to the customer as he handed him his sandwich. "Will there be anything else?"

The man shook his head, and Rocky rang him

up while Mardi and I glared at each other without speaking.

"How lucky for you!" I said too loudly as soon as the man had walked out the door. "How lucky for both of you!"

"Molly, please," Mardi said. "It's not what you think."

The truth is, I don't know what I'd been thinking. Only that it was really strange my sister and my boyfriend had both dropped off the face of the planet (or at least my planet). But here they were together, smiling and laughing; I felt sick.

I took a deep breath, concentrating on controlling my emotions. I wasn't going to give Mardi the satisfaction of knowing I was jealous, plus it wouldn't do to put on another display of errant magic in front of Rocky or I might have to kill him.

"So," I said when I was sure I could speak without screaming. "Mum's having a party this evening, and she needs some finger food. I was just going to go to Dispirito's, but of course I should totally be loyal to Sal, shouldn't I?

"I was thinking the Orson Welles," I said to Rocky, ignoring Mardi. The Orson Welles was a sandwich Marshall (when I still thought he was Marshall) and I had come up with one day last summer to pass the time. We tried to think of the grossest, most-impossible-to-eat sandwich possible—pesto, anchovies, and gorgonzola served between two slices of inch-thick pumpernickel slathered in pickled bitter melon–aji mayonnaise—which, for reasons that are more mysterious than the origin of magic, turned out to be a hit. What can I say? WASPs will eat, wear, or drive anything, as long as it's expensive enough.

The Orson Welles was also a particularly difficult sandwich to make, what with the number of ingredients and the generally disgusting odor most of them gave off, and Rocky made a bit of a face as he contemplated making them.

"Uh, sure," he said. "How many did you—"

"I think fifty would do it." I cut him off.

"Wow, fifty. Not sure we have enough, uh, bitter melon–aji mayo on hand."

"It's okay," I said. "I don't need them right now. You can make up a new batch of mayo and deliver the sandwiches to Fair Haven tomorrow. You know where Fair Haven is, right? It's where Mardi's boyfriend Trent used to live," I said pointedly. "Where you and I watched the Wimbledon final together? And then hung out together after."

Rocky's eyes dropped. "I don't know why you're mad at *me*," he said under his breath. Then, shaking it off, he said, "I'm going down in the basement to see if we have any more pickled bitter melon."

"There's a whole barrel of it in the back corner," I said, waving my hand. "It's the one with the Chinese writing on it."

I waited until Rocky had disappeared to confront my sister.

"What is going on between you two?" I demanded.

"Molly, nothing is going on. I swear. Come on."

We stared at each other. I believed her. She would never do this to me. "Fine, Mum has a message for you," I said.

"What message?" Mardi asked. She tried to sound nonchalant, but I could tell she was interested.

"Mum's playing in the Nassau Open starting tomorrow. She thought we could fly down with her and watch her play and do some of the touristy stuff afterward."

"Nassau?" Mardi said. "Like Nassau County, Long Island?"

"No, you ignoramus. Like Nassau, the capital of the *Bahamas*."

"Oh!" Mardi's eyes lit up. "When are you leaving?"

"Tomorrow."

"What time?"

"Whenever. Mum chartered a plane."

Mardi's eyes went wider. "For real?"

I shrugged. "Janet Steele has some baller moves."

I could see Mardi fantasizing about the trip. On the plus side: champagne in the plane, chilling on the beach where the weather and the water would both be a good twenty degrees warmer than the still-tepid East End. On the minus side: hanging out with the sister whose boyfriend she'd apparently stolen.

"I dunno," she said finally. "I kind of committed to helping Sal out."

"Whatever," I said in the most blasé tone I could

muster. "The limo heads to the airport at ten tomorrow. Be at Fair Haven if you want to go," I added as I walked out the door.

I heard Mardi sigh, and then the door swung closed between us.

* 22 *

LEAVING ON A JET PLANE

Mardi-Overbrook-Journal.docx

*I*van answered the door the next morning before I'd even rung the doorbell.

"Good morning, Magdi," he said, bowing deeply. "If you want to wait in the breakfast room, Ms. Steele and Mooi will be with you shortly."

"It's Mardi," I said, rolling my eyes. "Mar-dy."

"As you wish, my lady," Ivan said, and scurried away. It was only after he'd left that I realized he'd never said where the "breakfast room" was. The Gardiners were fancy people, but not quite so fancy that they'd ever set aside one of the twenty-five or thirty rooms in Fair Haven specifically for breakfast. If they took breakfast as a family, they ate in the dining room. Otherwise they scarfed down a bowl of cereal or some eggs in the kitchen, like normal people. I peeked into the dining room first, but not only was there nobody in there, there wasn't any furniture either: just faded spots on the parquet and on the wallpaper where rugs and pictures used to be. Dust bunnies swirled in the corners, suggesting that Janet had no use for this room at all.

I made my way to the kitchen then, but it was empty too, though filled with an intoxicating smell of fresh-baked pastries and coffee. Ingrid had of course made me breakfast before I left—you have to understand that that kind of thing is, like, part of her DNA—but whatever Ivan (or whoever cooked in Fair Haven) had made smelled so delicious that I was ready for round two.

I raised my head and sniffed, as if I could track breakfast like a dog on the trail of a rabbit, but whatever other abilities I have, the power of supersmell is not one of them. I had no idea where breakfast had gone, so I just pushed through the door closest to me.

I was pretty sure the hallway beyond the door was the one that led to the servants' quarters: in place of the elaborate parquet of the main hallways, there was simple wood, and the walls were plain white instead of covered in hand-blocked wallpaper, and the trim was unadorned instead of elaborately carved. But what made me pause was the dirt. I don't mean dust like I'd seen in the corners of the dining room. I mean mud, trampled into the floor and pushing up against the walls, where it had dried and crumpled and been trampled down again until the floor looked more like a tunnel than a hallway in a three-hundred-year-old mansion, with only a few glimpses of the floorboards visible where the inch-thick coating of dirt had accumulated. The walls were filthy too, with trails of dirt and food and other stuff I couldn't identify lining them in long streaks, as if someone had dipped their hands into muddy puddles or jars of peanut butter or molasses and deliberately dragged them along the walls. And when I stood next to the streaks, I couldn't help but notice that nearly all of them were either about five feet above the floor—which is to say, Ivan's shoulder height—or about six feet, which is to say, Janet's shoulder height. I mean, I knew she hated the Gardiners, but did she hate them so much that she had to defile the house she'd stolen from them?

And I knew I should probably turn around and go back into the, you know, not-crazy part of the house, but I couldn't help myself. This hallway was obviously in heavy use, and I wanted to see where it led. And so, doing my best to put my new Miu Miu studded patent-leather sneaks into the least dirty parts of the floor, I began to make my way down its length. It got darker the farther I went. There were only a few windows, but they'd been plastered with mud and let in almost no light. But I was still able to see that there were bits of green and brown things scattered about as I went, leaves and sticks they looked like, piling up more and more toward the end of the hall, which made it look even more like a tunnel or a path in a forest. There were also a few feathers and things that looked a bit like fur and bones, all of which made it feel like I was walking into an animal's lair, just like in my dream.

I came to the end of the hall and turned. There was only a little passageway left. It was darker than the long corridor I'd just walked through, not to mention about ten times dirtier, and there was a bit of a smell too, something not-so-fresh, maybe a little fishy. Here and there among the leaves and sticks, I thought I saw the glint of a bone.

From what I could see, the floor was wetter too, and I hesitated. Before I could decide whether or not to continue, a door burst open at the other end of the hall and Janet Steele appeared.

"Magdi!" she almost shouted, her face startled, guarded.

I caught a glimpse of the room behind her. It was dark but seemed quite large, and even filthier than the hallway. Then she hurriedly pulled it closed and locked it.

"Can you believe this mess?" she said as she turned toward me and began picking her way down the muddy hall in a pair of high-waisted flowy gold pants tucked into stiletto calf boots in black snakeskin.

"Are those Haider Ackermann?" I said. "They're so chic I want to die!"

"I know," Janet said. "And I have to walk through this mess in them. Can you believe it?" she said. "A staff of eight, a gazillion dollars in the bank, and yet they let this happen."

"What did happen?" I said as Janet put her arm

on my shoulder and steered us back toward the main house.

"Ivan said a family of weasels was camped out here. Living, breeding, eating, and—" She sniffed, made a face. "Everything else too, from the smell of it."

"But I thought you said the servants live here?" I said as we walked toward the kitchen.

"Did I?" Janet said, but didn't explain further.

We were walking past some of the streaks of finger- and handprints on the wall.

"Weasels?" I said. "Really?"

"That's what Ivan said. He cleared them out before I got here." She glanced at the stains on the wall and shook her head. "You know Fair Haven sits on a seam between Midgard and Hel?"

"I heard something about that," I said vaguely.

"Tyr sealed it all up hundreds of years ago, of course, but still, a little energy can't help but leak through. It attracts all kinds of weirdness," she said, waving a hand at the dirty floor and walls. "This is the newest part of the house, but I'm guessing we must be pretty close to the seam."

I knew that in fact the seam was located in the ball-room, which, if I had my bearings (and I wasn't sure I did), wasn't far from here. But I didn't point that out to Janet. If she was serious about this war-between-the-gods thing, I wasn't going to give her any ammunition.

"I'm tempted to have Ivan bulldoze it." Janet was still speaking. "Build something nice and modern. Glass and steel. Impregnable," she added as she pushed the door to the kitchen open. "But I don't know. These old places have their charms—literally, in the case of Fair Haven."

"Ha!" I laughed as we stepped into the kitchen.

"Mardi! There you are!" Molly's voice rang out. "Ivan told me you were here, but I was beginning to think he was having a joke at my expense."

I was a bit taken aback at Molly's seeming good cheer, after the frosty invitation she'd given me in the Cheesemonger yesterday. I guess she'd believed me when I said that nothing had happened between me and Rocky. Seeing her again made me realize nothing could happen between me and Rocky. Even if I was attracted to him, I couldn't do anything about it, and I wouldn't.

"Sorry, I just took a bit of a wrong turn, but here I am, ready and raring to go."

"Woo-hoo, Bahamas!" Molly said.

Now, I know I'm the dark, jaded sister and Molly's the bright, happy-go-lucky one. But not even she had ever said "woo-hoo" in her life. I found myself wondering who had kidnapped my real sister and sent this Stepford clone in her place. But all I said was:

"Woo-hoo." I couldn't bring myself to shout it, though, which didn't matter, since Molly had already turned to Janet.

"What were you doing in the servants' quarters, Mum?"

"Ivan told me the skunks were back. Thought I'd better check myself."

"Skunks?" I said. "I thought you said—"

"I'm going to get one of those humane pest removal services in here while we're in the Bahamas. Hopefully they can trap the little critters and cart them over to Hither Hills State Park on the big island. Well, is everyone packed? We don't want to be late."

"Late for what?" Molly laughed. "We're flying charter."

"Yes, and I'm paying for it. You miss a commercial flight and you pay a hundred bucks to change your ticket. You show up late for a charter and they charge you five thousand for the inconvenience. And I don't know about you girls, but I would much rather spend that money on boots," she finished up, lifting up one of her feet and flicking off a piece of mud with one golden-lacquered nail. "Not to mention bikinis!"

Molly and I looked at each other and smiled, and this time her joy didn't seem forced. "Yes, please!"

At the sight of the two of us looking all sisters-in-love, a big grin spread across Janet's face.

"Look at the two of you! My girls, together again." She extended her long strong arms and pulled us into a three-way hug. I felt Molly's arms snake around us as well, and after a moment's hesitation, I gave in and joined in the hug.

"We're going to have so much fun!" Janet breathed into my ear.

Mum climbed into the Maybach and I went to follow, but before I could, Molly's hand closed around my arm like a clamp.

"I know you want to sleep with Rocky, you little slut. I've got my eye on you."

"Molly, what the—"

But before I could even finish my question, she'd shoved me out of the way and climbed in next to Mum.

"Hurry up, slowpoke," Mum called to me. "We really don't want to be late."

I got in warily, trying not to make eye contact with Molly. Her rage filled up the back of the car like a toxic gas, although Mum seemed oblivious to it. I just hoped Molly wouldn't crash the plane.

✳ 23 ✳

CARIBBEAN QUEENS

From the Diary of Molly Overbrook

About a half hour after we took off from the East Hampton airport in Mum's chartered plane, a funny thing happened. Both my phone and Mardi's started buzzing like crazy. Voice mails, text messages, alerts from Twitter and Instagram and Facebook and a half dozen other social media feeds. At first, we thought something terrible had happened, and we started scrolling through them in alarm, trying to find out what it was. Then Mardi looked up, anxiety replaced by confusion.

"These are all old. Like two, three weeks old."

I hadn't been paying attention to the time stamps, but then I checked and saw that she was right. The most recent message was from yesterday; the oldest dated back almost a month to—

"The day I moved into Fair Haven."

Mardi shot me a look when I said that. We hadn't spoken a word to each other since I'd hissed into her ear outside Mum's Maybach, and I could tell she was biting her tongue so we didn't get into a fight.

"Look at that," I said sarcastically. "There are all the messages you said I didn't send you. *So good to see you yesterday. Let's hang out at the North Inn with F. Maybe you can come out to FH and show me where everything is.*"

"And all the messages you said I didn't send you!" Mardi protested. "*So glad we finally talked. I missed you! It's Jo's birthday tomorrow. Are you coming to the party?*"

"I missed Jo's birthday?"

"She wasn't happy," Mardi said. "Neither was Ingrid."

"Oh, look," I said, changing the subject. "Here are all the messages I sent Rocky. You remember Rocky? My boyfriend? *Yesterday was amazing. I miss you already. Where are you? Is something wrong? Are you mad at me? WTF?!*"

"Molly, please," Mardi said in a placating tone. "He didn't get them. Neither of us did. How were we supposed to know that you weren't having another one of your freak-outs?"

"'Another one'? Because freaking out is apparently something I do all the time?" I huffed.

"Come on. Even you have to admit you've been a little gun-shy ever since Alberich."

"I might use the word *cautious*. But I wasn't being cautious with Rocky. *As you know.*"

"Nothing happened! And I didn't know what was going on," Mardi said. "You have to believe me."

"Well, you should have tried harder to find out. You should have driven out to Fair Haven."

"You don't think I did? Three times! You were never there!"

"Well, then I was probably at the tennis club with Mum. All you had to do was look online."

"How?" Mardi said. "None of those pictures and posts went up."

"Bull," I said. "Look," I continued, holding up my phone to her. "Here's a picture from the club—that's the day after Mum got back from England. And there are more than three thousand likes from that day alone."

"But look at my phone," Mardi said, showing me her screen. "The alert from the picture didn't come until just now."

I was so mad that it was hard for me to focus, but when I'd stared at the picture and the responses below it, I saw that she was telling the truth. Somehow the picture had gone out into the Twitterverse—to everyone's phone in the world, except Mardi's.

"This smells like magic," I said.

Mardi nodded. "Like someone was playing a trick on us."

"Who was playing a trick on whom?" Mum said, emerging from the front of the plane, where she'd been hanging out with the pilot, who apparently gave her lessons.

Mardi glanced at me warily, discreetly shaking her head. "No one. Just this dumb Internet prank."

"Ugh," Mum said. "I try not to know anything about it. Ivan handles all my accounts, and I'm pretty sure he uses some kind of magic script to keep them going. Speaking of which." She clapped her hands twice. "Ivan!"

Ivan appeared from the galley at the back of the jet.

"Yes, Ms. Steele?"

"My daughters' glasses are empty."

"Begging your pardon, Ms. Steele. Mooi, Magdi, can I refill your champagne, or would you prefer something else?"

"Uh, champagne's fine for me," Mardi said, clearly uncomfortable at the way Mum was ordering Ivan around like a servant. I still found it a little off-putting, but it seemed to be their dynamic.

"Me too," I said.

"And my throat is dry," Mum added as Ivan collected our glasses. "Bring me a juice. Nothing too tart."

"As you wish, Ms. Steele," Ivan said, bowing low and backing out of the cabin.

With Mum present, Mardi clearly didn't want to talk about the situation with Rocky or the weird, possibly magical glitch in our electronic communications, and I decided to let it go—for now. Even if some magical force had hidden my texts and phone calls and social media posts from her and Rocky, and vice versa, she still should have tried harder to track me down before making a move on the guy I'd been seeing. But I didn't need to have a knock-down, drag-out fight with my sister the first time we hung out with Mum. Better to break her in easy.

Instead, we spent the rest of the flight sipping champagne and eating caviar, and before I knew it, we were landing in the Bahamas—or the BH as everyone called it—and then heading off in a waiting limo to the hotel.

The hotel was a bit like the Chateau Marmont in LA, with a large main building and a dozen or so "bungalows" scattered around it. "Bungalow" makes me think of a little building, but ours was bigger than Ingrid's house in the East End, a single-story U-shaped building that wrapped around a private pool, with bedrooms that opened right onto a private beach. I mean, my old room at Ingrid's looked out on the beach too, but it was on the second floor, and, well, as nice as the beach is in North Hampton, it's hard to compete with the tropics' perfect eighty-five-degree weather and seventy-five-degree water.

Seconds after we arrived, all three of us were in our bikinis (four if you count Ivan, whose Speedo was almost as tiny as our swimsuit bottoms—I guess he's European?) and splashing into the water. It was heavenly, and afterward, when Mum and Ivan went off to the tennis club to get in an hour of practice, it just seemed too peaceful to start fighting with Molly. And so it went for the next six days: every morning a pitcher of fresh-squeezed peach nectar appeared outside our door, served with a selection of croissants and fresh Caribbean fruits (gri gri, papaya, and chironja were my faves). They were so good they actually made me look forward to breakfast (and that's saying something).

But as good as breakfast was, dinners were even better. Normally, Mum said, she would've wined and dined us at the best restaurants in Nassau, but since she was playing a tournament, she had to be super careful about what she ate. So instead of going out, she'd arranged for a personal chef to come to our bungalow every night and cook for us. It was one of the few times I thought about the fact that Mum wasn't like me and Mardi and Dad—that she was human. We never worried about how healthy our food was, only if it tasted good. But Mum was mortal, and she had to be extremely conscious about what she put in her body to keep it not just looking as good as it could, but working as well as it could, and for as long as it could. Her chef, however, put any of those thoughts out of my brain because he served up an unbelievable array of grilled fishes that had been caught that same day in the Florida Straits— swordfish and octopus and shrimp and several things that came in shells that kind of grossed me out a little, but tasted *divine*. It didn't hurt that Sebastien, the chef, was gorgeous and spoke with a beautiful French accent (he was from Martinique).

Meanwhile, though, there was the tennis tournament itself. This was the first time we'd been seen in public together as Janet Steele's daughters. I started the week with 846 followers on Twitter. By the time Mum won the tournament the following Sunday, I had 13,351. Mardi scored almost as many. But of course the real star was Mum. There were paparazzi stationed outside the gates of our hotel to snap her picture in the morning, and sport photographers stationed at the practice courts to watch her warm up each day, and TV cameras at the matches themselves, to catch her in all her glory.

Crazily enough, even though our hotel was right on the beach, we never actually put on our swimsuits after that first day until our last day in the BH, the day after Mum won the tournament. Mum had scheduled an extra day at the hotel so we could all chill out and actually spend some time together without Mum being "distracted" by the tournament (although I have to say, when she wasn't playing tennis, she didn't talk about it at all, and seemed not to think about it either). And so, after another breakfast of croissants and guanabana (it tastes like the perfect marriage of a strawberry and a pineapple), we slipped on our bikinis and made our way to the beach, which in our case just meant walking out the door. Although just as we were finishing breakfast the phone rang, and Mum ended up getting called off to do an interview with ESPN Australia, who happened to have a correspondent in the Bahamas.

"They've promised to let me shill for my clothing line and my vodka, so I kind of can't say no. It pays the bills, you know."

"You have your own vodka?" Mardi and I exclaimed at the same time.

"Only in Australia and Asia at this point. But we sold a hundred thousand bottles last year, and we're getting ready to move into Europe and the US. It's called Fe, after the atomic symbol for iron. That's okay," she said to Ivan, who'd appeared in the room with the keys to the rented car. "I've called a cab. You stay here and look after the girls." She kissed us both and swooshed out the door.

Ivan stared glumly after her for a moment, then shook his head and turned to us brightly.

"So what're we starting the day with? Mojitos or margaritas?"

"Mojitos!" Mardi and I said without looking at each other.

"One pitcher of mojitos coming right up," Ivan said. "Go get your sun on, and I'll be out in two shakes of a fish's tail."

We've been to the tropics before—Dad's a big fan of Turks and Caicos, and took us there every January for four years in a row when we were in grade school, and we've also been to Anguilla and Cozumel and the Canary Islands—but every time I go to one of these fabulous beautiful places, I ask myself why I don't live there year-round. But I know the answer: it's because

I'd never do anything again. I'd just camp out in a lounge chair and have cute cabana boys bring me cold drinks all day long, basking in the sun (I'm a goddess, remember—no need to worry about skin cancer) and getting up once an hour or so to take a dip in the water. If there is a heaven, I can't imagine it looking like anything other than a Caribbean beach. And if that's not what it looks like, well, maybe I'll take Mum up on that whole Mimir revolt-against-the-gods thing after all.

"This is heaven, isn't it?" Mardi said to me at one point.

"Oh, my gods, that's eerie. I was thinking exactly the same thing. I want to die right here," I said. I couldn't really be that mad at Mardi for long. And I believed her that nothing had happened between her and Rocky. Of course nothing had happened. No matter what, we're sisters.

"Geez, morbid much?" Mardi laughed. "But I wasn't just talking about the beach. I was talking about being here with you. With you and . . . Mum."

"Really?" I said. "You're coming around to her?"

"How can I resist? She's been nothing but fabulous."

"Oh, I'm so glad! I knew you'd change your mind!"

Mardi took another sip of her mojito. "I'm not saying I'm ready to move in yet, but she's definitely winning me over. But really, I'm much more happy hanging out with you."

For six days, we'd hung out, taking all our meals together, shopping and watching tennis together, even sleeping in the same room like we had when we were little girls. But even though everything had seemed peaceful on the surface, underneath I had been seething with jealousy. No matter how much fun we were having, I couldn't get over the idea that she'd betrayed me with Rocky. And even though I believed her, I couldn't shake the thought. I still didn't want to shatter the peace, especially since it involved Mum, and so I kept on biting my tongue.

But suddenly, I realized that I didn't want to fight about it. Chances are something like this would happen again—and again and again—over the course of the hundreds or thousands of years that Mardi and I would be alive. If we got in a fight over every single boy or every single betrayal, whether real or accidental or purely imagined, we'd be fighting to the end of time.

I turned to her on her lounge chair. She was looking at me nervously, and I knew she'd been picking up on my mood.

"I'm happy we're hanging out too," I said, reaching out for her hand and giving it a squeeze.

We sat there like that for one more moment, and then Mardi grabbed her glass and drained it.

"Okay, enough schmaltz. Let's go swim!"

✳ 24 ✳

LEFT SHARK, RIGHT WHALE

Mardi-Overbrook-Journal.docx

I can't tell you how happy I was as Molly and I leapt off our lounge chairs and ran across the sparkling white sands toward the softly rolling blue water. I mean, I knew that at some point we were going to have to have it out about Rocky, but now I knew that we'd get through it one way or another. Sparks would fly, favorite items of clothing might mysteriously disappear, hair might even get pulled, but we'd survive this and get back on track.

We ran all the way to the water and splashed in without slowing. The Caribbean is amazing—warm but not balmy, so you don't have to take that minute or two to adjust before you dive in. We ran in until we were up to our waists and then dove straight in. The water was so clear that you saw every grain of sand on the bottom, every little brightly colored fish that flitted by. We swam and splashed each other and dove down to the bottom, pretending we were looking for pearls or gold doubloons from long-ago Spanish galleons, and generally behaved like seven-year-olds, for a good twenty minutes. When we were finally sated, we were a couple hundred feet offshore, where the water was still only eight or twelve feet deep, lazily treading water. And then I had to go and ruin it.

"It's true," I said.

Molly had been staring at the beach, and she used her hands to turn her body toward mine, rather than just look over at me.

"What is?" The look on her face was totally calm and trusting, and I could hear my brain scream, *Don't do it!* But I had to come clean. She was my sister.

"I liked Rocky."

Molly's face didn't change, didn't seem to move, but it hardened somehow, and I could've sworn the water got five degrees colder.

"I know," she said finally.

"I know you know. But I still had to tell you."

"How could you?" she asked, and what made her question so hard was that it wasn't angry. It was hurt, and I knew I'd put that hurt there.

"I don't know," I said. "I was just so confused after Trent dumped me, and there was the whole Mum situation, and you weren't responding to my texts, and—and he was just there. It was like he was as close to you as I was going to get. Like if I couldn't hang out with you, I could hang out with him."

"Okay, ew," Molly said, and I was relieved that she could make a little joke.

"I know! Although on some level, it didn't feel like it had anything to do with poor Rocky at all. It didn't matter what he looked like or said. It just mattered that he had this connection to you. I didn't mean to. I would never hurt you. I just needed to flirt with someone. He likes you."

"If he liked me so much, why was he spending all his time with you?" Molly said coldly.

"Maybe because I didn't give him a choice."

"What do you mean?" Molly said, looking at me sharply. "Did you use magic?"

"I mean, not consciously. But our powers are really acting up lately. Maybe I did something without realizing it."

"No offense, sis, but that sounds like a bit of a cop-out."

"I know it does, and I don't mean to duck responsibility. What I did was totally wrong. But as I float here in this beautiful, seventy-five-degree water and look back at it, it doesn't seem like it had anything to do with me. It was like something was acting through me. Making me do something I wouldn't normally do."

"What, like magic? You think someone didn't just hex our phones? They hexed you too?"

"Honestly, no. It feels . . . bigger than that. Deeper. I'm wondering if it has something to do with the Re-awakening. If it's not just our powers that are being affected. If our emotions are being changed too."

"The divine version of adolescence?"

"I guess so."

Molly was silent for a long time.

"I dunno, Mardi," she said eventually. "Part of me thinks you're just trying to get a pass for a low blow. But part of me knows what you're describing. This feeling of not being a hundred percent in control of what I do or say or even feel. Something weird is going on inside us right now. And who knows, maybe that did cause you to do what you did with Rocky. But, well, you did, and now things can never be the same between him and me again. Whatever Rocky and I might've had, it's gone now. And at least part of the blame for that is on you."

"Molly, come on. You know I'd never do anything to hurt you."

"But you did, Mardi. You hurt me. A lot."

Her voice was so quiet. So reasonable. She could have been explaining the rules of a card game to Jo. It terrified me.

"Molly, please. Don't be like this. Yell at me, trash my car, tell Dad to ground me for the next hundred years. But don't shut me out like this."

"I'm not shutting you out. I'm just not . . ." She paused, searching for a word. "I'm just not ready to trust you. I still love you, but I'm not sure I can ever trust you again. I know nothing happened, but liking the same guy as me still feels like a betrayal."

"Molly!" I said. "No!"

"The nice thing is, we're immortal," Molly said in a sad voice. "We've got eternity to figure it out. But I guess the bad thing is that if we don't work through it, we've got a really long time to feel awkward around each other."

She turned then and started swimming toward the shore.

"Mooi!" I called, using her Norse name. "Please don't leave it like that."

I wanted to swim after her, but I knew I couldn't. That if I did, it would just make it worse.

"Mooi!"

Something brushed against me then. At first, I thought I kicked myself with my own leg, but even before that thought was over, I felt a long scraping sensation and realized that whatever it was, it was way bigger than my own leg. And then I was being smacked aside by something that hit me like a baseball bat, sending me flying out of the water. But as I was soaring over the waves, I saw a dark shape beneath and a dark fin that was at least as tall as me piercing the water. The fin angled away from me then, and I saw the long black back and the gleaming white belly, the unmistakable markings of a killer whale.

"Whale!" I screamed just before I splashed beneath the surface.

As the water closed over me, I struggled to keep my body turned toward the whale. I wasn't sure how one fought off a killer whale attack, but I figured I had a better chance if I at least saw it coming. It was swimming at an angle away from me, and I saw the length of its body, from its rounded snout to its thick body with its wide pectoral fins spinning like a propeller to the muscular action of its fluke, which pumped through the water heavily. Within seconds, it had disappeared in the depths, and for a moment, I allowed myself to think that it was leaving. Then a dark shadow reappeared and grew quickly larger as the whale sped back for round two.

I kicked myself to the surface to grab some air, and for the brief second I was above water, I whipped my head in Molly's direction and called out to her. I was back under the water so quickly, however, that I couldn't tell if she heard.

Then the cool blue water closed around my ears, and I turned my attention back to the whale. I was trying to think of some magic that I could use to fight it, but before I could even gather my thoughts, it was on me. I couldn't believe how big it was. I'd always imagined killer whales to be only a little bigger than dolphins, but this monster's body was as tall as I was, and its gaping jaws looked like they could swallow a Saint Bernard whole. I paddled helplessly as it raced in my direction. At the last second, it turned on its side but continued heading straight for me. I started to ask myself why, but then it hit me: as big as it was, I was still too tall to fit in its mouth. It had to come at me sideways to take a chunk out of me. But if it could turn sideways, so could I.

I beat the water furiously to spin my body. The whale lunged for me, its jaws aimed squarely for my midsection. It turned, but I was able to grab its snout and turn with it, and then the whale's own momentum carried it past me. I rolled along the length of its body, one of its flukes smashing against one of my ankles as I propelled myself toward the surface to grab another breath of air.

As the whale sped past me, I thought I had time for a quick breather. Its body was too big for it to simply whirl around like a seal. But I didn't think about the tail. My head was just breaking the surface when I felt a push from beneath me. The next thing I knew I was flying through the air again. The whale had literally picked me up and thrown me with its massive flukes— in the same direction it was swimming! It was actually throwing me in front of its mouth!

"Molly!" I screamed. "Molly, help!" I was so disoriented I couldn't tell which way to look.

Then I was under again. I whirled around. The whale was right there, turning to take a bite out of me. I didn't even have time to spin. I just stuck out my hands and pushed at the big snout to keep my body out of the gaping mouth. I expected to roll along the side again, but this time, the whale was perfectly centered, and I felt myself being driven backward through the water as the whale swam. The pressure of the water against my back was so great that it took all my strength to keep from buckling and slipping into its mouth.

For the first time, I glimpsed the creature's eyes. I stared at it, and it stared back with pure hatred. If there'd been any doubt that this was a magic attack, that look completely erased it. This wasn't a wild animal hunting. It was here to kill me. Which meant one of two things: either it had been hexed to come after me, or it wasn't actually a killer whale at all, but some kind of shape-shifter that had taken this form. If that was the case, it was probably the same creature that had attacked Dad's plane.

The whale held my gaze for a moment, then suddenly its snout jerked downward to the sandy bottom of the sea. I knew what it was doing immediately: it was going to pin me to the ground. If it couldn't squirm around until it managed to get its jaws around me, it would just pin me underwater until I drowned. But it was moving so fast I couldn't see how to get out of its way without getting one of my legs snapped. And so, helplessly, I let myself be pushed toward the ground. As a goddess, I knew I could hold my breath two or three times longer than a mortal, but that was it. I just prayed something would happen before I ran out of air.

As if reading my thoughts, a pale form appeared in my peripheral vision. I looked over: it was Molly! She must have heard my call!

She swam up to the whale broadside, one hand curled into a fist. Before I knew what was happening, she struck it in the only vulnerable place on its body: the eye that was staring at me so malevolently.

It wasn't a hard blow, but a whale's eye is every bit as tender as a person's. And just like a person, it jerked away from the assault. The twist of its neck was enough to dislodge me, and I rolled safely out of the way. The whale arced off in the opposite direction. It smacked at me with its tail again, but this time I was ready, and all it did was push me a few feet closer to the surface.

I kicked upward to where Molly was already treading water and through to the surface.

"You came back!"

"No time!" Molly said grimly. "That thing's going to be on us again in seconds."

I nodded. "Let's link arms. If we can make ourselves too big for its mouth, it can't get us."

"Got it," Molly said. We grabbed each other's arms and dove under.

Just in time: the whale was barreling straight for us. Molly's elbow was crooked tightly around mine, and I could feel her legs swirling through the water. The sight of our conjoined bodies obviously confused the whale because it slowed down. I thought it might swim past us, when suddenly it rolled in for a bite. But we were too wide for its mouth, and with our two free arms and four legs, we managed to kick ourselves out of the way. The whale shot past us, and we kicked ourselves toward the surface.

"Start for the shore," Molly said as soon as we were in the air. "No way we can dodge this thing forever. But if we get into shallow-enough water, it won't be able to follow."

"Good plan!" I said, mostly because I wanted to be encouraging. The shore was still hundreds of feet away. It seemed to me that we'd be exhausted long before we managed to reach it.

"Back under," Molly said then, nodding toward the dark fin that was knifing our way. "Here it comes again."

We dove under and faced off another charge. The whale tried spinning this time and slapping us with its tail. But as agile as it was, it was still so large that it couldn't move in for the kill fast enough. It was able to send us rolling through the water, but by the time it had managed to turn around and charge us again, we'd regained control and were able to kick and push ourselves out of its mouth, then kick up to the surface again and snatch a breath.

Over and over again, it charged us. Over and over again, we managed to elude its grasping mouth. I kept thinking someone would see us, but that's the one drawback to a private beach: no gawkers or paparazzi, but no one to rescue you when a magical orca comes after you. The only person at the bungalow was Ivan, but he was apparently busy inside.

But with each attack, we managed to swim a few feet closer to the shore. I could feel my arms and legs tiring and could hear in Molly's ragged breaths that she was exhausted too, but if we could just keep this up for a while longer, we'd be out of the whale's reach. The water was only eight feet or so deep where we were. It wouldn't be long now until we could get to safety.

But as soon as I realized this, the whale did too, because it suddenly changed tactics. Before, it had been swimming out to the deeper water to turn around and charge us, essentially driving us toward the shore. But after its next attack, it swam toward the shallow water instead. When it turned around, its entire back rose out of the water, and its tail churned up clouds of sand. And then, when it came for us again, it swam slowly instead of charging. It didn't ram into us but managed to lodge its snout between our arms. Suddenly, its tail started churning: it was driving us back out to sea!

I looked at Molly. We had no choice: we had to let go of each other to get out of its way, and hope that we could rejoin our arms before the whale turned around and charged us. I nodded at her, hoping she understood. She nodded back, flashing me a grim smile.

I slackened my arm and felt hers slide away. We kicked off the whale's body, and it went speeding by us. It pivoted quickly, though, and swam back toward the shore to turn around.

"It knows we're trying to get to land!" I said as we broke the surface. "It's pushing us back to sea!"

"I can't keep this up much longer," Molly panted. "What are we going to do?"

"We have to keep fighting," I said. "Just a little longer. I think help is on the way." I could feel it.

"What do you mean?" Molly asked frantically, but there was no time to explain. We could see the whale's dorsal fin straightening out and beginning its charge. We linked arms and dove under to meet it.

But when we were up again, I pointed to the sky.

"Look!" I said.

"At what?" Molly said confusedly.

"Clouds!" I yelled just before I grabbed Molly and pulled her under to face another attack.

Molly's face was still confused as we dove under, but then I saw comprehension come into her eyes. She understood.

The sky had been crystal blue for the seven days we'd been here. But in the last ten minutes, it had begun to turn gray: thick dark clouds came rushing in, which seemed to form out of nothing. That wasn't normal weather. That was magic.

That was Thor.

Or at least that's what I told myself as, holding tight to Molly, my exhausted arms and legs fended off the twentieth or thirtieth lunge from our attacker. Because if it wasn't, we were done for.

"It's Dad!" Molly screamed when we broke the surface.

"It has to be!" I answered.

"What's he doing?" she said. "And why's it taking him so long to do it?"

I didn't have time to respond before we had to dive under again. I had no idea what the answer to Molly's first question was, but I was pretty sure the answer to her second had something to do with the huge distance involved. Dad was a thousand miles away. I'd never heard of anyone casting a spell from that distance. But Dad was the god of thunder. If anyone could do it, he could.

The whale came at us and I readied myself to fight it off. My legs felt like jelly. My free arm was numb, my palm scraped raw. *One more time*, I told myself. *I can do this one more time.*

The mouth was there, gaping open. I pushed at the side of the head weakly, barely keeping myself out of its jaws as I glimpsed one of Molly's kicking legs. It actually struck the whale right in the lip. The jaws snapped shut, missing her foot by a fraction of an inch. The whale snapped its head up, almost ripping Molly from my grasp. We rolled down the length of its back until our arms caught the dorsal fin, which we wrapped around like a piece of ribbon. The whale rolled, pulling us lower in the water, then jerked the other way. I felt Molly's hand slip down my arm, then pull free. I clutched futilely at her writhing fingers. I even opened my mouth and called her name, my voice sounding like a zombie groan beneath ten feet of water. As I watched helplessly, the whale's massive tail struck Molly full in the chest and stomach and sent her flying.

"Molly!" I screamed again, then choked as water rushed into my mouth. I barely managed to keep one eye on Molly and the other on the whale's dark form as it rocketed through the water. I clawed my way to the surface, whirling my head around, trying to find Molly. The glowering clouds cast dark shadows, and I could barely see anything.

Then I saw a flat form about fifteen feet to my left. It was Molly! Floating facedown in the water!

I began swimming toward her, screaming at my exhausted limbs to *move, dammit, get me to my sister!*

But even as I was heading toward her, a dark fin shot up out of the water and began racing toward her. It was farther away from her than I was but moving ten times faster than me.

"No!" I screamed. It was all I could think of. "No! No!" Like the whale was a bad dog I was trying to frighten away from a kitten.

But it ignored me and raced onward, its dark form cutting the water like a torpedo. Forty feet. Thirty. Twenty.

Suddenly, the sky exploded in light and everything disappeared. I heard a tremendous crash, but all I could see was pure whiteness, even behind my squeezed-together eyelids. And then: silence, as sudden and complete as the flash of light.

I pried my eyelids open. Everything was blurry and

suffused with a golden aura, but I could just make out Molly a few feet ahead of me, and another dark shape floating a few feet past her. It was far too small to be the whale, but I could smell the distinct aroma of charred flesh.

I raced to Molly with the last of my strength. Even as I got to her, her head jerked up, and she began coughing and choking.

"It's okay, Molly. I've got you. It's okay, it's okay."

"What—what happened?" Molly said. "Where's the whale?"

"I think Dad zapped it with lightning," I said. I smoothed her matted hair out of her face. "It's okay. It's gone."

"But what's that?" She was looking toward the dark mass floating about ten feet away. It had the unmoving quality of a dead thing, and it was completely flat in the water, but even so, we could tell it was human. Or at least human-shaped.

We pulled ourselves slowly toward it, but my eyes were still so singed from the lightning blast that it wasn't until we were right next to it that I noticed the stripe of red at its midsection, the distinct cut of a Speedo on a muscular man's body.

It was Ivan, and he was dead.

LOVE IS A BATTLEFIELD

From the Diary of Molly Overbrook

*I*t took all my powers of persuasion to convince Mardi to get on the plane back to North Hampton. At first, she told me that she didn't want to go anywhere near a plane that Ivan had touched—she was convinced that he'd booby-trapped it or something. Mum told her that it was unlikely we'd be in the same plane on the way back, since the charter company had been using it throughout the week, and Mardi reluctantly agreed. Later, though, when we were in our bedroom packing, she confessed to me the real reason she didn't want to get on the plane.

"It's not Ivan I'm worried about," she told me. "It's Mum."

It was about six in the evening. Seven hours had passed

since Ivan had attacked us. Mum raced back from her interview as soon as I called her. The first thing she did was make sure we were both unhurt, but aside from a few scrapes and bruises and being generally exhausted, we were fine. Then she stripped down to her swimsuit, grabbed one of those lightweight plastic kayaks that the hotel had provided, and set out to find Ivan's body. At that point, less than an hour had passed since the attack, but there was no sign of it. Still, neither Mardi nor I thought there was any chance he was still alive—not in that body, anyway. There had been a hole in his chest the size of a basketball. You could've put your head through it and looked out the other side.

"Sharks probably got 'im," Mum said, her accent coming out more strongly than ever with her anger. "And good riddance."

Mardi and I were still in too much shock to ask her the questions that were burning in our both our minds. Had Mum known Ivan was a shape-shifter? And if so, did she know if he was the one who had attacked our father's plane?

"When I think of the trust I placed in him," Mum growled. "My daughters' lives! I want to resurrect him just so I can kill him myself!"

We'd been due to fly out the next morning, but Mum called the charter company and told them she wanted to leave that day. There wasn't a plane on the island, which was why we had to wait till the evening. Mum told us that we should both lie down, and I reluctantly agreed. I was exhausted, but I was also so keyed up that I wanted to go for a run or pick up an ax and chop down a tree. I could tell Mardi felt the same way I did, but it was equally clear that she didn't want to be separated from me, and so when I trudged down the hall, she shuffled after me, and when I climbed into bed, she slipped in behind me and curled her arms around me.

"I can't believe how close I came to losing you today," she whispered in my ear.

I wrapped my arms around hers, interlacing our fingers together. "There was no chance of that happening," I said with a bravery I tried hard to feel, even retroactively. "Not when we work together."

Mardi pulled me even closer.

"Remember we used to sleep like this when we were little girls?"

I nodded. "Why'd we ever stop?"

"I dunno," Mardi said, and I could feel her shrug. I heard her open her mouth to say something, but all that came out was a yawn. It was infectious: my jaw fell open and a long, achy yawn sighed from my mouth.

"I've never felt this tired in my life," I said.

Mardi nodded but didn't say anything, and a moment later, I felt her breath come softly and evenly against the back of my neck. I thought about asking her if she was sleeping, but before I could get the words out, my eyes dropped closed, and I was asleep too.

The next thing we knew, Mum was shaking us awake.

"Come on, girls, let's get you packed and get to the airport. The sooner we're off this island, the better."

My body felt stiff as a board, as though I'd been in a fight—which I guess I had been. Mardi was stretching awkwardly, and I could tell she was sore too. She voiced her reservations about the plane, and Mum reassured her, then left us to go pack her own things. That's when Mardi dropped her bombshell:

"It's not Ivan I'm worried about. It's Mum."

I looked at her, first in confusion, then in disbelief.

"You think . . ." I found it hard to say the words aloud. "You think *Mum* was behind this?"

"Think about it, Mardi. Ivan was practically Mum's slave. He would never do anything against her will, let alone something as drastic as try to kill her daughters."

"But, but," I stuttered. "It's *Mum*."

"What does that even mean? We barely know her. About the only thing we know about her is that she wants us to kill our own father. So why shouldn't she want to kill her own children?"

"But it's Mum! Our mother!"

Mardi just looked at me for a moment. Then she shrugged helplessly. "Have it your way. But I'm not getting on a plane with her."

She grabbed her phone and, while I watched in disbelief, pulled up a number and pressed call. She held the phone to her ear for a moment, then pulled it away. "Huh."

"What is it?" I asked.

"I'm trying to call Ingrid's, but it's not going through."

It hit me then: Dad! We'd never reached out to him, to thank or tell him we were still alive, or just find out if it was him who'd saved us. I pulled my phone from my pocket and immediately called Ingrid's, but I got the same result as Mardi: nothing. No ringing, no busy signal, nothing. I tried her cell then, and Matt's, and Freya's, and the North Inn, and Mardi did the same. But none of the calls went through.

"Weird," I said.

"Weird?" Mardi said. "Or magic?"

"You think it's part of the same thing that stopped all our text messages and phone calls from going to each other?"

As an experiment, I called Mardi's phone, just to make sure we weren't in some kind of dead zone. The call went through immediately.

She turned to the bedside table then and picked up the hotel phone. It took some doing, but she finally figured out how to call the US. Once again, the phone on the other end refused to respond.

"If someone did cast a spell preventing us from communicating electronically," she said as she hung up the phone, "it wasn't just on our phones. It's on us."

"Or on the East End," I said. "Remember how all those

old messages came through about a half hour after we took off? Maybe someone cast some kind of perimeter spell that keeps us from communicating electronically."

"That's a very specific spell," Mardi said. "I have no idea how you'd cast it, but I suspect it's not easy. It'd take a seriously powerful magic-user to pull it off."

"That rules out Mum, then," I couldn't stop myself from saying. "As a mortal, there's no way she could cast a spell that powerful."

"Yeah, but Ivan probably could have. He was an elf, remember. And as his shape-shifting shows, he had some serious power."

"Which makes it that much harder to believe that he was following Mum's orders when he attacked us. If he had all the power, why would he demean himself by following a human's commands?"

"I don't know," Mardi said. "But he certainly didn't seem to have a problem with washing her clothes and fetching her drinks and all that."

"Whatever," I said. "We can talk about this more later. For now, let's just get home." Mardi opened her mouth to protest, but I spoke over her. "For the gods' sakes, Mardi. Mum's going to be on the plane with us. She couldn't hurt us without hurting herself."

Mardi just grimaced at me for a long moment.

"Fine," she said finally. "But I am not going to be happy about it."

Angrily, she began stuffing things in her suitcases.

• • •

The trip to the airport and taking off all went smoothly. Mardi might have been angry still, but she didn't seem to want to pick a fight, with me or with Mum. At least not yet.

Mum opened a bottle of champagne even before the plane took off. By the time we were at cruising altitude, we were already on our second bottle. We were drinking quickly enough that Mardi and I were feeling the effects of the alcohol, which, frankly, was a relief, because even though I'd told Mardi I didn't believe Mum was behind Ivan's attacks, I was still nervous about being thirty thousand feet in the air so soon after someone had tried to kill us. Just because I didn't think Mum was helping him didn't mean that he didn't have some other partner out there. At least this wasn't a seaplane—there'd be no whale rising out of the waves to smash us to bits.

As we were settling into the third bottle, Mum sighed heavily. "Well, I suppose I owe you girls an explanation."

My heart did a somersault in my chest. I looked over at Mardi to find her staring at me, looking equally startled.

"An explanation," I managed to spit out. "About what?"

"Well, about Ivan, of course," Mum said.

This time I didn't look at Mardi. I was afraid that she might flash me one of her I-told-you-so looks and I might short out the plane's electrical system.

"Well, I guess, sure," I stammered, "if you think you

have to, but, I mean, you could've hardly known he was going to do something like that. Right?" I added desperately.

Mum laughed. "Believe me, girls, I'm as surprised as you at what happened. But that doesn't mean I shouldn't have seen it coming. Ivan has always been jealous of my attention. He often professed to love me, not in a platonic way, but in a romantic way. It sometimes made our relationship . . . tense."

It took me a moment to get it.

"He wanted you to be his wife!"

Mum nodded, a modest smile on her face, but you could tell she also felt she deserved it.

"But Ivan was an elf!" said Mardi.

"Not just an elf, he was an elf prince," Mum corrected.

"And he still wanted to marry a human?" asked Mardi.

"You make it sound so degrading, Magdi!" Mum laughed. "And lest you forget, I'm not any just any human—I'm the mother of the Mimir. Elves have long awaited the coming of the new gods and the opportunity to restore the balance of power between the nine worlds."

"But," I cut in, "if being the mother of the Mimir made you so special, why would Ivan try to kill us?"

"I don't think he was trying to kill you, Mooi," Mum said. Before I could protest that if he hadn't been trying to kill me, he had a funny way of showing it, she continued: "He was trying to kill Magdi."

"What?" Mardi and I said at the same time, even as the lights in the cabin flickered on and off.

"Girls, please," Mum said calmly but firmly. "Control your emotions, or you're going to do Ivan's work for him."

I looked at Mardi and nodded. I took a couple of deep breaths and saw her do the same. I wasn't sure which one of us was sending out the energy that was messing with the plane's electrical system, but the lights stopped flickering, and we both breathed a sigh of relief.

"Thank you," Mum said. "I'd hate to go down in history as the woman who missed the Grand Slam because she died in a plane crash."

"You were saying that Ivan was trying to kill me, not Molly," Mardi prompted.

"He never told me this, but that's my suspicion. We had talked about your obvious discomfort with the information I gave you, and that Mooi seemed a little more receptive. When you two made up, we hoped that Mooi would bring you around, but Ivan was afraid that you were actually going to persuade her to distance yourself from me and the prophecies about the Mimir."

"'Bring her around'?" I repeated. "For the record, I don't remember ever signing on to the whole 'kill Dad' plan."

"Speaking of killing Dad," Mardi said coldly. "Was it Ivan who attacked Dad's plane? And did you know about it?"

Mum's face stiffened at Mardi's words. She turned slowly to her.

"Yes, Magdi," she said in a soft and somehow disappointed tone, "I knew Ivan attacked your father's plane."

Mardi shifted to me, but before we made eye contact, I shifted my gaze to Mum. Like I said, I had no need to see my twin gloat.

"Did you know before or after the attack?"

Mum took a long moment before speaking.

"I know you probably think I hate your father," she said finally, "especially after what I told you about the coming war against the old gods. But I want you to know that what your father and I had was real. It was love. And when you love someone once, you never stop loving them."

"With all due respect," Mardi said, in a voice that wasn't respectful at all, "that wasn't an answer to my question."

"Wasn't it?" Mum said. "Thor wasn't just the love of my life. The universe picked us out to be together. To conceive you. Don't think my spells to give birth to his children would have worked if we hadn't been destined to be together. If we hadn't been chosen to bring something wonderful into being. Something that could raise Midgard from the weakest of the nine worlds to the equal of Asgard or Jotunheim or Ljosalfheim. When you share that kind of bond with someone, you could never wish them dead. Never."

"And yet you said that it was our destiny to kill our own father, and Ingrid and Freya and all the old gods."

"I said it was the new gods' destiny," Mum said. Her

tone didn't really change but you could hear the scolding in it, and Mardi's eyes dropped to the floor of the cabin. "You two are the first. You will be the most powerful, and their queens, but that doesn't mean that the sword or the wand that finally strikes down Thor in a decade or a century or a millennium will be held in one of your hands."

Mum shrugged, as if to say these things weren't worth worrying about, and who knew, maybe for a mortal a hundred or a thousand years was such an overwhelming amount of time that it was inconceivable for her.

"Prophecies are a slippery business," she continued. "Much of their language is deeply symbolic, which means they're open to interpretation, and even then they often get some details wrong. According to all the legends, you two were supposed to be male, yet here you are, as beautiful and feminine as any two goddesses who ever lived. And yet the Council itself decreed that you were the foretold deities of strength and rage, and even your father agreed that you were the new gods that had been prophesied."

"Wait, Dad knows?" I turned to Mardi. "Did he say anything to you?"

"Nope," Mardi said in a closed-off tone. I wasn't sure if she was trying to suggest that Mum's statement wasn't to be trusted, or if she was trying to cover up the fact that she had had intimate conversations with Dad about our divine nature, which is something we'd never done on our own. I wanted to tell her it wasn't her fault. I was the one who'd run away, after all, at exactly the moment when there were all kinds of things we needed to learn from Dad. I could hardly expect her to wait for me.

"No doubt he didn't want to burden you, especially during the Reawakening."

"So Dad knows that Mardi and I, or our descendants, are supposed to kill him?"

Mum laughed. "I doubt he finds it quite as dramatic as the two of you did. Your father once told me that if he had a dollar for every prophecy about his demise at the hands of his father, his brother, his children, or some other of his relatives, he'd be a rich man."

"He already is a rich man," I joked.

"That's what I told him." Mum laughed. "At any rate, if he really was worried about the two of you killing him, he wouldn't have saved you this morning. Have you heard from him?"

"We can't get through," Mardi said. "We think someone—well, Ivan, I guess—cast some kind of spell that keeps us from communicating with other immortal beings, or at least the ones in the East End. Would a spell like that still work even with Ivan dead?"

"If he used an energy source like a lodestar or a moonstone to power it, it would. If he relied on his own energy, the spell should have died with him." At the last words, Mum's voice cracked. "I still can't believe he would do such a thing to my daughters. He served my family for so long—ever since the Council liberated us from our vassalage. In many ways, I knew him better than my own parents. I never once questioned his loyalty. But I guess the hearts of immortal beings are different." She looked up with a startled expression, as if just remembering that her daughters were also immortal. "Just promise me that when you come into your full powers, you won't forget about your poor old mum."

I felt a knot in my stomach. The lights flickered again, and I was sure it was me until I glanced over and saw Mardi's white knuckles gripping the arm of her seat.

I took a moment to calm myself, then I said, "Will he come back? Like we do, if our Midgardian bodies are destroyed?"

"I don't know," Mum said, a strange mixture of loss and anger and fear in her voice. "I know it's never happened before. But elves manifest differently. Their bodies are much more powerful, their magic more concentrated in them, and less dependent on material aids like wands and powders and all that. But to the best of my knowledge, he probably is really, truly gone . . ."

Her voice trailed off, and for a moment, she just sat there, her face sad at first, then angry again, and then she shook her head and smiled brightly.

"So you haven't spoken to your father at all?" she asked, clearly changing the subject.

I shook my head. "I told you. We tried calling . . . but if Ivan was behind this, his hex still seems to be in effect, even though we're not in the East End."

"It's probably because Troy's there," Mum said. "Hold on," she added, and got up and walked to the small table at the far end of the cabin. There was a set of cabinets behind it, and she opened one and pulled out a phone.

"What's Ingrid's number?"

Mardi and I looked at each other, then laughed. We may be goddesses, but neither of us had memorized her number, and I had to pull it out of my phone.

Mum dialed and a moment later sang out, "Ingrid Beauchamp. It's been years since I've heard your voice."

She grimaced then and held the phone away from her ear.

"They're fine," she said loudly, obviously speaking over Ingrid. "They're fine," she repeated. "They're sitting right here in front of me. I'm afraid they can't come to the phone. Ivan seems to have cast some kind of spell interfering with their ability to use electronic devices—no doubt he was piggybacking on Joanna's hexes around the East End." She sighed. "Girls, yell something so Ingrid knows you're all right."

"Hi, Ingrid!" we both yelled at the same.

"We're fine!" I added, grinning at the mental image of Ingrid's disapproving-librarian frown.

"Satisfied?" Mum said. "Anyway, we were calling to say we're on the way home, and to thank Troy for— what?" she interrupted herself, or, I guess, responded to an interruption from Ingrid. "Oh, my gods. Is he—"

I flashed an alarmed look at Mardi. Was Mum talking about Dad? Had something happened?

"I see," Mum said. "I'll tell the girls. We should be back in North Hampton in about three hours. I'll send them straight over."

She hung up the phone.

"What happened?" Mardi almost yelled.

"I want you to calm yourselves, girls. No need to bring the plane down."

"What happened?" I said, doing my best to keep my emotions under control.

"It's your dad," Mum said. "I'm afraid the spell he cast against Ivan was too much for his body to handle in its weakened state. He's fallen into a coma. Ingrid doesn't know if he's going to wake up."

26

GOD OF THUNDER

Mardi-Overbrook-Journal.docx

Girls!" Ingrid yelled in a voice louder than I'd ever heard her use before. "Oh, thank gods, you're home!"

She threw her arms around us in a bear hug that would have crushed a mortal's ribs and moved her lips back and forth from one of our cheeks to the other, kissing us over and over.

"I knew something was terribly wrong," she said when she finally let us go. "I just had this feeling. A pit in my stomach as though I'd swallowed poison. I called Freya and she felt it too, but when we tried to get ahold of you, all our calls went straight to voice mail. And then your dad—" She broke off. Her eyes dropped to the floor. "Your dad just screamed, 'Not my daughters!' The whole house shook. I mean *shook*." She pointed, showing us dozens of cracks in the plaster, as well as a half dozen broken vases and pots that had sat on shelves and on top of credenzas and sideboards. "I ran upstairs and he was in some kind . . . some kind of trance. His lips were moving, but I only caught the occasional word. 'Storm Caller' and 'Lightning Bearer,' which are some of your father's names in Old Norse. It sounded like he was summoning a storm, but the sky remained perfectly clear. It was where you were, wasn't it? He called a storm to save you, from whatever was threatening you."

"A killer whale," I said.

"A killer elf," Molly said at the same time.

"A shape-shifter!" Ingrid said. "One of the Fallen Elves!"

"The what now?" I said.

"Millennia ago, during the war between the Aesir and the Jotun, Odin called for allies among the nine worlds. The dwarfs took the side of the giants, but the elves took our side. All save a few, led by Johan, the king's son, who had the power of shape-shifting."

"Johan?" Molly said doubtfully. "Ivan maybe?"

Ingrid nodded her head. "After the Jotun and their allies were defeated, Johan was said to have taken refuge among the tribes of the east, which meant the Russians. Ivan is the Slavic word for Johan—John."

"Well, John or Johan or Ivan or whatever you want to call him is pretty dead right now," I said. "Dad's lightning bolt ripped a hole in his chest the size of . . . well, does it matter how big it was? It was a hole."

"Do you know if he'll come back?" Molly asked. "Are the elves like us?"

"I'm afraid so," Ingrid said. "Somewhere out there, he's invaded some poor woman's womb. He'll colonize a newly fertilized embryo before it has time to form a soul, and the parents will end up raising a demon as their own child. There are ways to find it, though. We can kill him before he's ever born. We'll kill him over and over again if we have to!"

Ingrid's eyes were so wide they were ringed by white. Her nostrils flared, and her lips were practically frothing. I'd never seen her like this. Who knew the goddess of the hearth had the heart of a warrior?

"Let's worry about that later," Molly said. "How's Dad?"

And all at once, the bravado was gone. Ingrid's whole body bowed as if someone had dropped a hay bale on her shoulders. I reached out to her, half afraid she was going to sink to the floor. But beneath my hand, Ingrid's arm was as hard as steel.

"I don't know," she said in a muted voice. "After he cast his spell, he never came out of his trance. He seemed conscious at first, though delirious, but then his eyes closed. I'd say he's in a coma, but that's a human term. Dr. Mésomier says it's more like a state of suspended animation. He's breathing about once per minute, and his temperature's barely seventy degrees."

"Is there some kind of magic that can help him?" I asked.

Ingrid shook her head. "It's not his body. His body's fine. Weak, but uninjured. Still he expended so much of his magical essence on that spell that he's . . . lost, is how Jean-Baptiste put it."

"Lost?" Molly repeated in a terrified tone. "What does that mean?"

Ingrid shrugged helplessly. "Jean-Baptiste says that your father's soul is wandering between planes right now. If everything works out, he'll find his way back to his Midgardian body. But if he takes a wrong turn or gets confused, he could end up in Niflheim."

"In Hel," I said.

"Wait," Molly interjected. "Do you mean *forever*? Do you mean Dad could . . . could actually *die*?"

Ingrid just stared at us miserably. "Oh, girls. I'm so sorry."

Molly and I didn't say anything, but I felt her fingers curl around mine and we took off for the stairs. Molly's hatred of exercise is boundless, but she ran so fast, Usain Bolt would have been left in her dust. It was all I could do to keep up.

But as soon as we burst into Jo's room, we came to a full stop as though we'd run into a wall. Dad's body on the bed just looked so . . . so . . .

"Is he dead?" Molly asked in a horrified voice.

"No!" I said harshly. "We'd know. We'd feel it."

Molly nodded, but she moved slowly as she approached the bed, as if she was afraid that I was wrong. Jo had a miniature peacock chair woven from white rattan with a tufted pink cushion on it, and Molly pulled this up to the bed and sat in it gingerly. Ingrid or someone had pulled the pink blanket up to Dad's chest, and his arms lay atop it. Tentatively, Molly picked up one of his hands.

Of course I wanted to run to Dad too, but I held back to give Molly her moment. It was the first time she'd seen him in a full month. As much as I needed to feel my father's hand in mine, she needed it more. Unlike me, Molly had gone off to live with Mum, but I'd stayed at Ingrid's with Dad.

"It's cold," Molly said in a hushed voice. She looked up at me with a small, determined smile on her face. "But it still feels like Dad."

I took that as my cue and grabbed a small silver gilded stool with yet another pink cushion and crossed to the other side of the bed. I sat down tentatively, not sure if the stool's thin, curly metal legs would hold my weight. When it didn't buckle beneath me, I relaxed into it and grabbed Dad's other hand.

Molly was right. It was cold. Not frigid, but chilly, as if he'd been walking outside in the winter with no gloves. But it was supple, and even though it didn't respond to my touch, you could still feel the strength in the muscles. This was the same hand that had once punched a hole through a brick wall and thrown a baseball a full mile. It was the hand that had held Thor's hammer.

"It definitely feels like Dad," I said.

For a long time, we sat there like that, Molly holding Dad's right hand, me holding his left, inhaling and exhaling in unison, as though we could fill his lungs with our breath. Then I had to ruin it all by speaking.

"This is what a real parent does."

Molly started at the sound of my voice, and I wondered if she'd dozed off.

"What are you talking about?"

"A real parent loves you so much he knows when you're in danger. He risks his own life to save yours."

Molly looked at me warily. "I don't get it. Are you saying Mum wouldn't do this for us?"

"Well, where was she when Ivan was trying to have us for dinner?"

"Have you for dinner, you mean? And you know where she was—she was giving an interview to ESPN Australia."

"Listen to yourself. 'Giving an interview to ESPN Australia.' She said on the plane that she knew Ivan wanted me dead. She should have never left us alone with him."

Molly looked shocked. "It's not like she thought he would actually try anything. He'd served her family for generations. Hundreds of years. Why would she think he'd betray her now?"

"Why?" I repeated incredulously. "Why? Because he *said* he would, that's why!"

"I can't believe this! After everything that's happened,

you still think Mum was in on it. You think—you think your own mother wanted you dead."

"That's not all I think," I shot back. "I think she wanted Dad dead too. I think she was trying to jump-start this whole god war thing, maybe get it out of the way in her lifetime."

Molly's knuckles went white around Dad's, and I was surprised I didn't hear bones crack.

"What are you even *talking* about?"

"Think about it," I said. "Mum knew Dad was weak. She knew he would sense that we were in danger, and that it would take an extra-strength spell for him to summon a storm from a thousand miles away. So she conveniently makes herself scarce, gets Ivan to take his killer whale form and attack us, and waits for Dad to do himself in. It's the perfect plan—no one can link it to her."

"That's because there's no link!" Molly almost yelled. "You just made the whole thing up! Mum told us—she still loves Dad. Maybe not in an I-want-to-get-back-with-him kind of way, but certainly not in an I-want-to-kill-him way either."

"My gods, Molly. It's staring you in the face, and you refuse to see it. When are you going to stop taking her side, and remember who your real family is? She tried to kill me! She tried to kill Dad!"

Molly's jaw dropped open. "How dare you suggest that I don't love Dad as much as you do! That I don't love you!"

"Well, if you do, you've sure got a funny way of showing it!"

"Oh, my gods! You're jealous! That's what it is. For once in my life, I have something that you don't have, and you can't stand it! You get the Ferrari, you get the rad tattoos, you get Freya, you get Tyr. You always get everything! Well, guess what? Mum likes me better than you, and you know why? Because I'm not a selfish brat like you!"

"Selfish!" I screamed, jumping up so fast that the stool rolled away across the room. "Selfish!" I screamed again. "All my life I've carried you, and you call me selfish! Talk about the pot calling the kettle black!"

"Really!" Molly said contemptuously, standing up so that she was on my level. She leaned over Dad's prostrate body and shoved her face in mine. "Were you carrying me when you tried to steal Rocky?"

"Ha!" I screamed back, leaning toward her so that our noses were practically touching and I could feel her hot breath on my face. "You can't steal the willing!"

"WHAT?" Molly yelled, and at the same time, I heard a tiny, sharp *pop!* followed by a little tinkle, and realized that she'd exploded all the lightbulbs in the room.

"You heard me!" I yelled back as a whiff of smoke filled my nostrils. Out of the corner of my eye, I could see thin tendrils of smoke curling out of the electrical sockets in the wall. "I didn't have to steal him because he liked me better!"

"OH!" Molly screamed, and stamped her foot so hard

that every single stuffed animal and book fell off the shelves in Jo's room. "HOW! DARE! YOU!"

"Girls, please," a faint voice said somewhere below us. "It would be terribly rude to burn down Ingrid's house after all she's done for us."

"I'll burn it down if I want to!" I yelled, and only after the words were out of my mouth did I realize who I was yelling at.

"Dad!" Molly screamed. "Dad, you're awake!"

"Girls, what's going on up here?" Ingrid's voice came from the hall. "I was using my brand-new KitchenAid mixer, and the motor just—Thor!" she interrupted herself as her flour-covered form appeared in the door. "Oh, thank Odin!"

She ran toward the bed, but there was no room for her to get in, because Molly and I had both thrown ourselves on Dad.

"Girls, please," Dad said, laughing weakly. "I just managed to get myself out of the astral plane. Please don't smother me and send me back there."

"You're okay!" I yelled. "Oh, Dad, you're okay."

"I'm fine," Dad said. "Or I will be, once I get one of Ingrid's smoothies in me. That storm took a lot out of me."

"You're going to get more than a smoothie," Ingrid said, beaming. "I've got a wild boar in the freezer downstairs. We're eating Valhalla style tonight! Assuming any of my appliances still work," she added, casting a baleful look at me and Molly.

"I'm sorry," I said. I tried to catch Molly's eye, but she refused to look at me. "I guess I was just overwrought and got carried away."

"It's okay," Dad said. "It was your voices that brought me back. The dulcet tones of home," he added, laughing.

"Overwrought?" Molly said, her eyes suddenly boring into me. "That sounds like a typical Mardi excuse."

"Molly," Ingrid said in a warning voice. "This isn't the time for fighting. Your father's very weak."

"Her father will be fine," Dad said. "But he wouldn't mind a slight reduction in volume."

"Things'll get a whole lot quieter when I go back to Fair Haven," Molly said.

"Molly, no!" Ingrid said. "You've only just gotten home. And I'm making a big dinner to celebrate your father's recovery."

"I'm sure it'll be delicious, Ingrid. Maybe I can have some leftovers tomorrow. But there's no way I'm sitting down at the same table with this traitor who calls herself my sister."

"Are you serious?" I said. "Dad, tell her she can't go!"

But Dad just looked at Molly with sad but respectful eyes.

"I'm afraid this is Molly's call. If she feels like she needs to stand by your mother, I'm not going to stand in the way of that."

"But she tried to kill you!"

"Maybe," Dad said. "It wouldn't be the first time

someone's tried to kill me. Hel, it's not even the first time this summer. But she's still your mother."

Molly looked as confused as I felt, as if she'd been expecting Dad to order her to stay.

"You're not mad at her?" she asked Dad.

"Whatever beef your mom and I have, it's between us, and you shouldn't let it affect your relationship with her. I hid her from you for seventeen years. I'm not going to keep making the same mistake."

My eyes flashed back and forth between Dad and Molly.

"Molly," I said in an urgent whisper, "get over yourself."

Molly's eyes jerked up to meet mine. I could see her brain searching for something to say.

"You get over yourself," she said finally, in a half-defeated voice, as if she knew how lame her comeback was.

And then she ran from the room.

* 27 *

SAVE THE BEST FOR LAST

From the Diary of Molly Overbrook

By ten o'clock the next morning I was at the Cheese-monger. It had been a miserable night. In the first place, when I ran out of Ingrid's house, I found myself standing in her front yard with no way to get anywhere. Ingrid lives a couple of miles outside of North Hampton, and a good ten miles from Gardiners Island, so I was not about to walk. I'm not Mardi. I could always call a cab, but I didn't want to just stand around in Ingrid's front yard for twenty minutes waiting for it to get there. So I ended up having to walk something like a half mile down the road to the next house, where I called a cab, and then I stood around like some crazy stalker until it arrived to pick me up.

Then, when I got back to Fair Haven, I discovered that Mum wasn't there. I went through the whole house looking for her. That probably doesn't sound strange to you, but Fair Haven is a really big house, and I'd never actually gone through the whole thing before, even though I'd lived there for more than a month now. I discovered that Mum's room was the only other furnished room in the house, although all the furniture was brand-new and looked like it had never been used. And who knew, maybe it hadn't? Or, like, only one or two times—she'd been on the road almost every day since she'd bought the place. What surprised me was that her suitcases weren't there. Ivan had left the Maybach at the East Hampton airport when we'd gone to the BH, and she drove me and Mardi to Ingrid's and told us she was coming back here. But even if the car was in the garage and its trunk was empty, and my suitcases were in my bedroom, there was no sign of Mum or her luggage anywhere. I looked in all twenty-seven rooms of the mansion. I even poked my head into the east wing. The part of the house that had been featured in my dream, which held the kitchen and the servants' quarters. I'd been in the kitchen, of course, many times, but I'd never ventured beyond it. Even though it was the servants' wing, I expected something pretty grand because once upon a time, it had actually been the original house.

But to my surprise, it was run-down and filthy. Not, like, dirty, but filled with dirt—and leaves and twigs and branches and a lot of little white things that looked like animal bones. And that was just the hallway. The rooms off it were even worse. The glass had been broken out of the windows and, judging by the piles of poop and fur and feathers, it looked like raccoons and crows and whatever else had been going in and out for who knew how long. But way before Mum had taken over the place. This surprised me, to say the least. It was hard to imagine Trent's mother allowing this kind of squalor in her house, even if it was a part she wasn't using. These were supposed to be servants' quarters. The Gardiners had employed a dozen people, and Mum had said she'd kept a few of them. Yet clearly they weren't living here, and after poking my nose in three or four rooms, I finally gave up and headed back to the normal part of the house.

Somehow I got turned around, though, and instead of coming out into the kitchen where I went in, I ended up in the ballroom. I guess I knew that the ballroom abutted the east wing, but I'd never realized the servants' wing actually "communicated" with it, as they used to say. But there I was, and as I stared at the doors on the opposite side of the room, the ones that opened onto the front hall, I realized that the last time I'd been in this room had been in my dream, and I had a sudden creepy chill that I'd somehow crossed into that other dimension, the one I'd felt in my dream. I made my way gingerly across the room, as if at any moment I might slip back into that strange place.

I got there without incident, closed the doors behind me and made my way back toward the kitchen. It was dinnertime, and the only thing I'd had all day was a few berries for breakfast and the champagne on the plane, so I was pretty ravenous.

When I walked into the kitchen, I got an answer to at least one of my questions. Because there, on the counter, was my favorite meal: a sushi platter with a small garden salad and a bowl of miso soup on the side. The food was laid out on the same china I'd been eating from since I'd moved into Fair Haven, and there were no take-out containers in the trash. The soup was piping hot, and the shrimp and unagi (that's eel, if you're not a big sushi eater) were fully cooked, but the stove and the oven were both ice cold. The food hadn't been delivered, in other words, but it hadn't been made here either. So Mum hadn't employed a staff, after all. She'd used magic. That explained why the servants' wing had been allowed to fall into disrepair, although I was curious why Mum had tried to cover up the fact that she was running the house with magic rather than with people. Maybe it contravened some Council ruling I didn't know about? Yet another thing I wanted to talk to my mother about, but unfortunately, she was nowhere to be found.

And, though I waited till two in the morning, she never showed up. Or at least I think she never showed up—Fair Haven is easily big enough that a whole crew of people could come and go without being heard. But I waited in Mum's room, picking at my sushi off and on and going through a couple of bottles of sake, until I finally fell asleep in the middle of a *Gilmore Girls* marathon.

Needless to say, I had the dream again. I mean, between the scare with Dad, the fight with Mardi, Mum's disappearance, and actually going into the east wing, it was bound to happen. I made it across the puddle-filled yard and negotiated the ruined floorboards in the hallway as before, pulled off the door to the ballroom and found myself faced with the same strange dimensional shift as before. This time I forced myself to go all the way into the ballroom, where once again it morphed into that strange curving tunnel. The light was burning at the end of it. The woman's shadow was visible, projected on the wall. Her voice echoed to me.

"Mooi, is that you? Mooi? Are you there?"

"Mum?" I called back. "Mum, is that you?"

"Mooi," the voice called to me. "Go back. It's not safe here."

I still couldn't tell if the voice was Mum's, but something about the way it said *go back* had the opposite effect on me. Whoever was saying it was in distress, was in danger, and for some reason, I felt like I had to help her. I went barreling down the hallway.

"I'm coming! Hold on, I'll be right there!"

"Mooi, no! Go back! You shouldn't have to see this!"

By then I was almost at the end of the hall, and I didn't bother answering. Just charged forward around the last bit of curve. The light was stronger there, but I still couldn't see the source. The shadow on the wall was at least twelve feet tall, but I couldn't see what was casting it. As I ran the last couple of steps, I could see bits of doorframe poking through the mud and roots, I knew from my experience earlier in the evening that I was running out of the ballroom and into the oldest part of the house. *This is it!* I told myself. *I'm finally going to figure out what this dream is trying to tell me.*

But instead of seeing the light source or whoever was casting that shadow and warning me away, all I saw was . . .

Mum's bedroom.

I was wide awake, standing in the middle of the room as if I'd been sleepwalking. But then, when I looked down at my feet, I saw it was more than that.

My feet were covered with mud and leaves, and when I scraped them off, I realized they were ice cold—my feet and ankles were so numb that I could barely even feel them.

I was so freaked out that I ran into Mum's bathroom and hopped in the shower and turned on the water even before I had my clothes off. I stripped and scrubbed myself with lavender-scented soap under the steaming water until even my Asgardian skin was tinted bright pink. Then I toweled myself off with one of Mum's six-foot-long bath sheets until I was bone dry, wrapped the sheet around myself and skipped back through the eerily empty hallways to my room. It was almost nine, I saw when I checked my phone, and I decided to head into town for a cup of coffee and a croissant. I dressed and headed downstairs to the garage, but I had to go through the kitchen to get there, and there, on the counter, was the cup of coffee I'd been craving.

"Uh-uh," I said to the steaming cup. "No magical food today."

The key to the Maserati was hanging on a peg in the garage, and I grabbed it and hopped in, pressed the garage door opener, and backed out so fast I almost ripped the top of my head off on the bottom of the door, which had only raised itself halfway up. I spun out on the gravel parking lot and shot down the mile-long driveway at a hundred miles an hour—or, if not exactly a hundred miles an hour, then fast enough that Mardi would've been impressed—and didn't slow down until I was back on the North Fork.

And it's not like I was heading to the Cheesemonger. The Cheesemonger just happened to be between me and the Last Cup Before Europe (which claimed to be the easternmost coffee shop on Long Island), the only place in North Hampton that can make a soy hazelnut latte that doesn't taste like a cross between a McDonald's milk shake and a Styrofoam peanut. But when I saw the Cheesemonger's awning, something made me stop. I don't know, maybe it was the empty angle-in parking spot right in front. In the past month, I'd gotten pretty good at driving forward and, you know, turning left and turning right, but reverse was like a whole other language. What I mean is, I can't parallel-park worth a damn, and when I saw the spot, I grabbed it.

As I marched up to the front door, I saw that it was

still dark inside the shop. I glanced at my watch. It was a few minutes before ten. When I was running the shop with Marshall, we always got here a half hour early so that we'd be good to go at ten. But I guess Mardi and Rocky ran a looser shop.

Well, screw that, I said to myself.

I pushed on the door. The lock held for a moment, but a teenage goddess in need of her first cup of java of the day isn't going to be put off for long. I felt a thump beneath my fingers as the dead bolt dropped out of its slot and the door fell open. The morning's bread delivery—baguettes and bagels and croissants and, if they were still getting them, the best apricot-ricotta Danish you've ever tasted—sat in a bag beside the door, just waiting for someone to come along for it. I grabbed it and made my way inside, past the shadowed tables covered with pine-scented crackers and jars of kohlrabi pickled in ginger, caraway, and pomegranate brine, straight to the counter. Though I'd only been in the shop once in the past year—and that just to fight with Mardi—I still remembered where everything was. I measured the beans, ground them, fired up the La Marzocco espresso machine and, while my double shot was dripping, poured some soy milk into a pitcher and frothed it into a fluffy cloud. Five minutes after I'd entered the store, I had a steaming latte in my hand. The first coffee I'd brewed in a year.

Nervously, I took a sip.

"Girl, you still got it," I said out loud. I took another sip. "Damn, that's good."

And of course I could've just grabbed a Danish from the bag and taken off, let Mardi and Rocky try to figure out why the door was open and the espresso machine was warm. Instead, I walked over to the light switches and flipped them on, and then I unloaded the bag of bread into its various baskets and fluffed some gingham napkins over them to keep them fresh, and then I wandered back to the walk-in and grabbed the spreads—a dozen different kinds of butters and cream cheeses and honeys, a dozen more kinds of jams and jellies and preserves—and set them in their slots on the cooler table. Somewhere in there, I must've grabbed an apron out of habit, and by the time I'd done that, I knew I was there for the day. Coffee in hand, I made my way around the shop, refamiliarizing myself with the store's exotic and esoteric comestibles and generally making things pretty.

Thank the gods I wore flats today.

My first customer came in at 10:05. I was halfway through his order—a toasted pumpernickel-raisin bagel with a cranberry cream cheese schmear—when the bell over the front door tinkled, followed a moment later by a hushed but still distinct gasp.

"M-Molly?"

I didn't look up, but I knew it was Rocky. In fact, I think I'd known Rocky was coming when he was halfway down the block because the bagel in my hand was smoking, and I hadn't yet run it through the toaster.

"Miss," my customer said, "that bagel seems to be burnt."

Just the way he said *burnt* annoyed me. Move to England if you want to say *burnt*. We're American. We say *burned*.

I looked up at the customer. He was a middle-aged man wearing a green pencil-striped button-down tucked over his huge belly into a pair of pleated khaki shorts. He only had about eight strands of hair, but he had at least as much product on them as I use, and his bronzer was sweating off his neck and staining his collar brown. In other words: a banker.

I hate bankers.

"Something tells me you like burned bagels," I said to him in a flat voice.

"I . . . like burned bagels?" he repeated in a confused voice.

"In fact, you probably wish this bagel was more burned. You probably wish it was on fire." I held up the bagel on its plate and it obligingly burst into flame.

"I like my bagels burnt," the man said.

"*Burned*. You like them *burned*."

"I like them *burned*," he repeated, nodding his jowly chin like a deflating air puppet.

I clapped the two halves of the charred bagel closed. The flames went out in a puff of acrid smoke, and I handed it over to him like that. No bag, no schmear.

"That'll be twenty—no, fifty—bucks," I said.

The man pulled out his wallet and dropped three twenties on the counter.

"I assume the ten is my tip," I said in my sweetest, snidest voice.

"I like my bagel burned!" the man sang out, and all but skipped out of the store.

Throughout all this, Rocky hadn't said another word, and I hadn't acknowledged his presence. But once the customer was out of the store, he turned to me incredulously and said, "What—?"

"Just happened?" I finished for him, even as he said, "—are you doing here?"

He added, "And yeah, what just happened?"

What just happened was that I'd broken at least half a dozen Council rules about using magic in front of mortals—and using magic on mortals—in a non-life-threatening situation, but all I said to Rocky was "Must've turned the toaster up too high. You know those banker pervs. They're all masochists—they love it when a pretty girl abuses them."

Rocky just looked at me for a minute, clearly disbelieving what he'd just seen, and I found myself contemplating putting a hex on him to make him forget what had just happened. I could do it gently, whispering a few words over some valerian leaves and dropping them in a glass of iced tea, or I could do it roughly, literally pushing the thoughts out of his brain with an image of my own making. But though one would leave a little psychic scar and the other would give him nothing more than a headache, both felt wrong to me for some reason. I had cared for Rocky. You didn't treat people you liked this way. Before I had to choose between two equally unpleasant options, however, he shook his head.

"Okay, then, that's one question. And question two?"

"The what-am-I-doing-here question?" I stalled. He nodded. "Didn't you get the memo? I work here."

Another long stare, followed eventually by another shake of the head. Without another word, he headed to the back room to drop off his backpack and came out wearing a Cheesemonger apron. You know the old saying about the tension being so thick you could cut it with a knife? Well, we were in a cheese shop. I'd say it was somewhere between a firm feta and a hard Havarti. But all Rocky said was:

"You started on Billy and Bruce's order yet?"

"Are they still getting all those Anthony Weiners?"

"A dozen. Plus a dozen Marilyn Monroes."

"How gay men can eat so much red meat and mayo and stay so thin is beyond me," I said, pulling out a platter of pepper-crusted roast beef and a tub of dill-infused aioli.

Rocky didn't say anything, but the corner of his mouth twitched.

"Was that a smile?" I teased.

Rocky's mouth twitched again. His lips actually curled this time, and I caught a glimpse of teeth.

He laid out twenty-four slices of rye bread and began

spreading horseradish mustard on every other slice. I followed along behind him with the aioli.

Rocky started to slice the roast beef into wafer-thin shavings, and I laid on the red and brown slices of prepared bread like a maid in a boutique hotel making the bed with Yves Delorme sheets. I tried to imagine what the name of this color would be. Lipstick-and-Tobacco, I thought, or Cranberry Iced Tea. Or who knows: Rare Roast Beef.

I laughed again.

"What's so funny?" Rocky said.

"I couldn't even explain it if I wanted to. Let's just say that if I can't build a career out of making sammies and coffee, I can always try to come up with product names for bedsheets."

Rocky looked at me like I was crazy, but crazy in a good way. He stared at me with a confused but gleeful, goofy grin on his face, framed by crescent moon dimples. And then the smile faded and his dimples disappeared, like a crazy double eclipse.

A line from that old Vanessa Williams song popped into my head. *Sometimes the sun goes 'round the moon . . .*

"Molly," Rocky said, "what happened to us?"

I knew he didn't mean the customer from ten minutes ago.

He meant what had happened to us after we'd watched the Wimbledon final and celebrated by losing our virginity to each other, and then I'd disappeared.

What had happened? I thought to myself.

I thought about telling him that what had happened was that he and I had met right when my mother had resurfaced in my life, and as great as he was, he couldn't really compete with her. Couldn't compete with any mother, but the fact that my mother just happened to be Janet Steele made it that much harder for him to stand out.

But I knew that wasn't true.

I thought about telling him that my mother's major-domo was so jealous of her daughters that he cast a spell on their phones so they couldn't contact anyone. Just to screw with them. But aside from the fact that I knew I couldn't tell Rocky that, I knew it wasn't true either.

I thought about telling him the truth: that I'd fallen in love with the sweetest, funniest, sexiest, good-hair-having boy I'd ever met, but he was mortal. A mortal who I knew was going to die one day, while I'd still go on living year after year, and no matter how powerful my magic grew, the only thing I'd have left of him was a memory.

All of a sudden, I was filled with incredible respect for Ingrid. Respect, and sympathy. Because I knew that as much as I loved Rocky, she loved Matt a thousand times more, and she was still going to lose him and keep on living.

"Molly?" Rocky said in a nervous voice. "The look on your face is scaring me."

I looked up at him. Wide jaw. Full lips. Stubbled cheeks. Hair that any member of One Direction would kill for. And right then I knew that if I spent all my time worrying about the future, I'd never be able to enjoy my present. Eternity was going to be really freakin' miserable if I lived it that way.

"Nothing happened," I said. "I freaked out a little bit, I guess. It was my first time, you know."

He nodded goofily. "I remember," he said in a hushed voice.

"You damn well better," I said, and gave him a little shove.

"It was my first time too," he said, his voice even more hushed—husky—now.

"I remember," I said.

"You better," he said, and gave me a little shove. But he didn't let go when he pushed and ended up pulling me closer than I'd been a moment ago, until the fronts of our jeans were just touching. His hands were resting on my hips, and I could feel them trembling slightly, as he fought off the desire to crush my body against his.

"If you don't kiss me, I'm afraid your hair's going to catch fire like that bagel did."

"What?" he said confusedly. Then: "Oh, never mind," and his mouth closed over mine.

Because I'm a goddess, I can tell you that our kiss lasted exactly ninety-eight seconds. It would have gone on a lot longer than that, but then three things happened.

First, the bells over the door rang.

Then the toaster exploded.

And then a familiar voice rang out:

"Oops."

28

WAKE ME UP INSIDE

Mardi-Overbrook-Journal.docx

At the sound of my voice, Molly and Rocky had broken their lip-lock. They both stared at me in shock for a moment. Then Rocky whipped his head around toward the flaming toaster.

"Holy crap!" He jumped toward the fire, whose flames were racing toward a shelf of boxed teas. His hand darted out and pulled the plug on the toaster. Then he reached under the counter and pulled out a box of . . . baking soda, it turned out, which surprised me, to say the least. But when he vigorously shook the box over the flames, they began to sputter. Within a few seconds, the fire was out, nothing but a thick white smoke emanating from the counter like the aftermath of a stage magician's trick.

I saw all this out of the corner of my eye. My gaze

was focused on Molly, and her eyes never left mine. She watched me warily.

"Mardi, what are you talking about? What's wrong?"

I didn't know what to say, but something about seeing them together made me want to summon my father's lightning and hurl it somewhere.

"Mardi, calm down, you're not really jealous," Molly said. "You were just into him to get back at me over Mum."

"That's ridic—"

I was cut off by the piercing shriek of the smoke detector. My hand jumped up of its own accord, my fingers curled into a claw. The smoke detector exploded off the ceiling in a dozen pieces.

"What the Hell?" Rocky exclaimed into the sudden silence. "What is going on with this place today?"

A look of concern replaced the anger on Molly's face. "Mardi, what are you doing? You're going to get yourself busted by the Council!"

"What council?" Rocky asked. "Like, the city council?"

"Uh, not exactly," I said. "The White Council, which oversees supernatural beings and the use of magic."

"Mardi!" Molly said, darting a look at Rocky. There was a confused expression on his face, but then he let out a little nervous snort.

"Okay, this is going from uncomfortable to just weird. Maybe I should take off for a while, let you two work this out?"

"Stay where you are!" Molly barked.

Rocky froze in his tracks, and his eyes glazed over as though he was hypnotized. He wavered back and forth slightly, as if a breath of wind could knock him over. Molly looked startled. I don't think she'd intended to use magic, let alone turn Rocky into a zombie.

"Now who's trying to bring down the Council's wrath?" I smirked.

"Oh, crap," Molly said, ignoring me. She hurried over to Rocky and walked him backward a few steps until he was leaning against a counter. "Rocky? Babe, wake up."

It was the *babe* that got me. Even as Rocky started to blink rapidly, I said in a deep, powerful voice:

"Yes, Rocky, wake up. Wake up and let Molly explain to you how she used her powers to make you fall in love with her, then kicked you to the curb as soon as she got what she wanted!"

"Wh-what?" Rocky said, his eyes clear now, but still dazed.

"Are you *kidding* me?" Molly said. "If anyone used magic to seduce Rocky, it was *you*."

"Magic?" Rocky said, his face rotating from Molly to me and back again. "Babe, what are talking about?"

There it was again. *Babe*. In that one word, I knew I'd lost and Molly had won.

I opened my mouth, but Molly spoke first.

"Mardi, think about what you're about to say," she implored, nodding at Rocky. "We can still roll this back without having to resort to . . . other means."

"What, like wiping Rocky's memory?"

Rocky looked completely at sea now. "I must've inhaled too much smoke. What the Hell are you two talking about?"

And of course what really pissed me off was that I knew I should have lost. Knew I shouldn't have been fighting for Rocky in the first place. I was the one who'd used Rocky as a toy, a stand-in, not Molly. But I was overcome by a rage that felt like it had been building in me all my life. Not just seventeen years, but seventeen hundred. Seventeen thousand. And now, finally, I was going to let it out.

I whirled on Rocky.

"Don't know how to break it to you, *babe*, but the pair of sisters standing in front of you are witches. And not your garden-variety, sold-my-soul-to-Satan bubble-bubble-toil-and-trouble witches, but card-carrying goddesses of the Asgardian variety. Your *babe* beside you is really called Mooi, the goddess of strength, and I'm Magdi, the goddess of rage."

Molly's jaw dropped. I could see Rocky fighting to disbelieve me, but I'd put just enough magic in my voice that it was impossible. As surreal as my words were, he had no choice but to accept the truth behind them.

"Witches," he said, the way the character in *Jurassic Park* says *dinosaurs* the first time he sees a living, breathing one. "Goddesses."

Suddenly, Molly raised her hand and pointed it at him. "Sleep," she commanded.

Rocky's eyes rolled back in his head, and his knees buckled. Molly must've been accessing some of her goddess of strength power, however, because she caught him as if he was as light and precious as a Balenciaga gown slipping off its hanger. As if he were no bigger than a sleeping infant, she kneeled and laid him on the floor behind the counter.

"I think I know what's going on here," she said as she stood up again. "I think this is the Reawakening! Our powers are manifesting."

"Really?" I said skeptically, not because I didn't believe her but because I felt like being a bitch. "Whatever it is, it feels good." I waved my hand at a shelf and watched as jars and boxes flew across the room and shattered against the walls and floor.

"I'm serious, Mardi. You've got to get yourself under control. It's like the magical equivalent of hormones. It's not you who's doing this; it's chemicals, or energy or something. And every time you use your power, I can feel it triggering mine too."

"I don't know why you're complaining. Isn't this what Mum wants? For us to embrace our identity as goddesses? The Mimir? The saviors of Midgard?"

"Look around you. Does this like you're saving anything?"

Molly waved a hand at the store, which was in shambles. As she did, I could feel a wave of . . . something . . . an energy . . . a force . . . a pulse away from her, and still more items went sailing through the air. A horrified expression took over her face, and she snatched her hand back as if it had been shocked.

"What's happening?"

I threw back my head and laughed, and was rewarded with the sight of the pressed-tin ceiling buckling and tearing like wet paper.

"You called it, sister. It's the Reawakening." I threw out my arms and felt the whole store shudder. "Embrace it. It feels wonderful!"

"Mardi!" Molly screamed. "Stop!"

Another wave of power hit me, hard enough to send me reeling backward. I managed to stay on my feet, but the overstocked table beside me wasn't so lucky. It went flying *Real Housewives*–style across the room, nearly going through the plate glass window at the front of the store.

"That's how you want to play it?" I said. "Okay, let's do this!"

I flung out my hands. Molly was still on the far side of the counter, which shuddered and lurched and then rolled toward her, sending bowls and buckets and knives and forks clattering to the floor. Molly screamed in fear and jumped forward to catch it. She ignored all the little things, throwing herself at the counter itself, catching it with both hands before it tipped all the way over. It must've weighed twenty or thirty times what she did, though, and she was clearly struggling to hold it upright—especially since I was still using my power to push it forward.

"Goddess of strength, huh?" I said. "What do you say we put that to the test?" Squinting my eyes, I concentrated all my anger at the counter. The glass sneeze-guard shattered, and the tubular metal frame began bending like licorice.

"Mardi, stop!" Molly grunted. "You're going to hurt Rocky!"

"What?" I said, confused, but not so confused that I stopped pushing at the lopsided counter. "Rocky?" I'd completely forgotten about him. "Where's—?"

I was cut off by a loud *crack!* The marble slab on top of the counter had shattered into half a dozen pieces and begun falling to the floor on the far side of the counter. *Crash! Crash! Crash! Thud!*

Thud?

I figured it out a half second before Molly screamed. "Rocky!"

Thud.

✳ 29 ✳

HIGHWAY TO "HEL"

From the Diary of Molly Overbrook

*C*rack!

The marble countertop broke into pieces and began falling to the floor, directly over Rocky's body. I wanted to swat them away, but I couldn't let go of the counter or it would fall on him and crush him. I tried pushing with my mind the way Mardi was, but I had to see the pieces clearly to affect them and there were too many and they were falling too fast. I managed to keep three of them from smashing into Rocky's chest and stomach and legs, but then there was a sickening thud at the other end of Rocky's body, and I whipped my face around just in time to see a massive piece of marble— at least a hundred pounds worth—falling off Rocky's head. His body twitched once, and then it settled into an eerie stillness.

"Rocky!"

I felt something move through me like a chill. My whole body shuddered, and the next thing I knew, the entire counter was flying through the air toward Mardi. I didn't see if it hit her, though, because I'd fallen to my knees next to Rocky.

"Rocky!" I screamed. "Rocky! Wake up!"

I could feel the magical force behind my words, but it didn't matter. Rocky didn't move. I snatched his wrist to feel for a pulse, but even as I did, I saw the . . . the dent in his forehead oozing with blood, and I realized it was hopeless. It was at least an inch deep, and bleeding profusely.

I whirled toward Mardi, who was extracting herself from the wreckage of the counter with a dazed expression on her face.

"What—what happened?" She seemed genuinely mystified.

"What happened?" I screamed. "YOU! KILLED! ROCKY!"

My voice was so loud that the windows at the front of the store shattered outward. Some part of my brain heard the squeal of brakes and a few startled shouts, but my rage was still focused on Mardi—who seemed to have no idea what she'd done.

"What? No. No!"

But the answer was lying dead at my feet.

Mardi stood up as if to run toward us, but one look at my face stopped her.

"Stay back!" I yelled, grabbing Rocky in my arms.

"What's going on in here?" a voice said behind Mardi. A sixtysomething woman in rubber boots and gardening gloves had appeared in the glassless window. "Is everyone okay?"

Mardi spun around.

"Fire!" she yelled.

I heard the magic in her voice and felt static electricity prickling the air around my skin. For a moment, I thought the whole store was going to burst into flame, but instead, it burst into smoke—thick, blinding bolts of black smoke that filled the entire space.

Suddenly, I heard Mardi's voice at my side.

"Out the back," she hissed. *"Now."*

Part of me wanted to hurl her away, but another part knew she was right. Rocky's body was still in my arms, and I turned and ran into the back room and then out the back door, Mardi hard on my heels.

The first thing I saw when I was outside was her Ferrari. I ran to it and propped up Rocky's body in the passenger seat.

"We've got to get him to Ingrid," Mardi was saying. "She might be able—"

"Haven't you done enough?" I snapped.

"Molly, please," Mardi begged, her eyes brimming with tears. "You have to let me fix this!"

"Fix this?" I sneered. "It's way too late to fix anything." I was already running to the driver's side of the car, but even as I reached for the door handle, I remembered: Mardi's car was a stick, and I had no idea how to drive it. I kicked the door in frustration, knocking a massive dent in the metal.

"What are you doing? Where are you going?"

"We've got to get to Fair Haven," I said.

"What? Why?"

"Because that's where Rocky's headed. Are you going to drive me, or do I have to destroy your transmission?"

"What are you talking about?" Mardi said, her face a mask of bewilderment. And then her eyes bulged. "Wait, you mean—"

I nodded. "The seam. Niflheim."

Mardi shook her head in terror and disbelief.

"What are you planning to do?"

"I'm going after him," I said. "I'm going to the Underworld."

I don't remember the drive to Fair Haven. I just remember squatting in the back of Mardi's car and reaching around the passenger seat to hold Rocky in place so that he didn't hit his head when Mardi screeched around a corner or stomped on the brakes. There's something really ridiculous about that, I know, given the size of the dent in his forehead. Given the fact that he was already dead. But although I didn't know if I'd be able to follow his soul through the seam into Niflheim—let alone drag it back—the one thing I could do was keep any further damage from happening to his body.

Then we were sliding to a stop on the gravel path. The first thing I saw when I got out of the car was the skid marks I'd left when I headed out that morning, less than two hours before. It seemed amazing to me that so much had changed in such a short time.

I swept up Rocky in my arms and ran for the door.

"Molly," Mardi said, running along after. "I'm sorry. I'm so—"

"Don't talk," I said. "Just—don't talk."

"I have to talk," Mardi said. "I have to apologize. I have to help. You have to let me make this right."

"You want to help? Open the door."

Mardi just stared at me helplessly for a moment, then turned and grabbed the door handle. I half expected it to fly off its hinges, but either Fair Haven was more sturdy than the Cheesemonger or Mardi was getting herself under control, because all that happened was that the door flew open and banged against the interior wall.

I ran in, heading straight for the ballroom. Mardi ran ahead of me and threw the door open.

"Do you even know where the entrance to the seam is?" she asked as I laid Rocky's body on the floor as gently as I could.

"I think we've already gone in it," I said.

"What do you mean?" Mardi asked, her head whipping from side to side as if the ornate walls of the ballroom might suddenly disappear, replaced by the ice sheets of Niflheim.

"You've seen it in the dream. I know you have."

A frightened look came over Mardi's face. "You mean the tunnel? With the light at the end."

I nodded. "I don't think it's a question of finding the seam. It's a question of knowing how to use it."

"And how do you do that?"

"Not me. Us."

"Us?" I could hear the confusion in Mardi's voice, the fear. But underneath that, I knew she understood.

"We've been having the same dream," I said. "We see the house, ruined. We come into the ballroom and find ourselves in a tunnel. We see the light at the end. But every time we go toward it, we wake up. I think it's because we can't go through it alone. We have to go together."

"Our power," Mardi said, nodding. "It's stronger when we're together." She glanced down at Rocky's body. I could tell she didn't want to, but she couldn't stop herself. "It's too strong."

"That's a risk we have to take. If we're going to save Rocky, we're only going to do it together."

I stared at her, a question on my face that I couldn't put into words. Finally, Mardi nodded.

"Okay," she said. She held out her hand, and I took it. I could feel an electrical charge run through my body.

"Now what?" Mardi said.

"Now we dream," I said.

Mardi nodded again and closed her eyes. I closed mine.

"I can see the tunnel," I said.

For a moment, there was nothing. And then I felt a cold puff of air on my skin. The ground seemed to soften beneath my feet, and then it went hard again, but it was a different kind of hardness. Before, it had been smooth, polished wood, and now it was slightly uneven, like rough-hewn stone or chopped ice. An odor came to my nostrils. It wasn't stinky or anything like that. It wasn't even unpleasant. It was just . . . cold.

I opened my eyes. The frozen mud walls of the tunnel were all around me.

"Mardi."

She opened her eyes.

"You did it," she breathed in awe.

We did it, I thought, but I didn't say it out loud because I was still too furious at her. But then I realized that if this was going to work, we would have to put aside our anger. For now at least.

"We did it," I said.

"We haven't done anything yet," she said, nodding at the far end of the tunnel. "We still have to go through."

Only then did I realize there was light at the far end of the tunnel, but no shadow. No woman. For some reason that felt wrong to me. Off. She should be here.

And suddenly it hit me. The female shadow I'd seen. It hadn't been Mum. It had been Mardi!

I could see the same thought occur to Mardi.

"Of course!"

We started forward. The floor grew colder and icier

with each and every step, and we slipped back and forth but pressed on.

"I don't know why I ever thought it was Mum," she said. "It was you, the whole time."

"Or you," I said. "In my dream. But . . . ?"

"What?"

"But if it was you, why were you warning me away?"

"I don't . . ." Mardi's voice broke off. "I don't understand. Was it you?"

That's when we heard the voice.

"Mooi? Magdi?"

There was no mistaking the voice this time, or the shadow that appeared on the wall.

"Magdi? Mooi?" Mum's voice called. "You shouldn't be here."

We rounded the corner, and there it was.

Niflheim. An endless, almost featureless plain of frozen snow lit by a pale, massive sun that cast almost no light. Yet that light was reflected by a billion crystallized snowflakes. A brightness relieved by only a single shadow.

Mardi's hand squeezed in mine. We were so in sync that I could feel her eyes slide with mine up the length of that shadow, until it reached a pair of delicate feet. Feet as white as the snow they stood on, and shod only in a pair of open sandals, and at least a foot and a half long.

Our eyes traveled up the endless length of ankle,

of thigh, up the short tunic that fell from her narrow waist and hung from one shoulder until finally we came to the face.

Mum's face. But it was at least twelve feet off the ground.

✳ *30* ✳

SEE YOU
ON THE OTHER SIDE

Mardi-Overbrook-Journal.docx

Girls, what are you—no, *how* are you here?"

I opened my mouth to answer, but Molly was faster.

"There's no time. Mardi kill—" She stopped and gulped. "Rocky was killed. Accidentally. We've got to grab his soul before it reaches Hel. He shouldn't be here."

Mum frowned. "Rocky? The human boy you had a crush on? How did he die?"

"It doesn't *matter*!" Molly pleaded. "We just have to—"

"I killed him," I cut Molly off.

This is not a sentence I ever imagined saying to anyone, least of all my own mother. Nor was her reaction anything like I might have expected. She didn't appear shocked, or angry, or scared. All she did was purse her lips for a moment, as if she was still trying to picture Rocky's face. Then: "Why did you kill him?"

Molly stamped her foot into the frozen ground. "Can we stop talking about this and start going after him? *Please!*"

Mum reached down and used one of her massive fingers to stroke Molly's hair.

"My darling Mooi. I know you're upset. But this is a serious matter you're talking about, and before we can even think about trying to intercept your friend, we first have to ascertain whether we have the right. So I ask again," she said, turning to me, "why did you kill Rocky?"

Mum had spoken gently, nonjudgmentally, but her words fell on me like hammer blows.

"It was an accident," I blurted. "I didn't mean to. I couldn't even see him."

But even as the words left my lips, I knew they were inadequate. Technically they were true. I hadn't been able to see him behind the counter, and I hadn't been thinking of hurting him when I pushed the counter over. I was thinking only of hurting Molly.

But we were fighting over him, and I knew there was a part of me that had been thinking, *If I can't have him, Molly can't have him either.* It was just like the time we were four years old, when we had talked Dad into buying us a one-of-a-kind Victorian doll we saw in an antiques store in Paris. We had promised to share, but inevitably we disagreed about what to do with it (as I recall, I had wanted the doll to go for a horseback ride, while Molly wanted it to serve high tea to its doll companions). The disagreement escalated into a screaming match, and the screaming match came to blows. Soon enough, we'd each grabbed hold of the doll, and seconds after that, the doll was in pieces, its cloth body ripped to shreds, its porcelain head shattered. And I still remember screaming, "If I can't have it, you can't have it either!"

"I wanted him, but he liked Molly more than me. So I guess I decided to hurt him. I mean, I wasn't thinking about it, but on some level, I must have wanted to do it. And then my powers just kind of took me over."

"It was both of us," Molly said now. "It didn't feel like we were in control of them. It felt like they were in control of us."

Mum nodded. "It's as I feared. The Reawakening is upon you."

I shot a glance at Molly.

"You knew this was going to happen?"

"I suspected it would. Your births are unprecedented, so no one could say for sure what was going to happen, but if my calculations were correct and you were going to turn out to be the goddesses of strength and rage, then your powers were going to descend upon you in one fell swoop. Your bodies and minds are still more mortal than immortal, which means that you are going to have a harder time assimilating your power than the Aesir or Vanir when they reincarnate. That's why I chose to reenter your life now," Mum finished. "I wanted to be able to help you through the process."

"I don't want to sound ungrateful, but can we finish the explanation later? After we've saved Rocky?" Molly stared at Mum hopefully. "We are going to save Rocky, aren't we?"

Mum shook her head, and Molly gasped, but Mum put a hand up.

"Not you. Me."

"What do you mean?"

"Rocky's soul is loosened from his body. As a consequence, it is traveling at a far greater speed than you could hope to reach without magical assistance, and we don't have time to prepare the necessary spells. Plus, someone needs to stay here to keep the portal open. Given how inconsistent your powers are, it's safer if both of you stay. For one thing, your powers tend to manifest more when you're together. They're also stronger that way."

"But I want to come," Molly said. "He's my boyfriend. I love him."

"Mooi," Mum said firmly. "Arguing is pointless, and juvenile. If you came, you would only hurt our chances of saving your friend. You and your sister need to stay here and keep the portal open."

"How do we do that?" I asked.

"Simply by standing in it," Mum said. "The energy that powers the Reawakening doesn't come from Midgard—it comes from the farthest reaches of the universe, in the infinite wastes beyond the nine worlds, and it enters Midgard through whichever seam happens to be closest to the two of you. In this case, that's the seam in Fair Haven. As long as you stand within it, or just on the other side of it, it will stay open."

Mum paused, looking at both of us sternly.

"I want to be clear on this," she said. "Under no circumstances should you come after me. If you step through the portal and I'm not there to reopen it, you'll be trapped on this side. And though there are other ways back, they are difficult and dangerous, even for goddesses—and there's no way a mortal would survive them. Do you understand?"

Molly and I nodded.

"Okay, then," Mum said, waving a hand at the darkened tunnel entrance behind us. "Go back in the tunnel, and wait for my return. It shouldn't take long."

She bent down and grabbed Molly, wrapping her in an enormous hug, and did the same to me. Her arms felt the same as they had when she was human-sized. Just bigger. So much bigger.

She kissed me on the top of my head.

"Go," she said.

She turned then, and started running. She looked

just like a normal person running, yet somehow the ground seemed to melt beneath her feet. The plain of ice was miles and miles long, but within seconds, she was out of sight.

"Wow," Molly said as we ducked back into the tunnel. "That was fast."

"That was insanely fast," I said, joining her inside the tunnel.

Molly stared across the ice field, as if Mum might suddenly reappear. After a long moment, she turned away, taking another step into the tunnel.

"So I guess now we wait."

"I guess," I said. "And try not to kill each other."

I heard it as soon as the words left my mouth.

"Sorry," I said. "Poor choice of words."

"Ya think?" Molly said sarcastically, before waving her words away. "I'm sorry. That was stupid of me. I know you didn't mean anything by it. Gods," she continued, "why is it we always feel the need to escalate things? Everything always turns into World War III between us."

"I know. Goddess hormones, I guess. They're like human hormones on steroids. Supersteroids."

To my surprise, Molly shook her head. "I don't think so. I mean, sure, we're wrestling with our new powers, so our fights are more destructive, but we've always argued, for as long as I can remember."

Somehow, I knew what she was getting it.

"You think it's because of our divine nature? I mean, I'm the goddess of rage. You're the goddess of strength. These aren't exactly gentle callings."

"I wonder," Molly said. "Do you think our whole lives are going to be one big struggle to hold them back? To keep from killing or destroying everything that crosses our path?"

"What if we can't control them? What if our powers win and we become something like Loki—agents of chaos, of destruction?"

"No!" Molly said forcefully. "I refuse to believe it. You're a good person. I'm a good person. I know that."

I nodded, but I wasn't as convinced as Molly. But then, she hadn't just killed someone. I had.

"Look at Freya, at Ingrid," Molly continued. "They have very specific callings like we do. Freya's the goddess of love, Ingrid the goddess of the hearth. And you can see how their divine natures influence their personalities, but they're way more complex than that. It's not like Freya's just a slut or Ingrid sits around knitting all the time. They do other things—lots of other things."

Despite myself, I snickered. "Freya is a bit of a slut," I said.

Molly laughed too, just a little, but it was so good to hear it in that cold dark place, especially after what had just happened between us.

"Rage, strength, they're not such terrible things," I said. "Especially when they work with each other rather than against each other. Look at Joan of Arc. She was full of righteous fury, and she used it to lead an army."

"Or the Rhinemaidens," Molly said. "And we're descended from them. I mean, assuming that Mum was telling the truth."

"Maybe not," I said. "The Rhinemaidens were human, and, well"—I waved a hand at the field into which Mum had disappeared—"the evidence is starting to look like maybe Mum's not actually human, after all."

Molly stared across the vast field, but the only thing that appeared was a small spray of snow and ice flakes, kicked up by a distant breeze.

"Maybe she's part human," she said after a while. "Or I don't know, maybe she's managed to acquire magical powers somehow. The Rhinemaidens were some of the most blessed humans of them all. Odin was supposed to have given them all kinds of gifts to help them defend the Rhinegold. Maybe some of those gifts were magical talismans or . . ." Her voice trailed off.

"I know," I said. "There are so many questions. I feel like I want to grill Mum for—" I broke off. I thought I'd seen movement on the horizon. A small shadow appeared above flat fields of ice, wavering but distinct. "Is that—?"

"They're coming back!" Molly cut me off, stepping to the edge of the tunnel.

"Careful," I said, taking her arm. "I don't know if the portal will just snap closed if we step across the threshold, but we shouldn't risk it."

I could see that it was taking all of Molly's willpower not to run across the field to the tiny form that was coming toward us swiftly, though not at the supersonic speed at which it had left.

"I only see one person," I said. "Where's Rocky?"

"She's carrying him!" Molly said, and then I saw it, the smaller body tossed across Mum's shoulders like a stole. "Oh, thank the gods, she's got him!"

Molly gasped then, and I was about to ask what was wrong when I saw it too.

A kind of wave or shadow crested the horizon behind Mum, stretching out on both sides of the field almost as far as the eye could see. At first, I thought it was a wall of snow tumbling toward Mum like an avalanche, but then I heard the faint growls and snarls floating across the field.

"Is that . . . barking?" I said.

Molly didn't say anything at first. Just nodded. Until: "It's the Hounds of Hel."

Mum raced across the field with Rocky's inert body draped over her shoulders. From somewhere, she'd procured a sword, as thin and pale as an icicle, and she swung it fiercely with her free hand, skewering any hound that dared to get too close to her.

"There must be thousands of them," I said.

Molly nodded. "Freya wasn't kidding when she said Helda doesn't like to lose one of her subjects." She winced as one of the hounds detached itself from the pack and launched itself at Mum, only to find itself impaled on the flashing ice sword and tossed away like a canapé.

"Holy crap, that was close!"

"I want to go to her," Molly said. "I want to help."

"Molly, no," I said, grabbing her arm again. "You can't. We have to keep this portal open. If it closes and we're stuck on the far side with that . . ." I let the image speak for itself.

"Damn it," Molly said, stamping her foot. "This is frustrating. Run, Mum!" she called. "Run!"

If Mum heard, she didn't answer. Just kept running and slicing and stabbing at any hound that approached.

My hand had slipped from Molly's arm to her hand, and we gripped each other tightly.

"Run, Mum!" I yelled. "You can make it."

Still no answer, but she was getting closer, barreling toward us like a wide receiver racing toward the end zone with the other team hard at his heels.

We could hear her footsteps now, each heavy tread smacking into the crystallized snow with a sound like breaking glass. Her breath sounded ragged like a wheezing car, and over that came the horrible barks of the hounds.

Suddenly, the dogs' barking changed. Before it had been just this cacophony, but now I heard little yips and growls in the middle of it all. It was like they were—

"They're talking to each other!" Molly said.

But they weren't just talking. They were giving directions. Because all at once, the two wings of the pack surged forward and began to fold around Mum and Rocky.

"They're trying to cut her off!" I yelled.

"No!" Molly screamed.

Before I knew what was happening, she'd pulled her hand from mine and shoved me backward, into the tunnel. Then she was off, racing across the field toward the pack.

"Molly!" I screamed. "Molly, come back!"

She ignored me, racing toward Mum and Rocky and the hounds. I took a step toward her, but as I did, I felt the walls of the tunnel shake. No, not shake: squeeze. It was like they were threatening to close in on me.

"No!" I screamed as Molly had. I threw my hands against the walls and pressed back. "You are not going to close," I yelled at the tunnel. "Stay . . . open!"

I could feel the walls vibrating against my hands. Showers of dirt and ice fell from them, but they didn't collapse.

And now Molly was reaching the horde. To my surprise, she ran not for Mum but for the dogs. Her fist raised above her head. A moment later, one of the hounds was flying through the air. Then another, and another, and another. Molly was beating them back with her bare hands.

"Do it, Molly!" I yelled. "Kick their asses!"

Molly and Mum made their way toward us, Molly clearing a path, Mum keeping the dogs behind them at bay. But the dogs were swirling around like water. It was impossible to get them all.

Suddenly, the dogs were on me, and before I knew it, a dark shape was lunging at me. My hands were practically buried in the wall. I reacted by instinct, lifting a foot and kicking the snarling beast right in the jaw. It went flying over the pack and disappeared in their midst.

But as quickly as the first dog was gone, another followed after it. Molly managed to grab this one by his tail, swinging him in a wide arc and tossing him away.

"There's too many!" Mum said, her sword slicing right and left. "I can't keep them all back!"

They were nearly at the entrance now, but there were at least a dozen dogs between them and me. Luckily for me, most of them were focused on Mum and Molly, and I only had to kick the occasional one away. But I couldn't see how they were going to get through. For every hound they held back, three more took its place.

"Mooi, go first!" Mum yelled. "I've got them."

"I'm not leaving you!" Molly yelled.

"Go!" Mum commanded in a voice that had to be obeyed. "Or we're all going to die!"

Molly turned from Mum and began beating a path toward me. As she got closer, I could feel the walls of the tunnel start to stabilize, and as soon as I thought it was safe, I let go of them and helped her clear the last of the dogs. A minute later, she was standing beside me.

I wanted to throw my arms around her, but there were still hundreds of dogs, snarling and snapping at us.

"I'm here, Mum," Molly called. "Just a few feet farther. You can make it."

"There are too many," Mum called back. "They'll come through after us. We're going to have to close the portal."

"What?" I yelled. "How?"

"I'll worry about how," Mum said. "You just worry about catching Rocky."

"Wha—" Molly yelled, then broke off as a dark form soared through the air toward us. She grunted as Rocky's body slammed into her, barely managing to avoid dropping him. Fortunately, he seemed to be unconscious.

"Now run!" Mum yelled, striking away the dogs with her sword and fists.

"Mum, no!" Molly yelled. "We're not leaving you!"

"Run!" Mum commanded, even as the walls of the tunnel started to shake more violently than ever.

"Molly, come on! The tunnel's coming down."

I grabbed her hand and yanked. I didn't want to leave Mum, but if the tunnel collapsed on us—on Rocky—then everything she had done would have been for nothing.

We ran across the shaking ground, dodging huge chunks of ice and frozen mud that fell from the ceilings. At the far end of the tunnel, I could see the hallway of Fair Haven, the bright light of Midgard shining on its polished floor.

We dashed for it, leaping over gaps that opened in the ground beneath us as the floor of the tunnel split apart. In the end, we had to jump across five feet of black nothingness, and we tumbled roughly into the hallway. But the ground was still shaking, and we heard the creaks and snaps of breaking timber and shattering plaster.

"What's happening?" Molly said, cradling Rocky in her arms.

"It seems like the whole house is coming down! We've got to get outside!"

"But Mum!"

"We can't help her, Molly. We've got to save Rocky!"

Before Molly could answer, the floor cracked and split in two, tipping up like the *Titanic* in the big final scene. We tumbled down the slope toward the front door, which obligingly cracked and fell off its hinges. We rolled across the steps and onto the lawn.

All of this couldn't have taken more than a few seconds. But when I looked back, I saw that the house had just broken apart.

"It's our dream," Molly said.

"Did Mum do that?" I whispered.

"I don't—" Molly broke off. "Where's Rocky?"

"What? I thought you had him!"

"I did. Then we rolled down the hallway and he was knocked loose."

She jumped up and started to run toward the house, but I grabbed her hand.

"Molly, no. It's still shaking. The whole thing could fall down."

"Mardi, let go of me or I'll—"

A weak voice to our left cut her off.

"M-Molly? Mardi?" We whipped our heads over to see Rocky sitting up in my car where we'd left his body earlier. He was rubbing a bruise on his head, but other than that looked fine.

"What in God's name just happened?"

RHIANNON

From the Diary of Molly Overbrook

$\mathcal{D}$ad sat propped up by pink pillows in Jo's bed, staring at the laptop resting on his thighs, which was open to the *New York Times*'s homepage.

> *Massive Earthquake Strikes Gardiners Island.*
> *350-Year-Old Mansion Destroyed. Janet Steele*
> *Feared Lost Among the Wreckage.*

"Girls, girls, girls," he said, snapping the laptop closed. "What kind of trouble have you gotten yourselves into?"

Twenty-four hours had passed since our trip to Niflheim. Rocky was recuperating from a minor concussion at Sal's house, and Mardi and I had both spent the night at Ingrid's. But there had been no sign of Mum. We had told him and Ingrid and Freya everything that had happened, and as far as I was concerned, he should have been the one answering our questions, not the other way around.

"Is there no way we can get through the seam to see if Mum's okay?"

Dad shook his head. "You heard Freya and Ingrid. It looks like your mother closed it from the other side. Unless someone opens it from that side, it's closed for good."

"That seems like a lot for a mortal to pull off," Mardi said from her perch across the room.

"It certainly does," Dad said, sighing heavily.

That sounded like a cop-out to me.

"Dad, come on," I pushed him. "Was Mum—is Mum really mortal? Or is she really a Jotun, like the legends say."

"Jarnsaxa," Mardi prompted. She glanced at me. "I looked it up last night."

"Jarnsaxa," I repeated. "Janet Steele. Sounds a bit like Mooi/Molly or Magdi/Mardi to me."

"Jarnsaxa," Dad repeated, a little smile playing over his lips, a mischievous twinkle coming into his eye.

"Dad! Spill it!"

"Sorry, girls. You're going to have to ask her yourself."

My heart started pounding in my chest. "Then you think she's okay! You think she's coming back!"

"Oh, I wouldn't worry too much about her. She's a resourceful woman. And she has a way of turning up when you least expect her. Now go find your aunt and ask her to whip me up one of her smoothies," he said, waving away any more questions. "I'm famished!"

ACKNOWLEDGMENTS

Thank you again to the wonderful team at Penguin, especially my editor Jennifer Besser and my publicist Elyse Marshall, as well as Kate Meltzer and Jacqueline Hornberger. Thank you to Richard Abate and Rachel Kim at 3Arts. Thank you to my family and my friends. Thank you to all the loyal WitchEEs out there who have followed this story.